Books by Elizabeth Engstrom

Novels
When Darkness Loves Us
Black Ambrosia
Lizzie Borden
Lizard Wine
Black Leather
Candyland
The Northwoods Chronicles
York's Moon
Baggage Check
Benediction Denied
Guys Named Bob
The Itinerant

Collections of Short Fiction
Nightmare Flower
The Alchemy of Love
Suspicions

Nonfiction Books
Divorce by Grand Canyon
How to Write a Sizzling Sex Scene

Praise for Elizabeth Engstrom's work

On *Baggage Check:*

"The author is so deft at creating interesting, 3D characters that I was instantly hooked into Sweetann's plight (yes, Sweetann). Even the bad guys have depth and lives beyond the story. This is not a typical thriller which makes it much more interesting than the average shoot 'em up, and Sweetann is not a typical heroine. A guaranteed fun time."

—Christina Lay, author of *Death is a Star*, editor at Shadow Spinners Books

On *Black Leather:*

...a darkly seductive page-turner by a writer who knows how to put the erotic thrill into a thriller.

—*DarkEcho*

...an artfully written and highly recommended erotic and psychological suspense from first page to last.

—*Midwest Book Review*

On *Suspicions:*

"This is where she's at her best."

—*Locus*

"A harrowing and suspenseful anthology filled with superbly crafted short stories about love, death, sex, and crossing the River Styx. Dark humor courses through these dramatic and sometimes horrific tales, in this blood-curdling anthology that leaves a fearsome chill in one's spine long after the last page has been turned. *Suspicions* is strongly recommended reading for those that prefer their literary entertainment with a decided flair for the unexpected."

—*Midwest Book Review*

"A spooky collection of tales."

—*Publishers Weekly*

"A hefty, genre-crossing pie spiced with images capable of snagging the imagination."

—*Booklist*

"Elizabeth Engstrom has selected twenty-five (four original to the collection) stories from the past twenty years of writing that reveal her as a suspicious sort. But then, aren't we all? We all suspect the unknown, death, sex, and "friends, family, love, work, technology, the government, and everything else." It's just that Elizabeth Engstrom can take her lack of trust and craft fine fiction from it. Like many fine writers, Engstrom's stories are across all genres. Some can be termed sf, others as mystery or fantasy or horror, still others are simply "fiction." A few are light and humorous. Most are quietly dark, slightly skewed, angled toward that indescribable place just at the edge of shadow. All are worth reading. Many are worth pondering. By the end, at least one suspicion will definitely be confirmed: Elizabeth Engstrom is one of the best. No doubts."

—*Cemetery Dance*

On *York's Moon*:

"*York's Moon* is so absorbing and unusual that you'll almost miss how beautifully written it is—almost. Elizabeth Engstrom's mesmerizing and unique style will draw you into a world of mystery, violence and heroic struggle. Ultimately, this story celebrates the uplifting power of the human spirit. Do not miss it."

—Susan Wiggs, bestselling author of *Marrying Daisy Bellamy*

"With quirky, engaging characters, *York's Moon* is as much about understanding the human condition as solving a murder mystery. I cannot imagine anyone but Liz Engstrom writing this fine novel."

—Terry Brooks, author of the *Shannara* series

"This book is most certainly not what you would call your average mystery. In fact, there are many facets of inspirational fiction, melancholy drama, and threads of romance scattered throughout, that mix in extremely well with the murder mystery that this novel focuses on."

—*Once Upon a Romance*

On *The Northwoods Chronicles*:

"Engstrom, a skilled horror fiction stylist whose novels include the biographical *Lizzie Borden* (1991), here gives us a deliciously creepy collection of interrelated stories. White Pines Junction is a quaint, sparsely populated tourist town that, along with its many outdoors-oriented charms, harbors some very dark secrets. Aside from a little-publicized history of hometown thugs and serial killers, the town trades deaths with its garbage dump on a one-for-one citizen-rat basis and hosts a motel whose residents' nighttime reveries become frighteningly true. Perhaps most disturbing of all, the town is tormented by an epidemic of mysteriously disappearing children. In one story, a preacher's pregnant wife becomes increasingly psychotic until an unearthly force literally steals the child from her womb. In another, a harried wife finds the grisly means to dispose of her troublesome husband behind the soon-to-be-remodeled walls of her kitchen. Engstrom's chilling scenarios will haunt readers' dreams for days."

—*Booklist*

"Dark fantasy writer Engstrom (*Black Leather*) starts on familiar ground, but rapidly turns this 'novel in stories' into a genre-blending exploration of love, aging, grief and sacrifice. In Vargas County, children under 12 occasionally vanish, but the locals have long viewed this as a tithe taken by the town in exchange for the happiness of the other residents. This theme is explored directly in stories like 'House Odds,' in which real estate agent Julia has to decide if her grandchildren would be in greater danger in town or away with their drunken father. Other tales merely use the disappearances as a backdrop, such as 'Skytouch Fever,' in which aging Sadie Katherine is forced to choose between her steadfast beau and a rakish visitor, and the wittily ironic thriller 'One Quiet Evening in the Wax Museum.' Fast-paced, melancholy and beautiful, the overarching narrative binds a collection of good stories into a superb if unconventional novel."

—*Publishers Weekly*

"*The Northwoods Chronicles* conjured up in me the same excitement and wonder I felt when I read Ray Bradbury's *The Martian Chronicles*. I was taken far away...inside my own heart, my fears, my hopes. I set it down to tend to life; forgot where I put it; got anxious just like Recon John when the monkey jawbone went missing. I finished it, but it's not over: I've been gifted with a life in a strange new world,

not without its shadows, and the glimmer of weird on the water. This one is a keeper, and I'm one of its kept. Brava, Elizabeth Engstrom."
—Nancy Holder, author of *Son of the Shadows*

"To read Elizabeth Engstrom is to be guided by the sure hand of an accomplished writer whose stories have the power to transfer readers to places both real and surreal. We believe in the unbelievable, marvel at worlds created between dream and reality, and reach for all that transcends the limits of our imagination."
—Gail Tsukiyama, author of *The Street of a Thousand Blossoms*

"From the ominous opening to the soaring conclusion, these braided stories—ubtle and spooky and smart—will keep the reader spellbound. The Northwoods is a scary place to live, but in Ms. Engstrom's hands, it's a fabulous visit."
—Karen Joy Fowler, author of *The Jane Austen Book Club*

"Were he still alive, Rod Serling would like Engstrom's book. Presented separately, each of her narratives would make a great segment of the classic "Twilight Zone" television program so popular in the 1960s. Taken together—and given Serling's absence among us—they give us another way to hold a book in our hands that gives our spines a tingle and makes us wonder if Serling is really so far away after all."
—*Eugene Register Guard*

On ***Lizzie Borden***:
"Marvelous stuff. The pressures on Lizzie were vivid and completely real. You know, I think I'd have killed him myself..."
—Mercedes Lackey, author of the *Heralds of Valdemar* series

"Every door in the Borden house is metaphorically locked, and each room holds the terrible secrets of the occupant... Engstrom [moves] the reader inexorably toward the anticipated savage denouement."
—*Publishers Weekly*

"Elizabeth Engstrom has woven a fascinating tale of a lonely, tormented and frustrated young woman."
—*Rocky Mountain News*

"A real page-turner and white-knuckler. The tension mounts without letup."

—*Maui News*

"Engstrom crafts a character with motivation, mental confusion and smoldering resentment, a woman who could stand unblinking in a shower of blood as she bludgeoned her parents to death."

—*Ogden Standard Examiner*

On **Lizard Wine**:

"*Lizard Wine* is the book your mother warned you about, sleek, nasty, perfectly focused, smart as hell, absolutely convincing, and utterly single-minded. This novel wants to buy you a drink, whisper in your ear, coax you into a dark room and there seriously mess you up. Because Elizabeth Engstrom is a magnificently talented writer, her novel not only actually does these things, it leaves you grateful for the experience. *Lizard Wine* is the kind of book which enlarges and enriches the genre of the thriller."

—Peter Straub, author of *Ghost Story*

"...*Lizard Wine* is a book that will make your skin crawl."

—John Saul, author of *The Blackstone Chronicles*

"...hard! Should carry a health warning: Just reading this could leave you bruised..."

—Brian Lumley, author of the *Necroscope* series

"Excruciating suspense!"

—Bryce Courtenay, author of *The Power of One*

"*Lizard Wine* is a disturbing vintage... With a true literary voice, Elizabeth Engstrom details the madness of human relationships... It is as if Franz Kafka, Tom Robbins and Shirley Jackson collaborated on a story which only Engstrom could write. A brilliant, page-turning read."

—Douglas Clegg, author of *The Children's Hour*

"Reading *Lizard Wine* is like sitting in a snowbound car with three very dangerous men and three vulnerable (yet-no-less-dangerous) young women, and watching in thrall as the balance of power trades hands through the night. Elizabeth Engstrom involves her readers equally with the pitiful and the pitiless, and as the sun rises on the living and the dead, we close this novel reminded that we can make our lives, or our lives can make us. *Lizard Wine* is a dark, rough draught, but it goes down as smooth as the grit will allow—and its after-effects are potent and lingering."

—Tim Lucas, author of *Throat Sprockets*

"Supertaut storytelling..."

—*Kirkus Reviews*

"I often stopped with a low mental whistle of awe at Engstrom's seamless style..."

—*DarkEcho*

"...Deliverance meets Misery..."

—*The Fiction Addiction*

"...Don't read this book alone at night."

—*Eugene Register Guard*

"...The message of *Lizard Wine* is clear. This could be anybody. This could be you."

—*AmericaOnline*

On *When Darkness Loves Us*:

"Engstrom's genre masterwork, comprising two harrowing novellas, exemplifies the rarest breed of horror stories: as tender as they are unsettling, as tragic as they are bloody, these are monster tales that sweep the reader along on currents of pained feeling rather than on the familiar beats of the ol' Creature Feature."

—*Los Angeles Review of Books*

"Finding the light when swamped in darkness is never an easy thing. *When Darkness Loves Us* is a collection of two novellas from Elizabeth Engstrom. One story follows a young farm girl as she is engulfed by an underworld and yearns to escape, and an old woman who is facing the monsters of her past. Two engaging stories make *When Darkness Loves Us* quite a pick."

—*Midwest Book Review*

The Itinerant

a novel by Elizabeth Engstrom

IFD Publishing
P.O. Box 40776, Eugene, Oregon 97404, U.S.A.
www.ifdpublishing.com

The Itinerant

ISBN: 978-1-7342978-9-8
Printed in the United States of America

Thanks to the best writing group ever for their exquisite insight and caring patience.

And to Machiventa Melchizedek, our Planetary Manager, for his calm, wise guidance.

The Itinerant

a novel by Elizabeth Engstrom

IFD
Publishing
Eugene, Oregon

. . .this is how it could be. . .

Prologue—October

Parker Montrose slouched on the sofa in front of the television, paying more attention to the tightness in his chest than the old football game rerun that his father was watching on television. It was a nice reprieve from the constant news updates on the flu pandemic that had ravaged the world's population. No one that he knew in Rowan had it yet, but everyone was scared. School had been out since last spring; his father no longer went to his office at the university. People wore masks for a while, but they didn't seem to help. The virus came in on the wind, and if it got you, you died, and died quickly. Some were immune, and science had yet to figure out why, as the virus cut a wide swath. There seemed to be no rhyme or reason why some were immune and some died within minutes. Scientists worked on a vaccine, or a therapeutic, but people in the laboratories died before making any headway, as the virus mutated quickly, and had now become so virulent, so infectious, that some people wondered if this would be the end of the human race. Governments were in chaos, blaming each other for biological warfare run amok. Some thought that the wealthier countries hoarded a cure, and as their governments collapsed, desperate rebel forces took control of the media and the militia.

In the Montrose household, things still seemed as normal as possible. Parker liked that his parents still tried to do everything as usual, so as not scare him or his little sister. But he knew they were scared. Everybody was scared. One of these days, the winds would change, literally, and the virus would come to Oregon. Maybe to their little town of Rowan. Maybe even to their home.

Parker never knew his parents could be scared; they always seemed so competent. He looked over at his father, a law professor, who was watching an old Green Bay football game, one he'd seen several times before. There hadn't been any live sporting events in almost a year. His dad leaned forward, elbows on his knees, as an instant replay ran. "Oh, man!" Victor Montrose exclaimed, then swiped his hand over his perspiring brow, wiped his sweaty hand on his pants and turned to Parker. "Do you believe this guy?" he asked. "What a catch!"

Parker shrugged.

The game was of no interest, not since the tight feeling had begun in his chest this morning before he got out of bed, and it had ebbed and flowed all day through his homeschool lessons.

"Victor, honey, would you please turn off the television? Parker? Sherilyn? Dinner." His mother's voice carried above the sound of the television, and Parker lifted himself from the couch, wondering if he ought to be exerting himself, wondering if he was having some kind of a heart problem.

Or worse, that he was the first in the family to catch the deadly flu virus. Fear flooded through him. He could infect his parents, his little sister. But then, if he had it, it was already too late to do anything about it. This thing was vicious and fast.

But from what he'd heard on television, the months of news reports, he didn't think this fullness in his chest sounded like any of the symptoms. It wasn't that kind of a tightness. His lungs felt as if they couldn't expand any further, not far enough even to take the next breath, and by the time he got to the kitchen, he felt a warm flush spread across his skin, up his neck and into his face.

"Are you all right?" his mother asked when she saw him. He nodded. She put her hand on his forehead, cool and damp from rinsing dishes in the sink. "You don't have a fever," she said dismissively, and turned back to the stove.

Parker filled four water glasses and set them on the table, then set the platter of fish filets and small roasted potatoes next to the colorful bean and corn salad in the myrtle wood bowl and took his seat. If his parents could act as if everything was normal, so could he. The potatoes were the last from his mom's little garden, and she had been waiting to cook the fish. There wasn't much left in the freezer after this. They hadn't been to a store in a long time.

The television clicked off and his father sat down at his customary place at the head of the table, perspiration darkening the front of his blue long-sleeve polo shirt. He shook out his napkin, took off his glasses, and mopped his face.

His mom sat in her customary place, opposite her husband, and for the first time, Parker noticed that her face was thin. She was losing weight, likely not eating much so she could feed her family what she could, trying to make it last until it was safe to go back to the stores again. Gray roots showed at the edges of her hairline, and she looked very tired. She looked at her husband with concern on her face. "Victor?" she said. "Are you hot?"

Just then, Sherilyn bounced down the stairs, her blonde ponytail sashaying with every step, holding something wrapped up in a wad of red tissue paper. She laid it on their mother's plate before sitting, and then she sat across from Parker, grinning and fidgeting in her seat.

"What's this?"

"A present," Sherilyn said, her eleven-year-old grin full of happiness and self-satisfaction.

Joyce Montrose very slowly pulled back the layers of red paper to reveal a hand-made ceramic dish painted blue with yellow polka dots. "Oh, my!" she exclaimed. "You made this?"

"In school," Sherilyn nodded. "before the shutdown. I was going to give it to you for your birthday, but I couldn't wait."

"I love it," Joyce said. "I'll put it on my dresser."

"You can put your earrings in it when you go to bed at night and stuff," Sherilyn said, her grin taking over her whole freckled face.

"That's exactly what I was thinking," her mother said, and leaned over to kiss Sherilyn on the cheek.

Sherilyn sat back, satisfied, and Parker picked up the salad bowl to pass it to his father, but as he did, his hands grew weak and he set it back down before he dropped it.

"Parker?" He heard his mother speak as if from a long way off. "Parker?"

Parker looked around at three worried faces, but the tightness in his chest moved up his throat. He cleared his throat, and then coughed, but there was something there, something stuck.

No, something coming up. He turned away, and coughed again,

then choked.

"Honey?"

He sat up straight, craned his neck, opened his mouth as if to gag, but instead, he spoke. "Be not afraid," he said in a clear voice.

His father's fork clattered to the plate and then to the floor.

Parker watched the family scene as if he were sitting in another chair, close beside his body, calm and interested, but not quite engaged. The tightness in his chest finally eased with the spoken words. His voice sounded foreign, yet familiar.

"Mama," Sherilyn whispered.

Joyce Montrose covered her daughter's hand with her own, looking every bit the controlled, calm school counselor that she was. "I know, honey," she whispered back. "Shhh." The three looked to Parker to see what would happen next.

A new feeling, a blossoming in his chest, took Parker by surprise. He felt as if his ribcage expanded by three or four sizes.

He wet his lips and struggled with a fresh concept. He was to say something else, but he couldn't put it to words. The thought was overwhelming in its scope and significance. He couldn't grasp it, couldn't make sense of it, could never put such an enormity into words.

And then he got it. The words came clearly as if spoken directly into his mind, synthesizing the concept succinctly. "You are not alone," he said.

The feeling left his chest, and he was back, looking at three amazed faces staring at him.

Sherilyn's mouth hung open. His mother covered her mouth in astonishment.

"Television!" his father choked out. "Sherilyn, run and turn on the news." He looked feverish and sunken in his chair. "The news," he barked out, then began to cough.

Sherilyn ran to the living room and a moment later, the nightly news anchor's voice came through loudly. "—suspects that the nuclear missiles came from rebels in Venezuela," he said, "who have taken over the military there. They believe that the U.S. has a vaccine for the flu virus that has ravaged the world's population and is unwilling to share it. Los Angeles, Mexico City, and Chicago were hit, all within minutes." He touched his earpiece. "Tokyo now, I'm hearing. We're expecting a statement from the Pentagon momentarily. Stay with NBC as we bring you updates—" his voice cut off, and all they heard was static.

"New York," Victor whispered. "I knew it."

"What?" Joyce asked, her voice high with alarm. "*What?*"

"Parker," Victor reached across the table, gripped his son's wrist, and stared intently into his eyes. "We have three months of food and water in the attic. Your grandfather's .22 rifle is up there, along with my .38 pistol and several boxes of ammunition. Your number one task, boy, is to take care of your little sister. No matter what."

Parker's heart began to pound.

"You get me?" A bloody tear pooled in the bottom lid of his father's right eye and then dripped down the side of his nose. He swiped at it without taking his eyes off his son. "*Do you get me?*"

Parker nodded.

"No," Joyce said, her face drawing pale as she began to understand. "No!" But then she looked at her son and she knew.

Something had happened. Something terrible, something wonderful, something unimaginable had just happened, because Parker, her sweet, beautiful son, in all his sixteen years, had never before spoken.

Not a single word.

Until tonight.

Chapter 1 – January

Willie McIntyre slammed the door of the red pickup truck and looked at his three passengers. Castile, his daughter, had dressed warmly in his raggedy old fatigue jacket over a Nordic sweater, and wore a wool cap down over her ears to ward off the pre-dawn cold. The two teenage boys in the back weren't dressed warmly enough, but the heater in the truck still worked like a champ. They would be all right. Alta, the black and white border collie that had adopted them sat, alert and attentive, between the boys in the back.

This trip was Castile's idea. Not Willie's.

Last night, when she brought two bowls of steaming rice with some bits of canned chicken and a few canned peas to his garage workshop, she brought up the subject again.

"I've got to go into Harwood. I've got to get some medicine for Rose and Lila."

"They're dying," Willie said. "There is no medicine for them."

"They're in pain," Castile countered. "Terrible pain. This is not like the flu, Dad. They have cancer."

"I know, honey."

"You will not win this argument tonight," Castile said, her mouth set in a grim line. "There are things we need."

She never looked more like her mother than when she was determined. Her dark hair and eyes and the set of her jaw was the absolute picture of her mother, his late wife, for whom he mourned every day. He, a former Marine, kept that pain private, letting it out only at night, and always when he was alone.

Willie chewed on a piece of chicken. He'd been thinking of going into the larger city of Harwood for a couple of weeks now, but the horrors of what he'd seen in their little town of Rowan were enough for him. He didn't need to see worse carnage from a bigger city. "I'm sure the hospitals have all been looted for their drugs."

"Maybe not for the drugs we need. There's also the VA hospital and several pharmacies."

"I'm sure—"

Castile cut him off. "I'm sure I'll find what we need. There aren't that many people left, Dad. We have to take care of the ones we have."

Willie put his chopsticks down.

"*I'm* going to town tomorrow," she said, her persuasion turning back into that characteristic determination. "I'll take Jamaal and Robby. We'll see what's left of Costco, too. It's time. It's been months."

"Jamaal and Robby are children."

"They're teens."

"*I'll* go with you."

"What about your work?" She waved her chopsticks at the workbench. "What about the wind generator?"

"I don't want you going into Harwood with just a couple of kids. I'll take you in the truck, and we can take Jamaal and Robby with us if you want, but you know that it's risky."

"What risk?" she asked. "We have immunity, or something. You know if we were going to die of the flu we would have by now." Like Mom, Willie knew she almost added, but didn't. "We need lots of supplies, not just medical. Toilet paper. Rice. Beans. Canned fruit. Dog food." She reached down and scratched Alta's ears, the border collie that had come along and been adopted into the community just like everyone else.

"Not that kind of risk, sweetheart. Bad guys. Crazies. We have no idea what might be out there."

"Yeah, well… We can't just hide here. If there are bad guys, we'll have to deal with them. There are things we *need*, Dad."

Castile was right. Their little community of one hundred and twenty-seven misfits—all that they knew that had survived in Rowan, Oregon—was running out of many things. They'd been living off of the contents of the homes and pantries of the neighborhood dead. Many people, especially the group of Mormons who lived to the north of town and the survivalists to the east, stockpiled food as the fear of pandemic and war grew, but those people all died. They had been the among first to be found, their bodies the first to be lightly wrapped in sheets and laid gently and respectfully in the park.

Willie's group had brought their stockpiled food back with them, and those stores were now running low.

Castile was right. It was time to go to town and see what was left. See *who* was left, if anyone.

Robby and Jamaal, both seventeen, sat vigilant in the truck's back seat, not dressed nearly warmly enough for the twenty-degree weather, but at least they knew their way around the shotgun Robby carried, and could help if Willie and Castile needed any extra muscle.

"Ready?" Willie asked.

Three heads nodded, even as heart rates increased. Nobody had any idea what to expect in Harwood.

Willie turned the key and after a rough start, the engine came to life. He let it idle and warm up. "We'll get gas," he said to Castile. "Don't let me forget."

She nodded. "I'll put the boys on it."

Gas was the easiest thing to find. Abandoned cars sat in the garages of empty houses all over town. Nobody drove. She'd put six five-gallon cans in the pickup, along with a siphon tube, and they'd forage for that while they were in Harwood foraging for other things.

Dawn spread an orange glow on the eastern horizon as they drove slowly out of the cul-de-sac that had become the hub of their encampment. The big truck moved easily across crusted snow that was pocked with animal tracks and dusted black with soot from the fires.

"Oscar showed me his preliminary spring garden plans last night," Castile said. "Very ambitious. I can't wait to start planting."

"I'll be happy when the days are longer," Willie said, "and I have more light for work." Though the garden needed serious consideration and very careful planning, it all sounded like petty and ridiculous small talk as soon as they turned onto the highway and saw a blue Honda pulled off to the side of the road as if the driver wanted to make a call or a U-turn. A corpse covered in hoar frost sat behind the wheel of his car. Clearly, the driver had been trying to make it home, and just couldn't manage it. He got too sick too fast.

That's how this flu worked. It came on quick. Horribly, mercifully quick.

"Mr. Jenkins!" Robby said, and then quieter, "my math teacher."

Willie's heart tightened. He didn't want to see that stuff, but he really didn't want teenage kids to see it. "I'll send the crew for him, Robby," he said. "I'm sorry."

"Doesn't matter," Robby said softly.

No, Willie thought, I guess it doesn't matter. Not after what these kids have already seen. Robby and Jamaal had buried their whole families. They'd done it together, as next-door neighbors, as high school football teammates, fortifying each other through that terrible October day by taking breaks, sitting together on Jamaal's front step, each with a bottle of Jack Daniel's. By the time the booze was gone and the parents and siblings all covered up in the back yard, they were not only drunk, but they had become brothers.

Every day, a detail of three men and two women from the cul-de-sac went door to door, bringing back food and any survivors who wanted to come along, and taking corpses to the park. At first, the women were very respectful, wrapping the dead in sheets from the houses in which they were found, and they made sure the men lay each body carefully side by side and record their names, but after the body count numbered in the hundreds, ceremony wasn't so important anymore. It was much more important to get the deed done before the thaw, and to find the survivors and get them to safety. Bodies began to be put in the park without identification, for the wildlife, the sun, and eventually the thawing earth to claim them.

Something would have to be done about the park when spring came, but that was at least a month away, maybe two. Willie would take that problem to the Committee and they would decide. Surely someone knew how to run a backhoe.

Some of the survivors who came to the cul-de-sac were so shell-shocked that they might never recover. Some of those put guns to their heads, others drowned themselves in the Silver River, too heartbroken and grief-stricken to live. Others wandered off, but some rallied, brought their personal items, moved in, and turned the residential subdivision around Willie's house into a compound, a community, a family. Together, they were building the new Rowan, Oregon.

Lila and Rose were among Castile's first concern. Best friends since high school, Lila and Rose became roommates in Willie's neighborhood when both their husbands died several years ago. Lila was diagnosed with pancreatic cancer and Rose with colon cancer mere months before the pandemic took a foothold. Now they were in the last stages of their lives and it was difficult to watch.

Willie drove slowly down the highway, everybody wary and alert, but there were no tire tracks in the snow all the way to the freeway. The landscape of the foothills of the Oregon Cascades, as familiar to Willie as the light in his daughter's eyes, looked completely foreign. Not because the snow was gray with soot and ash, but because now, everything was completely foreign. Even that look in his daughter's eyes had changed after she watched her husband and twin sons die of the flu.

"Smoke," Robby said. "Two o'clock."

A thin column of smoke rose in the still air off to the west, the direction of Harwood.

"Hospital first," Castile said. "If we do nothing else, I want drugs for Rose and Lila."

"Enough to put them out of their misery?" Jamaal asked.

"Maybe," Castile said softly.

"That'd be good," Robby said.

Willie didn't want to hear that kind of talk, especially from kids. He took a fresh grip on the wheel and kept driving. Harwood was ten miles up the freeway.

Along the way they saw two burned-out warehouses, one of which had scorched acres of trees and houses around it.

"What caused all the fires?" Robby asked. "Why were there so many?"

"Don't know," Willie said. "When people aren't tending to their things… I don't know."

In spite of Castile's request that they go directly to the hospital first, Costco was right at the freeway offramp, so he turned into the parking lot. A man dressed in camouflage, a thick wool cap, with a blanket on his lap, pulled off his gloves and picked up the rifle that leaned against the wall next to him. He stood up from his little folding chair by the door.

Willie stopped the truck and got out. "Stay here," he ordered his daughter and the two boys.

"Hi," he said as he approached the guard, holding his hands out to show he was unarmed.

"What's your business here?" the man asked.

"We're looking for painkillers for two of our people who are dying of cancer."

"Are you local?"

"Rowan," Willie said. "What is *your* business here, if you don't mind my asking."

"I'm rationing things. Some places have been looted clean, and I didn't want that to happen here."

"Self-appointed?"

The man hefted his rifle. "Self-appointed. Yessir."

Willie saw the black globe and anchor pinned to the collar of the man's coat. "Former Marine?"

"Sergeant," the guard said. "First Battalion, 23rd Marines."

"Gunny here," Willie said, "First Marine Logistics, Camp Pendleton. Semper Fi."

"Nice to meet you," the guard said. "It's good to know that some well-trained people are left."

"Indeed," Willie said. "Well, we mean no harm. We have people who are suffering."

"Tried the hospital?"

"Not yet. We're headed there now."

"I can give you a basket and you can go in and fill it full of stuff, but I doubt there are any painkillers left in the pharmacy. The opiates would be the first to go."

"What stuff is left?"

"Some toilet paper, but not a lot. I'm only going to let you get one package of that. There's some canned food, you can have two packages of that. All the fresh and frozen food is long gone."

"We're pretty good on the basics," Willie said, "but it's good to know this place hasn't been cleaned out."

"It's getting kind of thin inside."

"Any bottled water?"

The man shook his head. "Long gone. Try the hospital and some of the little clinics for your pain meds, and if you don't find anything, then come back. I'll ask around."

"Ask around? There are others?"

"Some." He volunteered nothing further.

"Thanks." They shook hands, then Willie got back into the truck.

"Do they have any dog food?" Robby asked.

Castile rolled down her window. "Is there any dog food?"

The man nodded. "Come and get it."

"Robby, Jamaal, take a cart and get some dog food. And a package of toilet paper. Rice if they have any." The two boys and the dog jumped out and a few minutes later, came back with four 50-pound bags of dog food, a 25-pound bag of rice, a twelve pack of Dove soap, and a package of toilet paper, all which they put in the back of the truck, then jumped back inside, blowing on their cold hands.

Alta paused for a scratch on the ears from the marine guard.

"That is one empty warehouse," Jamaal said.

"The pharmacy was a complete mess," Robby said. "Totally ransacked. That must have happened early on." He held the door open for Alta.

"Thanks for what you're doing," Castile called to the guard.

He nodded, then sat back down to continue his vigil.

"Hospital," she said to her dad.

~ ~ ~

A blue minivan had been driven through the emergency room doors of Harwood's Angel of Mercy Hospital, and left there, its front doors still hanging open. Frozen bodies lay all over the waiting room. It was obvious to Castile that most had come in vain, seeking relief from the flu, dead in their chairs or sitting on the floor lined up against the wall, too sick to even wipe away the telltale trails of blood that ran down their cheeks and out the corners of their mouths. The dog, shy and uncertain about everything in this place, stayed close at Jamaal's heel.

The bodies were all covered with frost, some had been caught in a gray snowdrift, which had blown in through the broken glass doors. The grayness made it easier for Castile to look at them as things, rather than as people—or worse, as patients—sunken into their bones, who hadn't begun to decompose until the power went out, probably a couple of days, maybe a week. The onset of winter put them and kept them in a horrific freezer-burned stasis. She couldn't bear to look close enough to see if any of them were recognizable. She didn't think she could handle that.

She had a mission and needed to stay focused.

Willie wound up his hand-generated flashlight and handed it to her. She cast the bright beam down the darkened hallway, then, heart hammering, proceeded carefully into the depths of the building where she had worked as an ER nurse for almost fifteen years.

It hadn't occurred to her until this very moment to wonder what had happened to all the patients in all the rooms who had been immune to the flu. When the ferocious virus landed in western Oregon, brought in on the wind that blew all the radiation from Japan to the north and east—thank God for tiny favors—doctors, nurses, and other staff got sick and died, or stayed home to take care of their families. As she had. Everyone, eventually, must have stopped going to work, leaving those in bed to. . . to. . .

She turned to her father. "Do you think there could be survivors here?"

Willie slowly shook his head. "Not anymore."

She couldn't think about it. She *would* not think about it. The last thing they needed was for her to bring home more sick and dying people.

The world had turned harsh and cold in more ways than she could have ever imagined.

She was here to get drugs and supplies and get out. "Right," she said, took a deep breath, and opened the door of the first supply closet she came to. Someone had been here already, of course, taking masks, gloves, surgical kits, intubation kits…whatever they needed. She ran the beam of her flashlight along the shelves, then grabbed an armful of fresh sheets and towels and handed them to Jamaal.

"Find a gurney or a wheelchair and follow me," she yelled at Robby, her breath pluming out ahead of her. They went through each emergency room bay, picking up all medical supplies they could carry: bandages, IV tubing, blood pressure machines, swabs, wipes, even tongue depressors.

She had to hurry up do what she came to do and get out of here. The air was thick with death.

Faster, she hurried through the dark, windowless hallways toward the first-floor pharmacy, the unmistakable sound of an empty gurney rattling along behind her. The deeper she went into the hospital, the thicker the cloying stench of death.

Vague, gray light shone through a few half-open doors, casting uncertain shadows.

A crowbar lay on the floor at the open door to the pharmacy, and the floor was covered in pills, broken glass and puddles of colored, sticky syrup ice that clung to her shoes. She stepped around the trash, scanning the shelves.

A half-finished cup of coffee sat on the pharmacist's desk. She'd had coffee at that desk with Andy many times. She hoped he wasn't here somewhere, and if he was, she hoped she wouldn't recognize him.

Her father had been right: all the opiates were gone. She grabbed two big bottles of penicillin, two boxes of syringes, a dozen tubes of cortisone ointment and a huge canister of vitamins and handed them to Robby, who put them on the gurney. She grabbed all the decongestants and big jars of prescription-strength Tylenol. Behind the decongestants, someone had tucked away two bottles of Tylenol with Codeine. Good! "Sometimes nurses keep a small cache of drugs at the nurses' stations," she said. But the last thing she wanted to do was wander through the cavernous hospital that, despite the months of cold, still smelled like the worst kind of hell.

She'd try just one nurse's station and see what was there. Second floor surgical.

"Each of you grab a pillowcase and follow me," she said. "Leave the gurney here. We'll come back for it."

The stairwell was completely dark except for the four flashlight beams that careened crazily around as they took the stairs two at a time. The nurse's station had been rifled, charts all over the floor, cabinets left open. No drugs. There were other nurses' stations, other floors, but what she saw in the beams of their flashlights was likely to be the case for the whole hospital, and all the doctors' offices, pharmacies and clinics throughout Harwood. They were not the only people trying to survive.

"Let's go, honey," Willie said in his discouraging tone, but the thought of Rose and Lila, trying to be brave in their best times and in desperate agony in their worst times, their eyes begging for relief—any relief—*permanent* relief—drove her forward.

"There's a nurse's station at the other end," she said, then pushed through the heavy door and moved slowly down the long hallway.

They entered the cafeteria, where floor-to-ceiling windows let in the winter light, and enough warmth to hasten decomposition of those sitting at tables with their lunches still in front of them.

Jamaal and Robby grabbed handfuls of snack-size bags of potato chips, cookies, and candy bars, then raided the cooler of soft drinks, and filled up one of the pillowcases.

Castile walked quickly through the horror show, pushed through the big doors, headed to the west end nurse's station. The boys would catch up. This hallway was much darker. She concentrated on her goal and refused to give in to the temptation to vomit.

The skin prickled on the back of her neck. A feeling that she was being watched was too strong to shake.

She heard the boys behind her, and everything slowed down as she walked gently, trying to make no noise at all. The three men behind her, following her lead, were equally as quiet.

She saw a blue shimmer out of the corner of her eye, but when she turned to look, nothing was there.

Nothing was *there*, but something was *here*. She knew it.

"Everything okay?" Willie whispered.

Everyone was subdued in the presence of so much death.

Castile stopped for a moment to collect herself and wipe the perspiration from the side of her face. This place was normally bright and full of happy activity, chatty nurses, recovering patients and their hopeful families. Now, the dark silence was as oppressive as the stench.

She heard her father and the boys breathing behind her.

Then the dog growled, and hair stood up along her neck and back.

"Alta," Jamaal tried to grab her collar, but she dodged him, growling louder, showing her teeth.

Castile took as deep a breath as the reek would allow and turned the corner.

The light she held in her hand flashed back at her in the form of three pair of glowing eyes.

Wolves, ripping at a frozen corpse in blue scrubs.

As one, they bared their teeth and growled.

Alta barked, a high-pitched hysterical sounding series of warnings.

Castile backed up so suddenly that Robby ran into her. She stumbled over him in her hurry to retreat around the corner as the low rumble of growl echoed a fair warning. Jamaal got a grip on Alta's collar and pulled her back.

"*Git!*" Willie yelled, waving his arms, and three sets of glowing eyes disappeared long enough for the four to make it back to the cafeteria, the "exit" sign still faintly glowing green from its diminishing battery. As soon as the door closed behind them, Castile felt her father's arm around her shoulders, and she wanted nothing more than to just sink to the ground and sob. One more disappointment. One more tragedy that Rose and Lila would have to die in excruciating pain because she couldn't find anything that could help them.

But she would hold off until tonight, when she could cry herself to sleep in private, like she did many nights. For now, they had errands to run, and they needed to be about their tasks.

As they made their way through the cafeteria, Jamaal stopped and whispered, "Listen. Someone's out there."

Castile ran to the stairwell and down to the first floor. She banged through the door, the others right behind her.

A man's voice echoed down the hallway. "Hello? Hello? Anybody here? Anybody alive in here?"

Willie stepped to the door to the emergency room and quietly pulled it open.

The man saw him and threw his hands up over his head. "I'm unarmed," he said. "My wife is in the car having a baby, and we didn't know where else to go. Can you help us, please?"

Castile pushed her father aside. "A baby?" A flush of hope, the first she'd felt in months, warmed her face. As far as she knew, all the infants had died of the flu. There was no one younger than five in their little community, and there were no pregnancies in their group. This child, this new life, born in a hospital amid wild animals in Harwood, Oregon, could be the beginning of the new world. "How close are her contractions?"

"She's been at it a long time," the man said. "We thought we could do it alone, at home, but we're both scared. Can you help?"

"Castile is a nurse," Willie said.

The man put his hands together and looked toward the sky. "Thank you, Jesus," he said.

~ ~ ~

Parker heard the knock on the door as he watched Sherilyn divide the last half can of chili into two small bowls. This was the end of the food. What his father had imagined was three months of food for the family turned out to be barely three months of food for the two of them.

And this was it. Now he'll have to do something else, think of something else to do to take care of his little sister, but he had only one option that he knew of, and it was a bad idea.

Someone was broadcasting over the little wind-up Red Cross

radio that he'd found in the attic with the cases of food and jugs of water. Whenever he could sneak away at 4 pm he went up into the attic to listen to the talk, assuming what he heard to be accurate news and calls for survivors to join forces in a growing list of cities and small towns. None of the places he heard mentioned were in Oregon, and Parker didn't have any idea how he'd get himself and Sherilyn to Kansas City or to Cincinnati. But if she knew about it, she'd want to go. For all Sherilyn knew, they were the only ones left alive, except the people who occasionally knocked on their door.

But all they had left now was a one-gallon jug of river water and a yard full of gray snow that he didn't want to melt, though they could. They had plenty of wood to burn—they hadn't yet burned the dining room furniture—but nothing to cook over the fire in their little hibachi.

He'd spent many freezing cold hours in the back yard with his .22 rifle waiting for a squirrel or a rabbit or even a bird, but only once did he shoot a squirrel out of a tree, and while they made that last almost a week in a soup, they hadn't had any luck with any other game.

He might try again, but he'd have to get out of this neighborhood, and he didn't want to take Sherilyn too far away from home. He had no idea what the world was like out there. They kept the draperies drawn and only went into the back yard to empty the bucket they used as a toilet into the pit he'd dug.

When the knock came on the door, Sherilyn looked up at him with hope in her face, and he knew that this time, he had no choice. They were out of food. He was out of options. People had knocked before, and Parker had shown them the barrel of his gun through a crack in the door and they'd been left alone. But now—now they needed to find out what these people needed, or offered, or whatever. He owed it to his little sister to hear them out.

He took a deep breath and went to the front door, giving her a hand signal to stay put. She followed him, of course, pulling her coat collar close around her neck.

Parker unlocked the door and opened it a little bit. A lone, thin man stood on the front porch, his eyes pale, his face lined and gray.

"Do you have food?" the man asked.

Sherilyn pushed her way to the door, opening it wider. "We're out of food," she said.

"How many of you are there?" the man asked.

"Just us. Two," Sherilyn said.

"Your parents?"

"They died."

The man took a step closer and stared long at them. "What's your name, girl?"

Parker pulled his sister back from the doorway, and pushed her behind him.

The man moved to look behind him at Sherilyn's face. "You look just like my little Cindy," he said, his voice catching. "You look exactly like her." He straightened up, brushed at the moisture in his eyes and squinted at Parker. "Come with us," he said. "We can take care of you. Bring some clothes and any medical stuff you have. Especially any old prescriptions."

"Okay," Sherilyn said, peeking out from behind Parker.

The man snaked out a hand and grabbed the front of her parka. Before Parker realized what was happening, the man had pulled her through the door.

Sherilyn screamed.

Parker caught her around the waist and pulled her back into the house and the man let her go, a look of horror on his face. "Oh God, I'm sorry," he said, backing away. "I didn't mean it, I just… you just look so much like her…oh God, I miss her so much…" His face began to sag.

Parker slammed the door and turned the deadbolt. He fell to his knees and enfolded his little sister in his arms, holding her tightly until she stopped trembling and began to cry.

"What are we going to do now?" she asked, hiccupping. "I thought he was someone we could go with. Isn't there anyone who can save us? Are we going to sit here and starve to death?"

Parker winced. He hadn't done much to take care of his sister, except to keep her alive. Their father had provided the house and anticipating something like this, he had stockpiled food and water and some wood. All Parker had done was to bury their parents in the garden before the ground froze. Then he brought the little barbecue in to the back bedroom and made a chimney to the window with aluminum foil and duct tape. They'd been living in that warm room ever since the first snowfall.

"There's got to be some place we can go," his sister said.

They'd find food, Parker knew it. He'd dreamed that he would find food, more food than they could eat. He had dreamed that their lives wouldn't always be like this, they would be happy, and healthy, with full bellies and friends, but he saw no way to get from here to there. Right now, he had to protect Sherilyn from men like that, men with desperation in their eyes.

Especially from that particular man, who could come back, now that he knew where they lived.

"Parker!" Sherilyn yelled at him, and his attention snapped back to the here-and-now. "We need to go out and find people. We can't just sit here and wait for them to find us." Her voice rose into hysterical territory, so he shook his head again and gave her the "case closed" look that their parents had so often given them, and returned to the kitchen, picked up his bowl of cold chili and took it to the warm back bedroom.

Sherilyn followed, as he knew she would.

An hour later, when darkness fell and Sherilyn had fallen asleep in his arms, Parker held her and rocked her and tried to make a plan.

But there really was only one plan, and that was to go out and find food.

~ ~ ~

The next morning, both the growling in their stomachs and the accusatory stare Sherilyn gave him prompted Parker to action.

He loaded the .38 revolver and left it on the table by the front door. He pointed to it. Sherilyn stood silently next to the table and stared at it, arms crossed, as if it might bite her. Then he loaded the .22 rifle, shrugged into his ski parka and a favorite blue and green ski hat and walked out the front door, waiting on the porch until he heard Sherilyn turn the dead bolt behind him. He took a deep breath of cold air and looked up and down the street.

Gray snow covered everything. Soot from the fires had fallen from the sky like black snowflakes, turning the world gray. There were a few human footprints in the snow on the sidewalk and the street, but no tire tracks. Lots of animal prints. Some bird tracks. None of the walks had been shoveled. The neighborhood was silent and seemed abandoned. On a normal quiet snowy morning, Parker could hear the freeway off in the distance, and now and then a train whistle. Not today.

He looked to the west, at the nice red brick house next door where the Zimmermans lived. Maybe they were alive. Maybe they had food.

He snorted. That was a fantasy. He knew they were not alive. If they were, they would have come over.

Nobody in this neighborhood was alive except him and his sister.

But maybe the Zimmermans had food.

With a last backward glance at his own front door, he stepped off the porch and walked down to the sidewalk and then up to the Zimmerman's front door.

Fresh footprints marked the snow, probably the man who had come to their door the day before.

Parker knocked, but of course there was no answer. He tried the knob, but it was locked.

When the Zimmermans went on vacation, Parker mowed their lawn and fed Socrates, their cat, so he knew where they hid a key to the back door. He stood on the front porch, knowing that they would want him and his sister to have whatever was in their kitchen cabinets, but the thought of going into their house to rob them of their food seemed so wrong.

His stomach grumbled, and he looked back at his own house.

Sherilyn, her face framed by the kitchen window, stared intently at his every move.

He waved, then made his own fresh tracks in the snow across the yard and opened the side gate.

Socrates, frozen and half eaten, lay on the steps to the back deck. He was a good cat, and for once, Parker was glad that his dad had not agreed to his and Sherilyn's continual pleas for a family dog. Parker could never have kept a dog fed these last three months. He picked up the dead cat by the tip of his tail, surprised at how flat and light he was, and walked to the back of the Zimmermans' garden and dropped the carcass, where it sank a couple of inches into the snow.

He looked back up at the two-story brick house and took a deep breath.

His little sister was hungry.

He picked up the fake rock by the rosebush and opened its secret compartment. The key was there, as always. He fitted it into the lock on the back door, turned the knob and slowly opened it.

A terrible stench wafted out, and Parker knew where the Zimmermans were. A fresh sadness weighed down his shoulders. They were the nicest people. Mr. Zimmerman was a retired general and his wife a retired librarian. Parker had earned spending money by doing odd jobs and little chores around their house ever since he was old enough. They were the only ones who never asked him why he didn't talk.

He held his nose and stepped into the mud room, although the dark, bitter taste of death clung to the back of his tongue. A bag of cat food had been torn open and the contents spilled out onto the floor.

Socrates had a cat door. Surely the neighborhood raccoons were well fed.

Parker wondered for a moment if he and Sherilyn could eat cat food for a week or so.

No.

Sherilyn deserved better than that. His father expected him to do better than that. He needed to go to the kitchen and see if the Zimmermans had some cans of soup or tuna or green beans or something. He'd go right in and come right out again, locking the house up tight and let Mr. And Mrs. Zimmerman alone in peace until someone else came for them, some other time.

Okay. Parker tried to still his pumping heart, tried to remember that his little sister waited at home alone—*alone!*—until he could get back to her with something to eat, so they wouldn't have to go with that man or anybody like him. Just a can of tuna. Just a box of macaroni and cheese. Just a tin of smoked oysters forgotten in the back of a cupboard, or a package of spaghetti noodles. Just something, please God. Pudding. Sherilyn would love some pudding.

He pushed the door open, and there they were, on the floor. Mrs. Zimmerman lay with a phone still held to her ear, frozen maggots spilling out from her eye sockets. Mr. Zimmerman had died kneeling at her feet, his arms wrapped around her legs, his cheek laid upon her ankles.

Parker felt his heart rip as tears spurted out of his eyes. He turned and ran, slamming the back door behind him, knowing he could never go back into that house, or any other house, no matter how much food they might have in their cupboards.

There had to be another way.

There had to be.

He sat in the snow on the steps of the Zimmerman's deck, not wanting to face Sherilyn empty-handed. He envisioned the disappointment on her face and the ache of failure made him want to scream and pound his head against the brick wall.

He could spend more time hunting. He could roam all over the neighborhood, looking for squirrels. Cats, even. He could put some of the cat food out as bait, and maybe catch a raccoon or a possum. They could eat that.

He turned to look at the back door of the Zimmerman's, and all the energy ran out of him. To fetch Socrates's cat food, he'd have to go back inside that house.

He took a deep breath and realized that there was real food inside that house, and that he just needed to man up, to steel himself and do it. He didn't have to look at them, the nice people who had been such good neighbors, he just had to go to the cabinets, open them, and take what was there. He could do that.

The Zimmermans had no more use for that food, and nice people that they were, they would want him to have it.

"Parker!"

Sherilyn.

Parker leaped off the deck and ran through the gate to the front of the house. A white van idled out in front. "They're here for us, Parker. Come on, let's go."

A woman dressed in a long skirt and leggings, wearing boots and what looked like a mink coat and hat, stood on the sidewalk outside their house. "We'll take you to safety," she said. A man sat in the driver's seat of the idling van.

"This is Sister Matthew, Parker," Sherilyn said. "C'mon. We have to pack."

"Just one small bag apiece," the woman said.

Parker stood his ground and stared at the woman. She looked to be his parents' age, her hair a little shaggy, but her eyes were bright and while not exactly soft and welcoming, they were not hard or cruel. Just very matter-of-fact. She didn't have a dangerous color about her, but kind of an ordinary beige.

He didn't particularly like her, but he didn't fear her. She meant his little sister no harm, he could tell that.

"We have a community outreach, a ministry set up in the high school," she said. "We have food, and there are other children. You'll be safe there."

Parker's face flushed with shame at the woman's inference that he couldn't keep his sister safe.

"What's your name?" she asked him.

"Parker," Sherilyn said. "He doesn't speak."

Without taking her eyes off him, she asked, "Why not?"

"He had a fever when he was a baby," Sherilyn said, then grabbed Parker's hand. "Come on, let's go."

"Is his mind right?"

"Yes, his mind is right," Sherilyn said with a touch of their mother's indignation. "He's very smart."

"All right then," the woman said, "but leave your technology and

41

firearms here. We're a Christian community."

"He hunts," Sherilyn said.

"No guns," the woman said. "No radios, no computers, no televisions, no cell phones. Technology is to blame for all this mess that we're in, and in the new world, we're not going to make the same mistake twice."

Sherilyn tugged on Parker's hand, and reluctantly, he followed her into the house and into her room.

She quickly pulled old schoolbooks out of her little pink backpack and stuffed it full with some clothes, underwear, her swimsuit, and her favorite little plush elephant, excited about the prospect of change and seeing some other people. She zipped it closed, then ran into their parents' bedroom and grabbed her mother's pearl necklace and threw that in. Her mother wore those pearls when she got married, and she'd promised Sherilyn that she could do the same. Then she stood at the doorway to Parker's room expectantly.

He began to pack his backpack, slowly, and with no such excitement.

First, he wrapped his revolver up tightly in the middle of four t-shirts and stuck it into the bottom. He looked at Sherilyn. She nodded her approval, and Parker relaxed. They had an agreement about going with this woman. She wanted to go, and he agreed, as long as it was a good thing for both of them. Parker, being mute, was used to isolation. He could be alone, but his sister was used to society, to school, to having girlfriends. She needed to be social, and she needed more than he could provide. They couldn't even have a conversation. He knew she was tired of doing all the talking, although with a lifetime of learned hand signals, facial expressions and body language, they communicated pretty well.

It would be good for her to be with this Christian group. They could always leave and come back here if it wasn't right, but for now, this was a good idea. Sherilyn would be safer in a group, especially if there were other kids her age. He put underwear in his pack, some shirts, jeans, socks and an extra pair of tennis shoes. He got their toothbrushes out of the bathroom that they shared, and gave

Sherilyn's to her, because she'd forgotten it. She went back and got her hairbrush, too.

Parker locked the house behind them and followed his sister into the van.

Ten minutes later, they pulled up in front of Jefferson High School. Sherilyn had attended the Three Oaks Elementary School across the street, and was looking forward to starting at South Lake Middle School. Parker had gone to a few science courses at Jefferson High, and he'd played on the school baseball team last spring. But because he was mute, his mom home schooled him for the most part. He knew some of the kids who went to Jefferson and was familiar enough with the school to not be afraid, so he took Sherilyn's hand as they walked up the steps and through the big front doors, backpacks in hand.

"Welcome," a man said. "I'm Reverend Elijah. Welcome to our community of grace."

The man looked very familiar, but Parker couldn't place him. He wasn't particularly tall, nor was he skinny. He looked very ordinary. They shook hands and his handshake seemed pudgy, limp and moist. Parker resisted the impulse to wipe his hand on his pants after the Reverend let it go. Sherilyn had no such resistance, and Parker smiled at the look of distaste on her face.

"Pray with me," Elijah said, then grabbed their hands. Sister Matthew joined in their little prayer circle just inside the front doors of the school. "Lord, look after these two young ones, the newest members of our flock. Help them to heal over the loss of their parents and speak into their hearts the knowledge that Jesus has welcomed them as you've brought them to me. We know these are the end of times, Lord, and we've been left behind to clean up the world. We ask your help in those endeavors. Amen." He smiled down at them. "Okay, kids," he said. "Sister Matthew will show you the ropes." He smiled, not a warm smile, and Parker saw a greasy fingerprint in the middle of his right lens. Elijah put his hand on the top of Sherilyn's head, and she grimaced. "Go with God, my children," then turned and walked away.

Sister Matthew picked up a black, zippered organizer from a nearby table, flipped a couple of pages, then with a pen, jotted down some numbers and handed them two slips of paper, one yellow, one blue. "Here are your locker assignments," she said. "Your beds have the same numbers. Girls in the science lab, boys in the gym." She handed the yellow one to Sherilyn, the blue one to Parker. "We meet in the chapel—what used to be the cafeteria—for lunch and worship at one. Do you know where those rooms are?"

Parker nodded.

"Any questions?"

"No, ma'am," Sherilyn answered.

"Then I'll leave you to find your lockers and your beds. Lunch is being served now, chapel in a half hour."

Sherilyn whispered as soon as they were down the hall and out of earshot. "Do you know who that guy is?"

Parker shook his head.

"He looks familiar."

Parker agreed. Reverend Elijah did look familiar. Chances are, the last time he saw the guy, Elijah weighed a good deal more.

But how could Parker run into a minister named Elijah and not remember it?

Perhaps he hadn't always had the name Elijah. Perhaps he hadn't always run a refugee camp in a high school.

These were confusing times for everyone.

~ ~ ~

"Get me scissors and some string or something to tie a strong knot," Castile said to the boys with skilled, urgent precision. "And alcohol from the pharmacy." She rolled up her sleeves. "Get me gloves! Size small. And more towels!"

The boys were back in record time, not wanting to miss a moment of what was taking place on a gurney in the middle of a freezing hospital hallway.

After patient and calm coaching from a practiced Castile, and with a final, mighty push from her mother, a slippery baby girl came squalling out of a warm, safe womb and into a frigid hospital foyer where the big windows afforded the best, if inadequate, available light. The boys held their flashlights so Castile could see, and Willie spoke comforting words to Daniela while Carlo held her hand and wiped perspiration from her forehead.

"It's a baby girl," Carlo whispered. "Ah, a girl." He shook his head in amazement. "Sophie. Daniela, it's our Sophie!"

"Please don't let her die," Daniela whispered to Castile, desperation on her face.

"She looks fine," Castile said, and lay the steaming infant on her mother's stomach. She watched as the child's skin pinked up with oxygen and the umbilical cord ceased to throb, then covered the baby with layers of fresh towels. A few moments later, Daniela delivered the placenta, Castile tied and cut the cord, wrapped the child in a blanket the boys brought back from the supply closet and handed the black-haired baby to Carlo.

Exhausted, Castile sat back in the wheeled desk chair and took off her gloves, then rubbed perspiration from her face with a fresh towel. This building was filled with dead people, and the whole world was filled with the flu virus. They could be inhaling it with every breath. Nobody knew. Baby Sophie had the benefits of her mother's immune system, but that hadn't helped any of the babies so far.

Time would tell.

"You'll come back to our place," Willie said. "We've got room, and food, and Castile can keep an eye on you."

Castile shot him a withering look for volunteering her time so casually. Yes, of course she'd keep an eye on them, but she had others to keep her eye on as well. And right now, she was exhausted.

She looked over at the two teenage boys who sat on the reception desk, kicking their legs back and forth. "You guys all right?"

They nodded. "That was amazing," Jamaal said.

"It's how you got here," Castile said, smiling. She patted Jamaal on the knee. "Good thing I did an OB rotation."

"All right, boys," Willie said. "Let's get those supplies loaded up in the truck and get home. Carlo and I will help Daniela to a wheelchair and then to their car." He looked at Carlo. "You three can follow us." He consulted his watch. "We've been gone almost all day and need to get home for the six o'clock broadcasts."

Castile smiled apologetically to Daniela. "Usually, you'd get to rest and relax for a while," she said. "But it's warm at our place. You can rest there."

Carlo was about to fall all over himself with gratitude, but Willie gave him a list of things to do instead, and soon everybody was in motion, everybody except Daniela, who lay quietly on the gurney, cooing to her newborn, wiping vernix and a little blood away from the baby's perfect head and face.

"Oh!" Daniela said, looking up. "I hear angels singing."

Castile whipped around, as comments like that were often symptoms of something dire, but Daniela looked up at her with a flushed face and clear eyes. "Can you hear them?" she asked, with wonder in her voice.

Castile listened, and as she did, a drop of moisture landed on her hand.

She didn't dare look, afraid that the flu had already clouded over baby Sophie's eyes, afraid that an angel had just shed a tear as she prepared to take that newborn spark of hope right back to wherever it came from.

Castile collapsed into herself a little bit more.

Then she pulled the blanket back from the baby's face. The child looked fine. No bloody eyes, no pallid complexion, no lethargy. She looked like a perfectly healthy newborn.

At least for now.

Still, Castile couldn't drop her guard and love this little thing. She hated that most of all, having to guard herself against the grief, the ongoing, ever-present grief that this virus, these times had brought upon the world, upon her loved ones.

Would the misery ever end?

Chapter 2 – February

Weeks of Elijah's twice-daily bullshit had begun to grate on Parker's patience. Elijah seemed to want to preach the gospel, but he never carried a Bible, he never really cited scripture the way Parker's pastor did on the rare occasions his folks took him to church, and in fact Elijah often contradicted himself. He was fond of saying, "There is no darkness but ignorance," which Parker wasn't even sure was a Bible quote, and then he would also say "It is better to be ignorant and correct than to be falsely taught." Which made no sense at all.

Parker couldn't figure it out. And yet, in the time he and Sherilyn had been here, everybody went about doing whatever they did every day, and he heard very little grumbling. The worst part was that nobody ever went outside. Poison, Elijah said. Air, water, and land, all poison. If there was one phrase his law-professor father taught him, it was to always ask this: What is the source for your information?

Elijah had no source for that information, not that Parker could see. He had no more source of information than anyone else.

So he, along with everybody else, endured these twice-daily prayer sessions, where Elijah preached nonsense and then prayed at them instead of with them, because what else were they going to do? Parker sat back by the door and wished he had a book to read.

"Amen." The Reverend Elijah concluded the evening service, then spread his arms open wide. "Are there any announcements before we all retire for the night?"

"I'm hungry," a man said, and a murmur rippled throughout the cafeteria. "There's plenty of food, why do you give us so little to eat?"

Parker's head snapped up at this unusual display of dissatisfaction. The energy in the room rose from its bored tolerance of the reverend's droning voice to alert attention.

"Brother Henry," Elijah said, in a condescending tone. He mocked them at every opportunity. "Please stand."

Henry, a small man, balding, looked thin and wan. "I've lost probably twenty pounds," he said, pulling on the loose waistband of his pants. "Some here have lost even more."

A woman stood up. "And we're cold. Look at us! We're all sitting here shivering in our winter coats. Why isn't this room heated?"

More murmurs from the group. Louder. People looked around at each other and nodded their heads in agreement. Parker's interest rose as he heard Elijah's dictates being challenged for the first time.

"It isn't healthy," Henry said. "It isn't right. There's plenty of food to go around, you know that. Enough to fill our bellies and then some."

"We know your *office* is heated," the woman said.

Elijah held up his hands to quiet the crowd. "I can't believe you are unhappy. We cannot use up all our stores before food makes its way to the stores again. If we eat everything in sight, then what? What would you have me do?" He took a step away from the lectern and leaned into Henry, who seemed to wither under Elijah's glare. "I provide food, shelter, and lessons for your children. You are safe and secure here."

"It ain't enough to live on," Henry insisted. "You want us to do stuff, but you have to give us calories if you want us to have any energy."

He was right, Parker knew. There was hardly more food here than he and Sherilyn had when they were alone at home. It wasn't enough. They'd been here with Elijah's group for two months, and he was hungry all the time.

The woman said, "Tell him what *you* had for dinner tonight, Elijah."

The crowd waited in silence. Parker noticed, and not for the first time, that Elijah didn't look thin like everyone else.

Elijah cocked his head and looked at the woman as if she were a traitor.

"If you don't, I will," she threatened.

Elijah took a breath and addressed the crowd. "I'm sorry it has come to this, Brother Henry," he said. "If you have concerns, please don't wait until they are unbearable. We are all trying to figure things out as we go. If the rations are insufficient, we'll increase them. It's that simple."

Henry sat down.

Elijah glared at the woman in the front row until she, too, took her seat.

Elijah raised his hands in benediction. "Go with God, my beloveds," he said in dismissal, and walked quickly down the center aisle, Sister Matthew behind him, hurrying to keep up, and out through the big cafeteria doors.

As soon as those doors closed behind them, people began to talk. Henry stood up, walked up to the lectern and held up his hands.

"Are we going to put up with this shit?" he said. "Do I need to have my food rationed? Good lord, there's an abandoned Safeway just down the street. We could have all the food we wanted, just by driving over there and picking it up."

"Half the classrooms across the street at the elementary school have been turned into pantries," a woman Parker knew as Molly spoke up. "They're full of canned and boxed food. Every day, people go out and bring back food. You know that, you've all been out doing it."

"Most of the Safeway is already over there at the elementary school," a man said. "We've cleaned it out. We've gotten plenty of food from there."

"And from the kitchens of the dead!" Rex yelled out.

Parker had noticed Rex right from the very beginning. He had a dangerous color around him. He was always the first to take a side, and it didn't seem to matter to him which side to take, only that he be vocal and obvious. Too obvious. He seemed a little off kilter. Someone to avoid.

Henry held up his hands. "That's not the point. The point is, who is Reverend Elijah to ration our food? Aren't we old enough to know how much we should be eating?"

"We've got no choice," a tidy young man on the edge of the crowd said. "He's taken charge, he's taken us in, he's made a place for us. This is his show. It's temporary, no doubt, but while we're here, we ought to be grateful for it, and be living by his rules."

"Why?" Rex asked. "Why his rules? Why not my rules? Or Henry's rules?"

"And until when?" someone else asked.

"Until there's somewhere else to go," the young man said. "You're not prisoners here. If you don't like the rules, you can leave."

"We could go to the coast. We could catch ocean fish," an elderly man said. "We could get boats and go out and get fresh fish."

"Poison," someone said. "The rivers and lakes are all poison, probably the oceans, too."

"We don't know that." Henry sounded desperate. "Just because Elijah says the world is all poisoned doesn't make it so. I've been outside. Everything seems okay to me, except for the soot from the fires. And it's cold, but it's *February*, for cryin' out loud."

The crowd quieted as people considered the option of moving to the coast. It was no option at all. There was no one to lead an exodus like that away from Harwood. Harwood was dead. Perhaps all of Oregon was dead. Maybe the entire west. Maybe they were all that was left. There was no other place to go.

"Options?" Henry pleaded with the group. "Somebody? Anybody?"

Several people got up and began to wander out, and a few moments later, Henry, shoulders slumped, stepped down and joined them.

Parker stood up and looked toward the back, where all the women sat, hoping to catch a glimpse of Sherilyn. She smiled and waved at him, then spoke to the woman sitting next to her, and Sister Ascot looked up at Parker and nodded. A moment later, Sherilyn's arms snaked around his waist and her sweet-smelling head was pressed against his chest.

Nothing ever felt so good as to have his arms around his baby sister. He had barely seen her in a couple of weeks, and then only in passing. "I miss you," she whispered. Parker closed his eyes and soaked up her little-girl energy.

A tap on his shoulder interrupted their reunion. Parker turned to see the young man who had spoken out earlier standing behind him.

"Hi," he said. "I'm Steven."

Parker held out his hand, his other firmly around Sherilyn's shoulder, and the two men shook hands.

"Hi," Sherilyn said. "I'm Sherilyn. Parker's sister."

"Hi," Steven said, and shook her hand, too.

"I'm in charge of trying to get electricity back," Steven said to Parker. "I saw you reading a book on chaos theory, and I think you could be of better use on our team and let someone else take their turn in the woodhouse."

Parker smiled and nodded. He was sick of monitoring the fire under the converted boiler all night.

"Great," Steven said. "Do your shift tonight, and by tomorrow I'll have someone to replace you. Then get some sleep and when you're up, meet me in room 203."

"Can I come?"

Steven smiled at Sherilyn. "You have your schoolwork, right?"

Sherilyn nodded. "*And* I work in the kitchen."

"That's good," Steven said. "You better be doing that and let us do the dirty work."

"*Sherilyn!*"

Sherilyn gasped at the sound of the disapproving female voice and hugged Parker tight for a long moment more before letting him go, and eyes down, moved away from the two men and toward Sister Ascot, the girls' teacher. "Don't be dallying with boys," Parker heard the woman scold his little sister as the two walked away in the company of the other girls.

"Okay then," Steven said. "Room 203 tomorrow after your rest."

Parker nodded and smiled. It would be good to put his brain to use. He wished he could attend classes like Sherilyn, but he was too old. Only children under thirteen were still in school. Everybody else had to work.

From the chapel, Parker stopped by the kitchen for a sack dinner and went directly to the woodshed, where he'd relieve Rachel, then feed wood to the boiler that heated the school until he was relieved.

Rachel greeted him at the woodhouse door, her backpack on and ready to leave. "Burn those first," she said, pointing at a bin of books from the school library.

Parker frowned.

"That's what I was told. I've been burning them all day. Lots of ash, not much heat. Best to mix them up with the wood. Okay, then," she said. "See ya."

Parker closed the door behind her, then checked the firebox, tossed in a few pieces of wood, and then sat down to enjoy his dinner.

Someone had rebuilt the boiler; the guts of the gas-fired system lay outside in a tangled heap of snow-covered plumbing. Now the boiler circulated water kept hot by what looked like an enormous fireplace insert. It wasn't so bad at night, when the air outside was very cold and the school didn't need much heat, but during the daytime, he had to open all the windows in the woodhouse so he didn't roast.

Rachel had kept one window open a little, and the room was toasty. Just right.

He opened the little handmade cloth bag and found a cheese sandwich with mayonnaise on wheat bread and a small handful of raisins twisted up in a napkin. Boy, Henry was right. This wasn't much to live on. He took the candle over to the bin of books and dug through it to see what Elijah had determined the best books to burn. *Fahrenheit 451* was in there, and titles by Mark Twain, Ayn Rand, Ken Follett, a whole pile of books by Dr. Seuss and Beverly Cleary. He dug through until he found a well-read copy of *Harry Potter and the Sorcerer's Stone*. He took it back to the table, picked up the first half of his sandwich, and began to read.

~ ~ ~

Sherilyn lay in bed, listening to the deep breathing and light snores of the twenty or so girls in cots or on mattresses on the floor of the science lab. She was lucky; her bed was right next to the window she had cracked open so she could feel cool air on her face. The grownups would not approve of her bringing poisoned air into the room, but she didn't care. She opened her eyes and looked out at the moon. It looked like it had been sliced cleanly in half.

Thoughts of her parents and their happy days of popcorn and pajamas on video nights, or summer walks with ice cream cones, or even the occasional frantic mornings while everybody was grumpy, trying to get ready for work and school, put a cramp of homesickness in her stomach. If she let her mind dwell on it, soon she'd be crying into her pillow. Again, like so many of the others who cried themselves to sleep. Sherilyn had done that several times but had determined that she wouldn't do it anymore. Her parents wouldn't like it. And she was too old for that. "What was done was done," people here kept reminding her. Time to move forward.

She watched the tops of leafless trees outside move in an invisible icy breeze, everything black and silver in the moonlight.

"Sherilyn?" The whispered voice was so close, as if a woman's lips were right next to her ear, but it was a voice she'd never heard before. She turned to look, but of course nobody was there. Had she dreamed it? She'd been thinking of her mother; maybe that was the way her mother had spoken to her when she was a baby. She smiled at that thought. Certainly nobody in this place spoke with such tenderness and affection. Sherilyn looked around, but the room was dark and silent, except for the various sounds of sleeping girls.

A shimmer of blue hovered by the door. Sherilyn sat up, rubbed her eyes and looked again. Nothing. She lay back down but thinking about her mom had rekindled the homesickness which now bubbled up into her chest. She tried to remember the words to a little song that Sister Monica sang to the littlest girls when they were sad.

When you're scared
And red haired
Don't be sad
Don't be mad
We're here too
And we love you.

But it wasn't the same if it didn't come from Sister Monica. And she was eleven now, too old for that little song, anyway. It was for the little kids. But Sherilyn was sad, she was scared, and she wanted her brother.

It wasn't right that the only time she got to see him was during chapel. Even then, they weren't allowed to talk but for a few minutes.

But she knew where he was now.

She slipped out of bed, grabbed her blanket and tennis shoes, and wove soundlessly between cots of sleeping girls, opened the door as quietly as she could, and left the big room. She put her shoes on, wrapped the blanket around herself, then hurried down the long, dark hallway, flanked on both sides by brightly colored lockers.

At the exit door, she paused for a moment, wondering if the door would lock behind her. It didn't matter. In fact, she kind of hoped that she'd have to stay all night in the woodhouse with Parker. She'd be punished, maybe they both would, but she didn't care. Maybe Sister Ascot would understand that sometimes she and Parker just needed to be together.

She pushed through the heavy door, and then held it until it gently closed. She tried it. Locked. Good.

A frigid breeze blew between the buildings. Sherilyn pulled the blanket tighter around her and ran through the moon shadows to the woodhouse, with its smokestack spewing, and a small yellowish light glowing in the window.

Parker gave her a look when she came in the door, disturbing his reading. She knew that look, it was half condemnation for sneaking out at night and half admiration that she had done so. She'd seen that same look on her father's face a million times. The homesickness surged, but then receded as Parker closed his book and pulled up a plastic chair for her to sit in. The room was warm and smelled like a campfire.

"What are you reading?"

Parker showed her.

"Where did you get the book?"

Parker pointed at the big, wheeled bin full of books.

She looked inside. "What are these?"

Parker picked up a handful and threw them into the fire.

Sherilyn gasped, then sat back in her chair. "Our parents would hate that."

Parker nodded, his mouth screwed up into a wry *I know* smile. He handed her a copy of *A Wrinkle in Time* he had dug out of the bin.

Sherilyn hugged it to her and rewrapped her blanket. "I couldn't sleep," she said, and then yawned.

Parker rummaged in the corner of the woodhouse and came up with some wool sweaters and a sleeping bag. He laid the sleeping bag out on the floor in front of the fire, wrapped a couple of books in several wool sweaters for a pillow, and Sherilyn laid down.

He tucked her in like Mom and Dad used to do, using the blanket she had brought with her. The woodhouse was warm enough, she didn't really need the blanket, but it felt good to be tucked in. He smoothed her hair and she closed her eyes, pretending it was her mom saying goodnight.

"You should tell Reverend Elijah that you can talk sometimes," she whispered, but knew without looking that he was shaking his head no.

Just as she drifted off to sleep, she thought she heard his voice. It was just like the voice that woke her up earlier, except it sounded like Parker. "Simply close your eyes and release all your troubling thoughts. Don't hold the energy of disappointment and the sad feelings of living in a troubled world. Go to the Father now and seek the peace that surpasses all understanding."

Is that something Parker would say if he could talk?

Not really.

It was all very confusing.

It didn't matter. She was ready to release all her troubling thoughts—like what Sister Ascot would say when she found Sherilyn's bed empty in the morning.

She didn't really care.

She thought of her dad, so calm, so competent, so in charge. What had Parker said? Go to her father now and seek peace?

Sherilyn snuggled up warm and cozy in her little nest at her big brother's feet and tried to picture her dad's face, but she couldn't, not really. That made her sad all over again, but she knew he would bring her peace if he could.

~ ~ ~

Parker gently put another log on the fire and poked at it with a piece of pipe. Sherilyn's visit had been a welcome surprise, and that she was sleeping quietly on the floor of the woodhouse made him feel even more like her protector. This was not a bad place, but he would rather be at home, taking care of his little sister by himself.

When the thaw came, they would go home.

If spring came. There had never been a winter like this in all his years, and apparently that was true for everybody else who talked about it, even the old people. Still, it had to end sometime. Surely spring would arrive. Eventually. Even in a normal year, spring was months away yet.

He listened to Sherilyn breathe, the sound of his own voice months ago still echoing loudly in his ears. How those words of comfort had come out of his mouth at the dinner table was a mystery. Someone else took over the part of his brain that was broken and used it to bring comfort to his family. How could that be a bad thing?

And yet he knew that Reverend Elijah would be threatened by this power, this gift, this… this message. He would think Parker a fraud and might punish him, or worse, exile him and keep him away from his sister.

Sherilyn was too young, too trusting yet. She didn't know that there was more to this Reverend Elijah that wasn't all that good, the way he had women running around after him, the way he rationed food, the way he laid down the law and threatened those who didn't go along with his plans.

How did he come to be in control, anyway?

He took it, that's how. Everybody was afraid, and he stood up and made a plan, and that's all it took for everyone to follow him.

Parker eventually remembered where he'd seen Elijah, a few pounds heavier. He was Sam York from Sam York Ford. Called himself Sam the Man, who sold used cars in stupid commercials on television. Well, Sam the Man had himself a new gig now.

Parker didn't follow him, didn't believe anything he said, especially his crazy religious talk. There was comfort here, minimal though it was, food and warmth, but Parker wasn't buying the whole "technology is to blame" thing. People were to blame.

He looked at the Harry Potter book, open on the table. If Parker had wizard powers, there was so much he could do.

What would you do? The female voice, clear and sweet, lips not even an inch from his ear, asked the real question.

What *would* he do, if he had the power of a wizard?

Parker quietly moved his chair around so he could put his feet up on a box of kindling, folded his arms across his chest and closed his eyes.

What would he do?

He dreamed of speaking to a large group of people in a park. He dreamed of teaching a classroom of children the same age as his sister. He taught them about how things used to be, and what happened, and how they needed to be in the future. He spoke, but the words were not from his mind, but from a higher authority, who knew the ending from the beginning, and who knew exactly how to approach those who were skeptical.

He dreamed of a new world, where love was the ruling power, where people were equal, where nurturing each others' life ambitions was the greatest job of all. He flew like a bird over forests and pristine lakes, small golden cities that stood on their own and traded with others for the pleasure of the social interaction.

The world was in balance, and Parker knew it could be, it would be. He had seen it and knew that he had a mission to help achieve it.

He relaxed further into his dream vision, wanting to never awaken from such peaceful splendor. But awaken he did, when the woodhouse door banged open. Reverend Elijah stood in the doorway, hands on his hips and fury in his eyes. Sherilyn sat up and scooted away from the door in sleepy-eyed fear.

Dawn had come, and the room was cold.

Parker glanced guiltily at the small bed of coals that should be a roaring fire. He quickly grabbed a handful of books and threw them in, splashing sparks and ashes into the room.

"Get to your bed, girl," Elijah said.

Sherilyn scrambled to her feet, grabbed her blanket and book, and ran out the door without a backward glance.

"I keep you around out of pity," Elijah said to Parker. "You are not breeding stock, clearly you cannot follow directions, nor are you dependable. It is good for us to have a mute in the community so people can see the power of the Lord when one misuses his or her gifts, as surely you must have done in order to be struck dumb."

Parker calmly picked up a handful of kindling and threw it onto the blazing books.

This guy knew nothing. He knew nothing about Parker or his family or his gifts or his potential, and he was clearly beginning to believe his own bullshit.

But what struck terror in Parker's heart was the phrase *"I keep you around out of pity."* Elijah would not hesitate to banish Parker, so until the thaw, he had to play by the man's rules. Maybe he just needed to play stupid in order to keep Sherilyn safe.

"You can't even apologize for fraternizing with a young member of the opposite sex and keeping her here all night long. You can't even apologize for being asleep at the switch and letting the boiler run cold. You can't apologize, you can't explain, but I will see that you atone for this." He smiled. "Oh yes, you will atone. We have uses for people who cannot talk."

He turned and left the woodhouse.

Parker stoked the fire and added more wood. He was wrong to have fallen asleep, but he was not wrong for watching over his little sister. He didn't want trouble with Elijah, but he wouldn't shy away from it, either. As long as Sherilyn was safe, Parker would do anything, even atone for sins not committed. He squared his shoulders as he walked. Her safety was up to him, and he was up to the task. He had promised his father, and he had promised himself.

The vision of the world as it would become still played in the background of his mind as he packed the Harry Potter book into his backpack and prepared to be relieved of his duty. He'd get some sleep, and then meet Steven and work on a better project than burning books to warm Elijah's feet.

~ ~ ~

Discouraged that they didn't accomplish more than they did on their trip to Harwood, Willie surveyed his workbench in the dimness of twilight and tried to put a positive spin on it. They did get big bottles of Tylenol, they did deliver a baby—who was miraculously still alive—they did get some dog food for Alta, and they did get a glimpse of life outside of Rowan.

Turns out, it was the same as life inside Rowan.

There weren't even enough people left in Harwood to loot the Costco.

And he got nothing done on the wind generator.

That's okay. Castile got codeine for the two in pain. She grabbed those two bottles and ran to the infirmary as soon as they got back. The boys fed the dog.

He checked his watch. They had missed dinner, but someone would have kept something warm for them. He got the wind-up radio from his shop and took it next door to the great room to listen to the broadcasts.

When he and his wife Alice had moved into the cul-de-sac two years before Castile was born, it was a nice, calm little neighborhood. When the pandemic hit, it became empty, vacant, and sad as everyone but he and Castile had died. Alice was gone, and Castile moved back in to her childhood home after she buried her husband and twin boys.

But as people found them, most likely by seeing the woodfire smoke from first their chimney, and then all the chimneys in their little neighborhood, the cul-de-sac and surrounding houses had found life. First, they gutted the house at the end of the cul-de-sac and turned it into the Great Room and the Kitchen. They found a beautiful nickel-plated wood-burning stove for Mary and her crew to use to cook, and brought in all manner of chairs and sofas for people to sit in at meal time and during the evening broadcasts. Willie still lived next door to the main house, Castile now with him, and his garage was his workshop.

There were other changes, too. As the houses around the cul-de-sac were cleaned up, had wood burning stoves installed, and were inhabited by new people, a crew tore down all the backyard fences, making a large common ground, that Oscar said would be perfect for the community garden, come spring. Just behind the main house, they built a brick, wood-fired oven for bread. The infirmary was in the house directly behind the main house, on the other side of the common. One house was used as a bathhouse. Each group of four houses had its own latrine. One house was nothing but a community closet. Every room held stores of food, clothing, towels, bedding and so forth they brought back from the houses where they'd taken the dead to the park. Everyone worked surprisingly well together, with different teams and their chores. Everyone worked, and everyone got along with nothing but tiny minor squabbles. So far, at least.

When Willie got to the great room, Kimmie was already there, teaching her eight-year-old son how to knit by the light of the kerosene lamps. Paul was finishing up a piano lesson for Kimmie's older son, and a half dozen others chatted about their day. A tray of fresh cookies was on the side table, and Willie's stomach rumbled at their fragrance. He handed the radio to Cliff, one of the teenagers, who began to crank it up.

The clock in the corner flashed 11:11, as it had ever since the power went off.

Mary brought in a bowl of rice with vegetables and handed it to Willie, who took it gratefully. "I hear we have a baby," she said.

Everyone stopped talking. "A baby?" Kimmie asked.

"Castile delivered a baby girl in the hospital emergency room in Harwood," Willie said between bites.

"Alive?"

"Still alive, far as I know," Willie said. "They're here, in the infirmary where Castile can keep an eye on them. Carlo, Daniela and their baby Sophie."

"Wonderful!" Kimmie said. "I'll knit her something warm."

"Does this mean it's over?" Russell asked.

Willie shook his head. "Who knows?"

"It's six," Cliff said, stopped winding the radio, turned it on and set it on the table in the center of the room.

The familiar crackling sound felt comfortable to Willie as others came in quietly and took seats close enough to hear. Parents settled young children in the play area and reminded them to whisper while the adults were listening to the radio.

"CQ, CQ," the familiar voice said. "This is Roger Miner, broadcasting from Boulder, Colorado. A baby was born here last night and is thriving today."

Cheers went up from the small group.

Castile sneaked in quietly and sat next to her father. "What are they cheering about?"

"A healthy baby in Boulder," Willie said, the smile on his face feeling odd, as if he hadn't used those muscles in years.

Castile clapped her hands. "And one here, too. I just checked on them."

"Perhaps we *have* turned the corner," Russell said.

"We can only hope."

"As of today," Roger Miner continued, "we know of one hundred forty-seven communities in the United States, and we have heard from sixty-three others in Canada, Mexico and Europe. I will broadcast the locations of those groups at the end of this message. I encourage all who hear this to find one of those groups and establish community. Before that, we will hear from Mitchell Green with a simple way to purify water, Mike Burrell will tell how to keep your chicken flock healthy during the coldest part of the winter, and Monica Edmunson will take you through tonight's next step of building your transmitter so we can hear from all the groups out there. We want to hear from you. We need to hear from you. We want to know how you are making do with what you have, we want to know how you are governing yourselves, we want to know your lessons learned so we can share them with one another. There are other broadcasts from others on other channels. Be sure you monitor them all. And now, here's Mitchell."

Cliff picked up the radio and gave it another thirty seconds of vigorous cranking.

Willie didn't need to hear about purifying water, as that had been broadcast before, and they were doing all they knew how to do in that arena, but he did want to hear the next step in building a transmitter. Maybe then he could transmit his needs for some help with the wind generator. And he needed to tell the world that they were here, too.

He picked up his empty bowl and chopsticks and signaled for Castile to join him in the kitchen while the others listened. It wasn't the information that kept a few dozen people glued to the radio every night, it was the sound of society, of life in faraway places. They clung to it as to hope.

"How are Lila and Rose?" Willie asked.

"Sleeping peacefully for the first time in months," Castile said. "Grateful for the respite, but you know, Dad, something has to be done."

"I don't know what." He looked at his shoes, then up directly into her eyes. "You want to kill them?"

Castile shook her head. "I don't know. Something. We have to do something. I can't stand it. They can't stand it. They ask to be put down every day."

"Put down," Willie said softly.

"I'm taking it to the Committee," she said.

"You've done it before. Nobody can agree on what to do."

Castile planted her feet and put her hands on her hips. Mary set a steaming bowl of rice with vegetables on the counter in front of her. "Why is it up to the Committee? Why don't Rose and Lila have control over their own lives and their own deaths?"

"Because they have no way of taking their own lives," Willie said. "You know this. We've been over this again and again."

"We have guns," Castile said.

"You want to give Rose a gun so she can shoot herself?"

"Yes." Castile picked up the bowl of rice but didn't eat it.

"Would she use it?"

"She might. I don't know. Having the option would be a comfort to her, I think."

"Okay," Willie said. "Take it to the Committee. Not that you need my permission to do that."

Castile nodded and took a bite of her dinner.

Willie looked at the resolve on her face and knew that she was going to do whatever she had in her mind to do, no matter what the Committee said. Maybe that was a good thing. Who said these particular people on this particular Committee always knew the best actions to take? And furthermore, how would they decide, other than a majority of opinions based on…what?

There ought to be some type of a standard test against which every decision was weighed. The Committee was comprised of all good people with good hearts, but they were anchored in their opinions, which caused a fair amount of tension. That hadn't been a big problem so far, but it also didn't mean that their majority-rule decisions were always sound ones. And Lord knew that he didn't want to be the one making all these difficult decisions.

There had to be a better way. They needed a constitution of sorts, a creed, a code, a document that could see them all through this time and the times to come, a method of making decisions that would sustain the community and—if babies were going to again be born—see the community through the coming difficult years.

Maybe the next two hundred years. Five hundred years.

But then there were lots of wars started over misinterpretations in the Bible, in the Koran, even in the Constitution of the United States. Writing things down was dangerous, as hundreds of years down the line, unforeseen changes tended to take place. Writings tended to become crystalized and revered, when really they were just basic guidelines, and they ought to be open to reinterpretation on a regular basis. So maybe writing things down wasn't the best idea.

And yet, couldn't they do better than the world leaders had done in the past? It seemed that this group here, and the ones Roger Miner from Boulder was in touch with had a fresh canvas to work with.

With a drastically reduced population, the planet had an opportunity to heal itself, to right its equilibrium. And people had an opportunity to not pollute, to not overpopulate, to be gentle with resources and use them wisely.

A vision of how the planet could be began to form in Willie's mind. This could be a world of lushness, of abundance, of small, productive villages with educated children, with the best of technology not taken to its limits of ridiculousness but used wisely for the enhancement of all. Healthy, organic farms that respected the soil and produced nutritious food, calm communications with those far afield who compared notes and worked together to solve whatever problems that arose.

In a vision as clear as if he were looking across the planet from a low-flying airplane, he saw it all as it could be, saw that he could make a difference with this vision here in his tiny little community.

And perhaps it started with the whole idea of how to help Rose and Lila in their hour of need.

~ ~ ~

Castile awoke in the early hours and lay quietly listening.

The compound was absolutely silent. No traffic sounds, nobody up and rustling about. She and her father lived in his house, each with a bedroom to themselves. Mary, who was in charge of the communal kitchen, slept in the third bedroom with her eighteen-year-old daughter Katy, who tended the library and organized all the educational materials for the children. Katy also taught language arts to the younger ones. Everyone took a turn in the classrooms, officially teaching their specialty, but most of the youngsters learned by doing their chores, and those chores were rotated sufficiently to find out who had what talents and interests.

Jamaal was interested in medicine. He shadowed Castile when she visited the infirmary. They even did an autopsy once, with the help of books that Katy brought back from the local library, and they spent many hours together talking about the physical systems of the body, how they worked and what happened when things went awry. He was always first on the scene when there was an accident in the compound, whether it was a bump on the head, a cut that required stitches, even a broken finger. He tended to Rose and Lila as if they were his blood relatives.

Castile, with Willie's support, made sweeping decisions about the nutrition in the compound, no more than five percent animal protein, and after a little grumbling, everyone got used to it. She and Jamaal spent hours poring over books on nutrition and vitamins and micronutrients and minerals and what happened to the body when the nutritional needs were out of whack.

Once a month, they sat down with Mary and discussed their findings and the best way to nourish their community. They had plenty of food, that was not a problem, but maximizing nutrition was the goal, and a lot of what food they had on hand was nothing but empty calories. Mary had a lot to add to their knowledge base of human nutrition.

Mary had founded and run a world-renown five-star restaurant in Portland. She was smart and talented, ran her kitchen crew with a calm hand, and seemed to revel in the role of keeping inventory of foodstuffs, making menus, and fixing delicious, nutritious meals for everyone with very limited resources.

In the spring, they would begin to work the garden, and Oscar knew about that, so now and then he joined in on the nutrition meetings. Until it was time to break ground, Oscar spent time working on the composting systems. Just their small community generated an extraordinary amount of human waste, and he was convinced it could be turned into usable fertilizer. He had Lois working with him on that, and the garden plans. Castile couldn't be certain, but she thought Lois and Oscar had made a love connection while reviewing all their springtime plans. Castile saw how Oscar looked at Lois when they were going over the garden layout and lists of seeds they needed to acquire. It was a look of genuine affection.

Witnessing little baby Sophie's birth had been a life-changing event for Jamaal.

Witnessing Sophie's continued breathing was a life-changing event for Castile. New life, finally, after so much death. She had the little family stay in one of the bedrooms in the infirmary for a couple of days while Sally Jane readied family quarters for them, and once moved to their new quarters, the baby was not to leave there for thirty days. Soon, Willie would take Carlo and one of the boys to fetch whatever household things they needed from their previous home, as Carlo and Daniela were thrilled to be invited to move into the compound.

Once her mind had turned to the infirmary, Castile began to worry about Lila and Rose. Were they awake? Were they in pain? She threw off her covers and pulled on leggings and her shearling boots, then wrapped herself in her down coat—all scavenged from nearby houses, from people who no longer had earthly use for their things. She walked quietly through the moonlit house and out the back door, across the well-worn path in the snow to the infirmary.

At the front door, she lit a candle and carried it quietly through the kitchen, into what used to be the family room, now Rose and Lila's room. Carlo, Daniela and the baby were in the far bedroom, so it wasn't likely she was going to make enough noise to wake them.

Rose slept noisily on her back, her mouth open, her breathing ragged and uneven, but at least she was asleep. Castile put a hand on the woman's foot and wished her peace, wished her a peaceful journey, hopefully sooner rather than later.

Across the room, Lila was too quiet in her bed. In the moonlight coming through the filmy draperies, Castile saw the big bottle of Tylenol with codeine on the nightstand, the cap unscrewed, an empty glass next to it.

Castile touched the woman's neck and felt no life, no pulse. Lila's flesh was cold and dead. This was what Castile had prayed for, and yet now that it was here, she was sorry.

Lila, in pain enough to scream at times, had been a gentle, gracious soul, and she and Castile had talked into the sleepless night on many occasions.

Lila had the wherewithal to take the pills when offered. Castile only wished she'd had the courage to do what someone else had done. This was the Tylenol with codeine that she had brought back from the hospital just yesterday. Nobody else knew about it except her dad, Jamaal and Robby.

Jamaal.

Had he held her head while she drank the pills down? Did he count them out in her hand? Did he know how many she could tolerate without throwing them up? She had been so weak, her liver so compromised, it couldn't have taken many.

Did he hold her hand and talk to her while she fearlessly made her transition? Had he spoken soft words of love and encouragement and his vision for her afterlife? Had he cursed Castile for leaving this difficult task to a teenager the way she was currently cursing herself?

Had Rose been given the same offer and refused?

Maybe not. Maybe one merciful death at a time was enough for Jamaal.

Bless him. Bless him. She could hear Lila's tiny, thready voice: "Bless you, boy,"

Regret. Regret burned like acid in her solar plexus.

Regret that she hadn't been a better mother to her dead sons, regret that she hadn't been a better wife to her dead husband, a better nurse to her patients, a better daughter, friend, sister... caregiver.

Regrets.

Castile screwed the top back on the bottle and returned it to the cabinet of medications in the kitchen.

Then she went back to Lila, sat on the edge of her friend's bed, stroked her lifeless hand and cried.

It had taken a teenage kid to teach her how to act like a woman, but from now on, she would stand up for what is right. Committee or no Committee.

Chapter 3 – March

Amanda knocked softly, then opened the door to Elijah's office. The calendar said it was her night to sleep with him, and she hoped that he was distracted enough to want to be alone.

He moved chairs around and then pulled out the sofa bed, then sat on its edge, slumped and apparently exhausted. "Don't they see what we're doing here? Don't they see that we have the opportunity to do things differently this time?"

Amanda sat next to him. Maybe the best she could hope for was that he got this over quickly and she could go back to her own bed. She put her hand on his back in what she hoped was a reassuring gesture. "They're struggling with many changes, Sam. They're not angry with you."

"Seems like it. Seems like they're all ungrateful jerks. They have no idea how stressful it is to lead like this."

"They need a strong leader."

"Well, of course they do. That's the whole point. Nobody else stepped up. I'm happy to do it, leadership is one of my God-given talents. This role is both a blessing and a burden, but I am happy to shoulder it for the new world."

Amanda squeezed her eyes shut. She was playing a role here, just like he was. Being Sister Matthew was no easy task. She was here to assure a place of safety for her daughter, Reyna. And for that, she would do whatever she had to do. Leadership was certainly never one of Sam's talents, and neither was preaching. In fact, she could never quite put her finger on what it was that he wanted. To rule the world? To save mankind? He had no clear message, not like he had when he sold cars, when "Bad credit, no credit? no problem. Come see us!" Was his battle cry. Short and sweet and it had made him a lot of money.

But this. This was something else. He had a taste of whatever power he thought he wielded over his little "flock" as he called the residents in the high school, and he wanted more.

"They will come to see your sacrifices," she said. "Everyone is still grieving their lost ones, their lost lives." She rubbed the back of his neck.

"We all are, but that doesn't mean they need to sabotage my efforts."

"I don't think they're sabotaging. There are lots of opinions. Some will leave come spring."

Sam snorted. "I would like to see them try to strike out on their own. I would like to see them try to set up a community that is run as well as this one." He took her hand. "We've done a good thing here, but it's so hard." He rubbed his hands through his hair. "It's so damn hard." He looked up at her. "Are we really feeding them too little?"

Yes! she wanted to shout. *You are a cruel and power-hungry fraud.* But that would not get her what she wanted, which was to be safe, and being Sam's number one woman was the safest place she knew of at the moment. "Excess was one of the reasons that the world collapsed," she said.

"I could never do this without you next to me," he said. "This being Elijah is one tough job."

"We're making good progress," she said, whatever that meant. She just knew that he liked to hear it. She had no idea why he picked religion as his crowd control mechanism. He didn't know anything about the Bible. There were a few women who had his ear, she knew, and she assumed he was getting all his preaching lessons from them. They should be in his bed, then, not her.

"And soon we'll start having babies," Sam said, his hand slipping under her blouse. "The next generation will know how to do things the right way. We'll teach them."

Amanda was glad she had found that cache of birth control pills in the Safeway pharmacy, and she never failed to take one. And she handed them out freely to all Elijah's other women, and any other woman who wanted them.

Sam would shit if he knew.

Amanda would do anything to survive, and see to the safety of her daughter, Reyna. The flu had taken her husband and son, but she and Reyna survived, and if she needed to bed Sam York, from Sam York Ford, aka Elijah, then she would. And she would see that Reyna was safe and warm and fed, even if it meant a misguided dose of Elijah-speak and warped scripture. Reyna was thirteen, and Amanda got to spend a lot of extra time with her in the kitchen where she could work to contradict some of the ideas Elijah and a few of these religious cult people were putting into her head.

Susie was one of those religious people. She was the one who came to Amanda's door, looking for survivors and food, and Amanda had bundled Reyna up and gone with her. Now Susie was in charge of the kitchen, and Amanda was the one going out searching for survivors and stocked pantries that they could raid.

Amanda knew exactly what she was doing when she shed her knickers for Sam. She didn't want to, but everything had a price.

Sam pulled her back onto the uncomfortable mattress, climbed on top of her, and began his rooting around and huffing, the acrid stink of his unwashed sweat sharp in her nostrils. She turned her head to the side and made little noises to make him think that she was enjoying herself. In reality, she was counting the days until the sun melted the snow and people from everywhere came out of their isolation and began to travel.

As soon as there were buses, she and Reyna would be on the first one out of town. Headed south where the weather wasn't out to kill them on a regular basis.

~ ~ ~

Parker pulled his file from the cabinet in the science lab, found his mechanical pencil, sat down at the big table, and looked over the work he'd completed the day before. The schematic looked good, and he was pretty sure it was not only accurate, but the tweaks he'd put in would make the building's electrical system more efficient.

Steven came in, set his backpack on the table next to Parker's, unzipped it and unloaded a bunch of textbooks. "Hi," he said.

Parker nodded his head.

"Hey, do you mind if I ask you a few questions?"

Parker shrugged, put his pencil down and leaned back in his

chair. Steven was probably thirty years old, very smart. Had some kind of a degree from some fancy college, but Parker couldn't quite remember which one, nor could he remember what Steven had studied. He looked like a professor, slim and tidy with round glasses and a receding hairline.

"You can read, right?"

Parker nodded.

"Can you write?"

Parker screwed up his face, and waffled his hand as if to say, "sort of." He shrugged and then shook his head no, not really. Whatever took his power of speech had also taken that aspect of communication from him.

"And yet you understand these schematics and can modify and draw them?

Parker nodded.

"I guess we all have our talents."

Parker opened his backpack and pulled out a heavy textbook titled *Basic Electrical Theory*. He pushed it across the table toward Steven.

"You finished this? I just gave it to you last week."

Parker nodded. He pulled the book back and thumbed through until he found a dogeared page, the beginning of a chapter on alternative power sources. He pushed the open book back toward Steven, who picked it up and sat on the edge of the table.

"This is exactly what I've been reading about," Steven said, and grabbed the stack of books he'd brought with him. He picked up a blue one and handed it to Parker. "There's a whole chapter here on zero point energy."

Parker shook his head. That was a waste of time. He flipped pages to a page on solar panels.

"Solar. Yeah, of course, but we don't have any of those. I don't know how to build one of those."

Parker gestured broadly at the windows, taking in the whole city.

"Well hell yes," Steven said, finally understanding. "There must be thousands unused on rooftops all over the city."

Parker nodded.

"Good thinking, buddy. Can't believe I didn't think of that. Duh. So much for a philosophy major." He pointed at the schematic Parker was working on. "Will this work with solar panels?

Parker shook his head no, but pulled other drawings from the file folder in front of him. He shuffled through them and handed one to Steven. It was rustic, but the basic information had been sketched in on solar panels and how to hook them into the school's electrical system along with a series of car batteries.

"Well done!" Clearly excited, Steven handed the sheet back to Parker. "Pretty this one up, and I'll get permission to go harvest some panels from around town."

The door opened and Don, the third member of their team came in. Older than Steven, Don sported a thick, heavy beard and a thin ponytail. "Elijah wants us to go provisioning."

Steven stood up. "Us again? Now?"

"Yep. The three of us."

"Isn't it too soon? Too much exposure to the poisoned air and so forth?"

"I don't know," Don said. "I told him we had plenty of provisions, and what was more important was figuring out how to hook up electricity to this building."

"And?"

"He didn't care. He doesn't seem to think electricity is a priority."

"For cryin' out loud." Steven shoved books back into his backpack.

"You know when Elijah speaks…"

"Yeah, yeah. Okay. You driving?"

"Sure."

Ten minutes later, the three were in the brand-new pickup truck that Elijah had donated for the express purpose of running around town and getting everything they could find and taking it back to the elementary school across the street. What Elijah called "provisioning." Don, the oldest of the three, who used to be married before his wife died of the flu, jumped into the driver's seat with a list. He handed the list to Parker, riding shotgun, with Steven in the back seat behind him.

Flour, sugar, corn starch, yeast, sheets, pillows, blankets.

Parker handed it to Steven.

"We've already cleaned out the Safeway," Steven said, adjusting his green John Deere hat. "I think we have the entire store over in the grade school buildings. There isn't any flour and sugar in there?"

Don started the truck and they pulled out of the parking lot and headed into Harwood. "Looks like they are going to be baking some fresh bread," he said. "I love me some fresh baked bread."

It felt good to get out of the school and out on the road, in the fresh air. March brought with it some drizzle which melted most of the snow, but February had not had its two weeks of what his mom used to call "pea planting" weather. Every February, she counted on two weeks of sun and mild temperatures that got people outside and too eager to exclaim that winter was over. Afterward, March came in with its cold fog and drizzle, and literally dampened spirits all across the region. But the peas were always in, and it wasn't long before they germinated and showed faith that spring would eventually arrive.

Right now, Parker was happy to see rows and rows of daffodils up everywhere, in rows, in clusters, in front yards, and singly in surprising places, like behind the abandoned and ruined gas station.

Was there a gardening committee at the school? Where was the garden going to go? Had they prepared the beds? Had they planted peas yet? He hadn't heard anything about it. Was the ground really poisoned? Too poisoned for a garden? Was the air really poisoned? He rolled down his window and took a deep breath. Smelled clean and fresh. Felt good on his face.

He remembered the daffodils and other bulbs that came up around the base of the big tree in their front yard. His mom had worked so hard to make a pretty spring petticoat for that tree, and the memory threatened to sink him.

Maybe he should take Sherilyn over to their old house and see if their mom left any pea seeds, or other vegetable seeds they could plant in the back yard raised beds. That would be good to have when they moved back there.

The idea that he and his little sister would move back into their house brought with it both a feeling of homesickness and a real knowledge, however much he didn't want to consciously admit it, that they would never go back there to live. He couldn't manage it, and Sherilyn enjoyed the new friends she was making in her classes.

But what did that mean? They would be stuck there for… how long? He had no way to get her back to their house anyway.

As if summoned by his suddenly downcast mood, rain began to fall.

Don slowed the truck down as they passed through downtown Harwood. They didn't see a single other working vehicle on the road. Saw no other people. The world had been abandoned.

"Starbucks," he said, and smacked his lips. "Boy, what I wouldn't give for a grandé latte right about now."

"No coffee for us," Steven said.

"I know. Elijah is an ass," Don responded. "If I had a way to make it, I'd bust into that store and come out with a dozen pounds of that good coffee."

The Starbucks merely looked closed. Nobody had molested it. Clearly, coffee was not a priority for any survivor.

"Let's get that electricity going," Steven said from the back seat. "Then maybe you can be our little bootlegging barista."

Parker reached over and turned on the radio. Thin static. He pressed the "seek" button, and the digital numbers went up, pausing now and then for more static, through the whole range, and then back to where they started. Nothing.

"Well, lookee there," Don said. He stopped the truck and backed up, looking down a side street. Two people were loading a big chair into the back of a pickup truck. A man and a woman and a black and white dog.

"Let's go talk to them," Steven said.

"Do you think we should?" Don asked. "And say what?"

"I don't know. Let's just be neighborly. They don't look very dangerous."

Don put the truck in gear and drove slowly toward the pair, who were pulling a tarp over the chair and a table they had already loaded.

Parker and Steven both rolled down their windows. "Hi," Steven called.

Willie gave them a glance, then kept working to tie down the tarp as the rain was beginning to pick up. "Hi," he said. He tied off the knot. "Get in the truck," he said to the woman.

He took a couple of wary steps toward them. "What can I do for you?"

"Nothing," Steven said. "Just surprised to find other people out and about is all. I'm Steven, this is Parker and Don is driving. We're from the group over at Jefferson High School on Lansing Road."

"Big group?" Willie looked in at them, paying particular attention to Parker. Not liking being scrutinized, Parker looked down at his hands, but not before he noticed the warm color around the man.

"Maybe seventy," Don said. "Maybe more. Run by Elijah. Do you know about it?"

"Nope," Willie said. "What are you fellows out doing?"

"We have a shopping list," Steven said, and held it up.

Willie took a step closer and took the list. "You'll find all that stuff over at the Walmart off 99. People have been pretty respectful there, not like at the Safeway, where some greedy assholes went in and totally cleaned it out. At Walmart, the pharmacy's empty, but there's still a lot of stuff on the shelves. Probably sheets and blankets, too." He handed the list back to Steven.

Don leaned across Parker. "Have you been to Costco?"

Willie nodded. "There's a self-appointed guy monitoring it so it doesn't get looted like Safeway."

"You got people? You got a group?" Don asked. "Are other people alive?"

Willie squinted at them, looked again at Parker. "It's time we got going," he said and turned back toward his truck.

Don turned the truck around and headed out toward the Walmart store. "Good info," he said.

Parker couldn't stop thinking about the man's sparkly blue eyes.

They were kind. They were compassionate. It seemed that the man investigated him, and him alone. What was that about? He wanted to get out of the truck and go with that guy and the woman. He didn't know why, he just wanted to be with them.

~ ~ ~

When they pulled back up at the high school, two men came to help them unload. Sister Matthew came out and told Don that Elijah wanted to see the three of them.

He rolled his eyes at Parker and Steven. "Elijah beckons," he said, "as always." Clearly, he had been through this routine before. He handed the truck keys to Sister Matthew.

As the three mounted the front stairs of the school, Parker carrying the little battery-operated radio he had found, Don said quietly, "I'll do the talking."

Elijah was in his office, which used to be the principal's office, but was now his bedroom, too. All the shelves which used to hold textbooks and reference books were now bare. Parker knew where the books were, and it made him sad.

Elijah immediately came around to the front of his desk as the three entered. "Who did you see while you were out?" He seemed extraordinarily aggressive and defensive at the same time, crossing his arms over his chest.

"Nobody," Don said.

"Did you retrieve the necessary items?"

"Yes."

"From where?"

"There's still some stuff at Costco."

Elijah narrowed his eyes in suspicion. "Costco has flour? Sheets? What else did you get at Costco?"

"Everything you wanted." Don looked the shorter man squarely in the eyes.

Parker was surprised that Don could lie so easily to Elijah.

Elijah moved to Parker and grabbed at the box in his hand. "What's this?"

Parker looked to Don, who nodded, and let go of the box.

"It's a radio. And some batteries. The kid wanted it, I thought it was okay."

"*No technology*," Elijah said forcefully, squarely into Parker's face. Parker kept his eyes on the empty bookshelves until Elijah passed by and stood in front of Steven, trying to catch one of them in a lie. "You saw no one out there? Is this true?" he asked Steven.

"Why would we lie to you?" Steven said, meeting the man's suspicious gaze.

"You only went to Costco?"

"Now what did Don just say?" Steven responded as if to a child.

Elijah turned back toward his desk, still holding the radio and package of batteries. "Get out," he said.

The three filed out. Parker and Steven went back to the lab to continue their work. Don went somewhere else.

Parker sat in front of his drawings and picked up his pencil. Was a little radio considered technology? Maybe the broadcasts he used to listen to were still happening. They could learn things from others who were out there.

"Those people we met were good people," Steven said. "There's no reason for Elijah to know about them. You know that Safeway he was talking about? We were the assholes that looted the entire store and are hoarding all the stuff, leaving nothing for anybody else. We know there are others out there. I didn't want that to happen to the Walmart."

Parker nodded.

"Elijah is not a good guy," Steven continued. "Most of us will leave when the thaw comes."

Leave? Parker's eyebrows went up.

"We'll take what we need from the community stores and head south. There's a small group of us. You and your sister are welcome to join us."

Parker tapped his pencil eraser on his paper. He liked Steven. He liked Don. He liked most of the people here, but he wanted to be with the guy who had the sparkling blue eyes. He nodded noncommittally and picked up his ruler.

~ ~ ~

"There was a kid," Willie said to Castile as she put a bowl of hot soup in front of him on his garage worktable.

"You saw a kid? How old?"

"I don't know. Fifteen, sixteen, maybe. He was with two adults. Two guys. They were looking for some supplies. Said they were with a group at the high school."

"I didn't know there was a group at the high school. Which high school?"

"Lansing Road?"

"Oh yeah, over there. Jefferson." She poured herself a cup of coffee, pulled up a stool and sat next to her sweaty dad. "You did a good job of bringing Daniela and Carlo's stuff over."

"We only got some furniture. Daniela wants to go back for some personal stuff."

"So what about the kid?"

Willie stopped eating, stared off into the distance. "I don't know. There was just something about him."

"Something like what?"

"Can't put my finger on it, Buttercup. They all seemed to be nice guys... I don't know. Something unusual, maybe special about that kid."

"Did you tell them where we were?"

Willie raised his eyebrows and looked at her over the top of his glasses as if he couldn't believe she had asked the question. "What's the first rule of Fight Club?"

"Don't talk about Fight Club."

"Precisely."

"Two things happened while you were gone. First, Rose died."

"I'm sorry," Willie said.

"It was her time," Castile said, taking a deep breath. "It was maybe past her time. The crew took her to the park, and now the infirmary is very empty."

"You nursed her well."

"I did what I could. I always think I could have done more."

"And the second thing?"

"Oh, yeah. The gleaning crew found a small herd of starving

goats," she said.

"Goats?"

"Five. One billy and three nannies. Robby found some grain in the barn and fed them, then went back with water and filled their trough, but he wants to bring them here."

"I don't know…"

"We should do it, Dad," Castile said. "Robert said he could fence in a portion of Emerson Park, and there's even that little shelter for them. In the meantime, the house across the street has a completely fenced yard."

"More mouths to feed," Willie said.

"You want to just leave them to starve to death?"

"We can't save everything, and everyone, honey."

"Robby wants to put the little kids in charge of taking care of them. And you know there's plenty for goats to eat. Everywhere."

As usual, Willie knew he wasn't going to win. The tide was against him with this one. "Fine," he said. "Whatever."

She gave him a hug. "It'll be good for Robby, good for the kids, and Mary will like having goat's milk on hand. Said she'd make cheese."

"Cheese?" Willie wiggled his eyebrows at his daughter and made her laugh.

He gave her a big smile and looked at his watch. 5:58. Time for the broadcast. He picked up his bowl of soup and chunk of bread and went into the great room to join the rest, Alta at his heels, as always.

"CQ, CQ," the familiar voice said from the little wind-up radio. "This is Roger Miner, broadcasting from Boulder, Colorado. We are still in the middle of a deep freeze here with twenty-four inches of snow, but we understand that spring is approaching some of the low-lying lands to the west and to the south."

It was true. The rains had melted the snow, and Willie smelled spring when he went outside. Little flowers were blooming all over town as if they had no idea what was happening with the human population.

"We hope you have been working on your compost piles," Roger went on, because today we're going to start a series of high-intensity gardening sessions from Nancy Neff, our Master Gardener. But first—"

Roger was interrupted by loud knocking at the front door.

Alta barked and charged the door.

Willie's heart immediately began to beat harder. He looked around the room. Almost everyone in the community was here, except ()Daniela and Carlo, still sequestered with their baby.

Robby turned down the radio. Oscar grabbed it. "I need to hear this," he said, motioned to Lois to follow him, and took the radio into the back room.

Willie stood up, along with Ned and Dusty, two of the larger men, and the three went to the front door. Ned held onto Alta's collar.

Willie turned the knob.

Three masked ruffians pushed their way through the door, one carrying a baseball bat, catching Willie off guard and off balance, and he took steps backward, pushing Ned and Dusty back to the wall. "Everybody down!" the interlopers yelled.

Most of the people in the great room complied, sliding from their chairs or their seats on the sofas to the floor.

"Now what's this about?" Willie asked.

Alta growled.

"Control that dog," one of them said, "or I'll shoot it."

Ned took a firmer grip on Alta's collar.

The oldest one, couldn't be more than twenty, pushed Willie back. "We told you to get down, grandpa."

"I'm too old to get down on the ground. Why don't you tell us what it is that you need?"

"Get the fuck on the ground! Now!" He pointed at him with what he clearly hoped looked like a gun pushing through his jacket pocket, but Willie knew it was just his fingers. These guys were desperate.

"Stuff," the apparently self-appointed leader said. "We need stuff. We need food. You have it, we're going to take it."

"You could ask nicely," Dusty said. "We have food to share."

Mary stood up. "I have a nice pot of chicken and rice soup and some fresh bread. Would you boys like a bowl?"

The three desperados looked at one another.

One pulled down his bandana. He couldn't have been more than eighteen. "Yes, ma'am," he said. The leader scowled and jabbed his elbow at him. "These are nice people, Mac. I'm hungry." He looked at Willie. "We're all hungry."

The other one pulled down his mask as well. "It smells so good it makes my belly ache," he said.

All the wind out of the leader's sails, his shoulders slumped, bravado failed. He followed the other two who were beckoned by Mary toward the kitchen.

"Check for weapons," Ned said quietly to Willie, who followed them.

Willie watched Mary dish up three steaming, fragrant bowls of her good hearty soup and put them in front of the boys at the kitchen's breakfast bar. The leader, Mac, had to pull down his mask in order to eat.

They were all skinny, unwashed, with long, stringy brown hair. Willie could smell that neither them nor their clothes had been washed in months.

At first, Willie thought they might be part of the Lansing Road high school group, but those people he saw didn't look like they were starving. These kids were desperate to eat. "You boys on your own?" he asked.

"Yes, sir," one of them said around a mouthful of Mary's delicious bread. "We ate all our food weeks ago." He picked up his bowl and drank down the broth, then held it up for more. Mary ladled more into it.

"There's food in all these houses," Willie said. "Why are you so hungry? Why are you so desperate?"

"Dead people," the youngest one said. "Mac says it's a desecration to see their dead bodies and to take their food."

"Those people have no more use for the food," Mary said. "They would want it to go to good use."

"I can't look at the dead people," the eldest said. "I can't smell them, either."

"It's just biology," Willie said. "Sad, but biology just the same. We've been taking bodies out of their homes and putting them in the park, to let nature have its way with them."

"Whew!" one of them said. "I ain't going anywhere near that park."

Oscar and Lois had brought the radio back from the bedroom, now that the drama had settled down and everyone was back in their seats. Half the people were listening to the conversation in the kitchen, and the other half listening to the gardening lesson.

Mac's ears perked up at the sound of voices on the radio. "There are others, then?" Mac asked. "Where?"

"Little pockets all over the place," Willie replied. "This group that we're listening to is from Boulder, Colorado."

"Our sister lives in Boulder," Mac said, suddenly alert. "Well, she used to. I wonder if she's still alive." He looked at his brothers. "We could go there."

"We could stay here," one of them said.

"I'm Willie," Willie said, and held out his hand. "This is Mary. She's in charge of the kitchen."

"Troy," one said, took off his knitted hat, and shook Willie's hand. "Thank you for the food."

"Owen," the other one said, and also shook Willie's hand.

"I'm Mac." He was too busy eating to shake hands.

"Mac's our older brother," Troy said. "He's done a good job taking care of us, but it just got too hard."

"No need to be ashamed of desperation," Willie said, noting the family resemblance for the first time. "Most of us here have felt that to some degree. Are you armed?"

Troy and Owen shook their heads. "Just the ball bat. We've met with resistance, though, with people who have food and don't want to share, so we thought we'd try something different this time," Troy said.

"One guy ran us off with a shotgun," Owen said.

"Someday I'm going to go back for that guy," Mac said.

"He's just desperate and scared, too," Willie said. "Don't harbor feelings of resentment. He's just trying to protect his own."

Castile came into the kitchen and watched the way the boys shoveled food into their mouths. When they had had their fill, they sat back.

"You're welcome to a bath and some fresh clothes," she said.

"Seriously?" Troy looked as if she had offered him riches.

"Of course. I'm sure we have extra clothes that will fit all of you."

Against the whispered dissent from some of the other members, Castile took the boys to the bathhouse, the community closet, and then to the Olson house, just a block away. She got a fire going in the woodstove and made sure the beds were made. Mac got the master bedroom, and Troy and Owen got the twin beds in the kids' room.

"Fresh sheets," Troy said quietly, surveying the room with what appeared to be worship. Owen couldn't stop running his hands through his clean hair. Mac frowned at both of them. "Don't get too comfy," he said. "We ain't staying here."

"You boys sleep well," Castile said. "Breakfast is at seven. There's lots of work to be done around here if you do decide to stay."

"That front door have a lock on it?" Mac asked.

"Of course," Castile said, sad but not surprised that the boys had such feelings of insecurity. At least Mac did, but then he was the elder, the caretaker of the group. "This is a regular house. We want you to feel safe."

By the time Castile went back to the Great Room, most everybody had gone to bed. Willie sat up waiting for her, with a cup of tea and a cookie to share.

"The young ones want to stay, but the older one wants to hit the road."

"You invite them to stay?"

Castile took a bite of the cookie. "Yes. Good, strong boys who need a community. Our teens could stand to have a couple of friends."

"After you left," Willie said, "Oscar and Lois presented their detailed plans for the garden. Lordy, you should see what they have

85

in mind. They're going to need a lot of help." He paused, thinking about those three boys. Would the elder one be a problem? Maybe. "Oh! Oscar has a solar panel hooked up, powering a dehydrator. It's already working over at the Dodge house. He dehydrated a can of mandarin oranges and passed them around in a little bowl. They were like candy. Everybody got pretty excited about that."

"If we can get real electricity going, we can power up a freezer," Castile said. "Or two, for all that produce."

"I know, I know," Willie sighed. "That was mentioned, too. I'm working on it. You know I'm working on it."

"You'll get there, Dad," Castile said. "We'll all get there, eventually. One step at a time."

Willie smiled a weary smile at his beautiful, competent daughter who favored her mother in more than just looks. "Time for this old man to hit the sack."

"I'm right behind you."

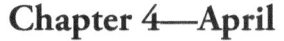

Chapter 4—April

The tightness in his chest woke Parker in the early hours. He lay quietly, listening to the squeaking of cots, farting, and snoring of the other men in the gym. He turned over on his side to look at the moonlight coming in the window. Oregon trees were silhouetted in black and silver perfection against the bright night sky. He took a deep breath. He knew this tightness, this heart pounding feeling of impending... impending something, and he didn't like it. Didn't want it. Hoped he could wish it away.

It lasted through breakfast. He saw Sherilyn, and they waved at each other across the cafeteria, but he was unable to smile. He tried to eat but had little appetite. He sat alone at a table, the worry turning into faint nausea, and afterward tried to get to his desk instead of staying for Elijah's preach /fest. He'd rather be working on his drawings. Halfway down the hall, however, people turned him around, patted him on the back, and one dreaded step at a time, he followed along and took a seat near the back door, not exactly ready to hear Elijah's version of religion.

Again, Sherilyn smiled and waved. He nodded.

Elijah got up and addressed the crowd. "Never forget," he started. "Never, ever forget what brought us to this point, to the brink of disaster, to the collapse of civilization. Evil. Sin. Technology. Those are the three legs of the stool of doom." He paused to mop his sweaty forehead. "It was evil, sin, and technology that killed our family members. Evil, sin, and technology that poisoned our air. Poisoned our water. Poisoned our land." His voice rose in passion.

He was not a natural preacher, and Parker paid more attention to the discomfort in his chest than he did to Elijah's message. Others in their seats had obviously heard this before, as there was a lot of shuffling, coughing, and impatience in the crowd.

"You are lucky that the Lord has brought you to me, to this refuge, to live a Godly lifestyle. We will have no sin, no error, no blasphemy here in this community. We will have no technology, no evil thoughts, no evil acts. This is exactly what God wants of us, and we will praise his name and give him his due."

The intensity in Parker's chest got so heavy, his heart pounded so hard he was sure everyone around him could hear it.

It was unbearable.

Stop resisting. The soft female voice in his ear was as gentle and clear as fresh water. He looked around to see who spoke to him, but there was no one there.

Trust.

All right. He would do as he was told. He stopped resisting, tried to relax, and the clamp on his chest eased.

Elijah was talking with someone in the front row, and Parker, against his will, against everything he wanted in the world, found himself standing up. And then, horrified by his own actions, he moved to the center aisle and walked up toward the front.

"Well!" Elijah said. "What is this? Go sit down, young man, you've no right to come up here."

But Parker was no longer in control of himself. Heart thumping, perspiration oozing out of him, he stood in front of Elijah, then turned and faced the people sitting at the cafeteria tables. He had their full attention, his greatest nightmare.

And then abruptly his heart slowed, the band around his chest completely relaxed. He took a deep breath, accepted what was about to happen, and no longer fighting it, he began to feel as though he was in the flow.

He cleared his throat. "Be not afraid," he said, his voice gravelly and unpracticed.

A loud murmur came up from the audience.

Sherilyn stood up. "Hush!" she yelled at everyone.

Elijah walked to the side to confer with the two men who provided his personal security.

Parker spoke, each word clearer than the last, each word with more confidence, more authority. "There is in the mind of God," he said, "a plan which embraces every creature of all his vast domains, and this plan is an eternal purpose of boundless opportunity, unlimited progress, and endless life. And the infinite treasures of such a matchless career are yours for the striving! The kingdom of heaven is within you, and the keys to that kingdom are sincerity, more sincerity, and more sincerity."

One of Elijah's goons grabbed Parker's arm. Parker shook him off. Two men in the front row threatened to stand up, ready to defend him.

"Empathy, compassion, and a love for humanity is what will rebuild this world," he said. "Nothing more, and nothing less. All the tools to achieve this are yours for the asking."

All the energy ran out of Parker, his knees weakened, and for a moment he thought he would fall to the ground.

The two men in the front row saw him falter and stood up to help him to a seat. He was barely cognizant of the spontaneous applause that arose from the crowd.

"Blasphemy," Elijah yelled. "Blasphemy! And lies! We've all been duped. Clearly the boy can speak!" He seemed to cast about for something else to say. "Everyone go to their chores!" He looked at his two henchmen. "Bring the kid to my office." He turned and stormed away, Sister Matthew hustling after him.

People crowded around Parker until Sister Ascot brought him a glass of water, which he gratefully drank down. She shooed all the rest of them away. "Give the boy some space," she said. "Give him some air."

Everyone seemed to want to touch him before they walked away. His shoulder, his head, his cheek, his knee.

Parker handed the empty glass back to Sister Ascot and put his head in his hands. He didn't understand any of this.

"Feel better?" a man asked.

Parker nodded.

"Elijah wants to see you."

Parker was not surprised. He stood up, solid again on his feet, and followed the man. Sister Ascot stood watching with the empty glass in her hand and a worried expression on her face.

Parker opened Elijah's office door and walked in with his escort. Elijah's face was red with fury.

"Talk to me!" he demanded.

Parker stood silently.

"I know you can talk, you fraud. It's either that, or you've been touched by God, and I don't believe that for a nanosecond. How dare you preach to my flock! How *dare* you! I don't know what your game is, but it is over here at this haven. You will rue the day that you stood in front of *my* congregation in *my* sanctuary. Pack your things and be gone by nightfall."

Parker's head snapped up. Gone? A thousand things ran through his mind. Should he take Sherilyn with him? How to get her away? They could go back to their old house. Is that even a good idea? What would they eat? What would be different than before they came here? Spring. Spring was different. It was April, and the snow had melted. They could go south with Steven. He wasn't even certain what he had said, but it seemed to have made an enormous impression on almost everyone.

He took a deep breath, lifted his head and looked Elijah straight in the eye. In a flash of insight, he realized that Elijah was powerless over him. He nodded.

"By *nightfall*," Elijah repeated.

He nodded again.

Just as he was about to turn and leave the room, Timothy and Russ, two of Elijah's young faithfuls, rushed through the door without knocking.

"What is this?" Elijah demanded.

"There's another community," Timothy said breathlessly, perspiration beading on his forehead.

"Not far from here," Russ said.

"Where?" Elijah demanded.

Timothy seemed to realize that Parker was in the room. He jerked his head toward the boy.

"Never mind him," Elijah said. "He's not talking to anybody."

"They're in a cul-de-sac a couple of miles north, just off Spring Creek road," Timothy said. "We were getting water from the river and saw them doing the same. We followed them. They've taken over all the houses on the cul-de-sac and down the street. Looks like there are a lot of them."

"What do they have?"

"A windmill, a big garden plot, new cars. A baby." Russ said.

"A windmill? A *baby*?"

"Playing on the front lawn of one of the houses. Looks Mexican."

"Mexican!" Elijah rubbed his chin. "All of them?"

"No, just the baby and the mom."

"Did they see you?"

"I don't think so," Timothy said. "We parked and got out for a better look. They look pretty organized."

"Okay, then." Parker could see Elijah's mental wheels turning. "You can go."

Timothy and Russ turned to leave. Elijah looked up, surprised to see Parker still in the room. "Get out!" he said.

~ ~ ~

Willie fitted the blades into the second windmill chassis and secured them with pop rivets. These weren't as sturdy and as durable as he would like, but it would do until he could figure out how to fabricate heavier metal.

The first, smaller windmill was powering two refrigerators and a freezer. He had them hooked up to a bank of car batteries, so they would keep cold on still days. Oscar had added a solar array in the side yard to power an oven, a stove, and several dehydrators, so food preservation was no longer an iffy proposition. Mary knew how to can produce, and if the stove worked, she would be canning all summer and into the fall harvest. They already had more eggs than they could eat as the hens had begun to lay again in the expanded chicken coop down the street. He was happy with the food confidence that Oscar and Lois and Mary exhibited.

The whole community was working well.

He put his rivet gun down and sat on the stool, looking out at the garden. A half dozen people were out there, weeding, planting, fertilizing, hauling fresh soil in from other gardens in the neighborhood, putting wood chips in the pathways, doing whatever

Oscar directed them to do. The garden, even in its earliest days, was a wonder. It took up six back yards, and the raised beds were laid out in a very pleasing geometric design. Most were for vegetables, Oscar told the group one evening, but there was also plenty of room for flowers. One of the houses had a beautiful rose garden, and Oscar had incorporated that into the design. He calculated that this garden, with a little extra help from the gleaning committee that went out daily to find orchards and fruit trees, and the chickens, would feed a hundred fifty people. More than that, they would have to take over another set of houses and replicate what they'd done here.

Lois walked over to Oscar, and he put his arm around her waist, tipped up her broad-brim gardening hat, then brought her in for a kiss. Willie had long suspected a love connection there, but this was the first evidence he had seen. They were both in their early thirties, and to his knowledge, neither had married, so they had not lost spouses or children. There were no other couples in the community except for Carlo and Daniela, but there were certainly young people, and he'd even seen a little flirting going on. Jamaal, for example, seemed to enjoy Anne's company, and more than once, Mary had to remind Anne that her free time was after the bread came out of the big ovens. Maybe it was time to implement those classes Castile had talked about—parenting and child rearing, so these kids made good, solid, eyes-open decisions, and didn't let hormones make their decisions for them. Maybe she had already had a talk with Anne and Jamaal, put them on birth control. He didn't know.

As if on cue, Castile knocked twice, then opened the shop door, carrying her cup of coffee. With her came the tantalizing aroma of baking bread, and Alta, who went immediately to her bed in the corner. "Mmm," Willie said. "Smells like Mary has upped her bread baking game."

Castile sat in one of the chairs. "She has indeed. Sourdough today. In the outside ovens." She looked at the enormous windmill parts on Willie's bench. "How's it going?"

"Good. I guess. Big but maybe fragile. I want it to pump water, so we can have running water."

"Flush toilets?" Castile asked.

"Well, that might be a while yet. The sewer system is complicated. The outhouses are working, are they not?"

"They are…"

"Hey," Willie said. "I've seen some springtime flirting going on among the teens. Remember you were going to start holding some classes on adulting or some such?"

"Think it's time?"

"I do. Do you need to pass the curriculum by the Committee?"

Castile scowled. "I'm up to *here* with the Committee."

"I know, but if not the Committee, then who?"

"Why pass a science curriculum by anybody?"

Willie looked at her over the top of his glasses.

"I know. I know." Castile sipped her coffee. "There's another situation, and it's going to be touchy."

"Great," Willie said. He crossed his arms over his chest, knowing that if Castile thought it was going to be touchy, then it was likely to be mightily controversial in the community, and the Committee was going to have a time of it.

"Oscar and Lois want to take over the Spencer house."

"That's good," Willie said. "Setting up housekeeping."

"Lois told me they wanted to try for a baby."

"Better yet!"

"Not so fast," Castile said. "Lois has some medical issues, which she has told me about, which I don't think anybody else knows."

"Fertility problems?"

"No, genetic problems. Her mother died of Huntington's Disease."

"I don't think I know exactly what that means."

"It's a terrible thing, Dad. It's genetic. Loss of motor control, dementia, all at an early age."

"Does she have it?"

"She hasn't exhibited any symptoms. She watched her mom die of it and she's scared that she might have it. She has the gene."

"Is this one of those things where Oscar has to have the other gene?"

"Maybe, but not necessarily."

Willie closed his eyes, worked his neck back and forth. He took a breath. "You want to keep them from having children?"

"To keep them from passing on those genetic traits, yes." Now Castile folded her arms across her chest. Willie knew that gesture, so much like her mother. This was not something that Castile was going to budge on.

"But what are the odds? Realistically."

Castile set her coffee down. "Listen," she said. "We have an opportunity here to cleanse some of the worst genetic strains in our species. I know we're just one small community, and I can't possibly know what other people are doing in this situation, but as a species, we've bred ourselves into a pit. This is a chance to start rectifying many things in society, and this is one that needs to be addressed."

"The Committee won't like it."

"Fuck the Committee," she said. "Oscar and Lois won't like it."

Willie looked out the window again. Oscar and Lois were talking over in the corner of the garden. Lois smiled at something Oscar said, and if Willie were closer, he was certain he would see the blush in her cheek.

"What's your plan?"

"Well," Castile said. "This is where the Committee might actually do some good. Oscar and Lois have options."

Willie shook his head. This girl. She had her head on straight, that was for sure, and she was going to cause no end of trouble for this group. "Make your case, then, but I think you're opening a can of worms. There used to be privacy laws about medical information."

"I'm trying to put a lid on a can of worms. Are you with me?"

"Don't lobby me."

"I'm not lobbying. I want to know if you see my point."

"I see it, and as a member of the Committee, I will hear your position."

Castile stood up. "Thanks, Dad."

"You're in for a rough ride on this," he said. "I hope you know that. Oscar and Lois might leave us."

"They might," she said. "But I don't think they will. I think they're smart, and I think the Committee will do the right thing."

~ ~ ~

Castile took a fresh cup of dandelion tea to her office in the infirmary. Since Carlo, Daniela and their healthy little Sophie had moved into their own home, and both Rose and Lila had died, there were no injuries, no sicknesses, nobody in the beds in the two sick rooms or in the great room. This was the one place she could come for peace and quiet.

The Committee meeting had gone much as she had expected. There were high emotions all around, as they debated reproductive rights and eugenics. Castile felt good about her presentation. She thought she had made her points clearly and dispassionately. The hard part was the look on Lois's face when she realized what the topic was. Castile had blindsided her and Oscar, even though she never mentioned them by name, and she felt bad about that.

She made her case, then sat down and let the debate rage. The ultimate decision was easily reached by everyone on the Committee: This was none of their business. This was for Oscar and Lois to decide.

Castile slipped off her shoes, put her feet up on her desk, and leaned back in her chair, hot tea in hand. Maybe they were right. Maybe this wasn't something that should or could be legislated. Maybe this was truly an educational issue. People, having the facts at their disposal, should be able to make the right choices.

But would they? History showed that they wouldn't. They certainly hadn't.

Oh well. The fate of nations did not rise or fall on the decision of one couple, nor did it depend on Castile's point of view. The rock in the pit of her stomach had to do with Lois believing that Castile had gone behind her back to do harm to her new relationship. That was something Castile was going to have to talk with Lois about.

She took a deep susurrating breath, closed her eyes. She'd talk with Lois after breakfast. That decision made, she tried to relax and wait for peace to wash over her, so she could go to bed and sleep well.

Tomorrow was going to be another challenging day, as were they all.

The front door opened, and footsteps made their way toward Castile's office.

She righted her chair and set her tea on the desk, ready to do some nursing.

But it was Lois who knocked softly on the office door and then pushed the door open. "Hi," she said.

"Hi," Castile said.

"What you did was brutal," Lois said, sitting in the chair next to Castile's desk. "It was mean-spirited and unfair. You took something I told you in confidence and broadcast it to the entire community." Her voice rose an octave as tears closed her throat. "I feel betrayed. Betrayed by you, Castile. I trusted you."

Castile handed her a tissue. "I'm sorry."

"Oscar is furious. We fought over this, Castile. We *fought* over this! He wanted to pack up and leave. He wanted to come over here and make a big scene. I made him go for a walk to cool off instead. He feels even more betrayed than I do, because you made this about me and suggested that I was making poor life choices. I don't like the feeling I have inside, Castile, and I don't know what to do. About you, who I thought was my friend."

"I should have talked with you and Oscar before bringing this up at Committee tonight," Castile said. "I'm so sorry about that. You didn't deserve to be blindsided."

"Yes, you should have," Lois said. "We may be a small community, but that does not give you the right to bring our personal business—my *medical* business—out in front of everybody."

"I will apologize to Oscar as well."

Lois sank back into the chair and cried quietly for a long moment. "What I came here to tell you is that you're right. I won't be having any babies. I didn't think about it exactly the way you presented it, although it has been in the back of my mind for a long time. My mom died a horrible death, but I always thought, "What are the chances of me marrying someone with the other gene?""

"Don't know," Castile said.

"Exactly." Lois's voice cracked, and she paused to control her emotions and blow her nose. "We owe it to the future generations, the future inhabitants of his world to give them the best." A tear fell out of her eye, and she brushed at it. "Somehow, for some unfathomable reason, we were left alive, immune from this horrible virus. Us. We're challenged to make all the right decisions."

Castile opened her arms, and her friend fell into them, sobbing, letting the dreams of having a family shatter and fall onto the ground at their feet.

"Just because you don't carry a child doesn't mean you can't be a mom," Castile said, whispering into her hair.

Lois took a deep breath and then sat up, wiping her face. "Well, that's a discussion for another day. Meanwhile, Oscar and I are going to get married."

"Wonderful," Castile said. "I'll tell Willie. He'll do the ceremony."

"He has already agreed," Lois wiped away a final tear. "Oscar asked him this afternoon. We're going to do it in the garden. In June, when the roses bloom."

"Perfect!" Castile said, feeling the rock in her belly begin to dissolve. "Our first wedding."

~ ~ ~

Steven took the van without asking and gave Parker and Sherilyn a ride back to their old house. It was twilight when they arrived, and the old street, and all the empty houses looked vacant with their dandelion lawns and dark windows.

It seemed unbearably sad.

"Thank you," Sherilyn said, as she got out of the van.

Parker tapped Steven on the shoulder.

"I'll come get you when we decide to leave," Steven said.

Parker nodded, knowing in his gut that Steven would never leave, or if he did, it would be in some kind of an emergency situation, and Parker and Sherilyn would be the group's last consideration. No, Parker had to take charge now, like an adult.

They waited on the sidewalk, avoiding even looking at the house, until they had waved Steven away and he went back to the warmth of the community in the high school.

"I don't know why you had to do that," Sherilyn said, fighting tears. "Why did you have to go and do that? Now what are we going to do?"

Parker took a deep breath. There was no way he could explain to her that he wasn't the one who was speaking. Someone was speaking *through* him. He wasn't the one who spoke at dinner that night, and he wasn't the one who spoke at the school cafeteria. He took his little sister's hand and led her up the walk toward the front door.

The house felt abandoned. There was no life in it. It still smelled like stale wood smoke from the fires he had set in the little hibachi in the master bedroom to keep them warm.

Sherilyn dropped her flowered backpack on the floor, rummaged around in it and came up with a candle.

Parker gave her a thumb's up. That helped.

He had learned things in the months they had been at the high school. He knew where to go to find food. He knew he could find a car to drive to go get the food. And he knew there was a place, in a cul-de-sac just off Spring Creek road, where there were other people. Maybe better people, maybe not. Maybe the guy with the blue eyes was there. Maybe not. But for now, they were fine.

He and Sherilyn wandered through the house before darkness took over. The house was exactly as they had left it. Dishes still in the kitchen cupboard. Bedding still on the beds. Sleeping bags and blankets still in the little room where they spent their time trying not to freeze to death during the winter. Tomorrow, they would wake up in this house, put their energy into it and it would be theirs again in no time.

"I hate it here," Sherilyn said. "But I hated it there, too."

Parker put his arm around her and started making a list in his head of everything he needed to do in the immediate future.

Sherilyn didn't even bother to light the candle. She handed it to her brother, then went to her room and closed the door. Parker knew she was due for a good cry, and he'd leave her to it.

He, too, went to his old room, but before he could go to bed, before he could send his sister to her bed with an empty belly, he had to get some food, and he knew where to go to get it.

He sat on his bed and mentally went through all the steps he was going to have to take to raid the Zimmermans' pantry. He should have dealt with their bodies when they were frozen, because this was going to be a completely different situation. Messy and awful. But he was no longer a kid, and he could no longer leave his sister's life up to the whims of whoever came driving by. He had to take charge.

He took a deep breath, stood up and went to the kitchen. All the flashlights were dead, of course, but he did have the candle. He put it in his shirt pocket, then got peppermint extract, poured some onto a dish towel and tied it around his face. Almost strong enough to gag him, but better that than what was coming. He got a pair of gloves and a tarp from the garage.

While there, he looked over his parents' car. Dusty, but probably full of gas. If the battery was still good, tomorrow he'd teach himself to drive on his way over to the Walmart to get some groceries. He'd take Sherilyn and she could get some new clothes while there. Maybe some new shoes. She'd like that.

He pulled the disengagement cord on the automatic garage opener and pulled up the big door. Night was coming on. He had to hurry.

The key was still in the lock of the back door to the neighbor's house, just as he had left it when he had run away from his promise to his father.

He took a deep breath, held it, and opened the door.

Dear God.

He ran, gagging, to the nearest bathroom and got as many towels as he could rip off the towel racks, and covered the fly-blown bodies.

He went outside to puke off the edge of the deck, deeply breathed in some fresh air, bolstered his resolve, then resettled the peppermint mask. Holding his breath as well as he could, he went back inside, where he covered Mr. and Mrs. Zimmerman with the tarp. Slowly and carefully, he tried to roll them onto it, so he could drag them out the door and down to the back of their property.

But they were juicy and loose, full of maggots, and they kept falling apart.

Eventually, he got most of them onto the tarp and then grabbed the end of it and pulled it out the door, across the deck, down the steps and into the cooling night. He kept going, all the way to the back fence where he had thrown the corpse of their cat. Was that just a couple of months ago? Seemed like years.

He went back to his garage for a shovel and a bucket to clean up the rest, mopped up with more towels, and then poured bleach all over the kitchen floor where they had been.

Then he went around the house and opened all the windows.

It was hard to imagine that he would ever be able to eat again, but he had a mission here, and he was going to see it through. This place would be better in the daylight, and he could come over and actually take inventory. He bet their car was full of gas, too.

The kitchen cabinet had lots of canned goods. He found a brown paper bag under the sink, and filled it with canned salmon, peas, beans, corn, potatoes (who would buy canned potatoes?), and some beef stew. That was enough for now.

He left the back door open so the flies could find their way out and went back to check on his little sister.

~ ~ ~

The trip to the big Walmart store went better than he anticipated. The best part was that the car started right up, which made Sherilyn squeal with happiness. Driving wasn't all that difficult since there were no other cars on the road. It didn't take him very long to get the hang of it.

He drove slowly down Spencer Road, trying out the brakes, trying out the accelerator, making various turns to figure out how the car worked. While he drove, they both looked for signs of life, but he didn't see any. If there were signs of people, Sherilyn would see them. She hadn't been out of the house or off the high school grounds since October. She was eager to be looking around. Oregon was beautiful in the spring. Even the dandelions looked good, along with blazing azaleas, budding rhododendrons, bright tulips and daffodils. Spring didn't know there'd been a disaster. A pandemic. Scraping clean the slate of human stupidity.

"Look!" Sherilyn said, pointing down a side street. "Dogs!"

A pack of dogs was tearing at something in the middle of the street. He didn't want to know what they were eating, and didn't want Sherilyn to know, either. He stepped on the accelerator and kept moving.

He ran over a curb when he pulled into the store driveway, making Sherilyn laugh. Then he drove right up to the front door and parked on the walkway. "There aren't even any other cars here and still you can't park," she said, her mood more jovial than he had seen it in months.

That mood turned wary when they got out of the car and stepped through the broken glass door. The stench of rotting meat and fish filled the air. Even as she held her nose, Parker took his sister by the hand and led her to the girls' clothing section. He pointed at the dress rack and held up three fingers.

Sherilyn hopped up and down with glee.

He pointed at the shoe department and held up two fingers, then tapped his wrist to indicate that she needed to waste no time. She nodded.

He went back for a cart and began going up and down aisles, looking for things they could use. All the usable things like lamp oil, candles, batteries and so forth were gone. But there was plenty of canned and dry food. He filled the cart, but not to overflowing. He remembered what the blue-eyed man said about people looting. He just wanted to take care of the two of them, and now that he knew how to do it, he could use the pantries of everybody on their street, although the thought of encountering more bodies made him queasy. The clothes he wore last night were airing out in the sun, but he could still smell the Zimmermans on them, and on himself. The smell was in his nose, perhaps permanently. He needed to bury the Zimmermans, because no matter where he was in his house or yard, he could still smell them.

He went to the garden section and loaded up three bags of

potting soil, and grabbed an assortment of vegetable seeds. He could cover the neighbors up with the soil, and then plant the seeds in his mother's raised beds. He didn't know much about it, except pulling the weeds she pointed out to him. He picked up a gardening book while he was there. Maybe Sherilyn would take a liking to the idea.

He got some soap and shampoo and that was enough for today. They'd stop at the river on the way home and wash themselves. Sherilyn would want to wash the rotten meat stench out of her new clothes.

Sherilyn found him before he made his way back to her. She had an armful of colorful dresses, was wearing new shoes, a pink headband on her blonde hair, and her eyes were bright and shining with delight. "I also got some jeans," she said. "Mine are too small now."

Parker realized that she'd had a birthday last month and was now twelve. Elijah didn't allow personal celebrations, and she'd been cheated. On the heels of that realization was another. Soon she'd be getting her period, and he had no idea how to help her navigate that. He doubted their mom had had time to have the talk with her the way their dad had had the talk with him.

Maybe he could find a book on that. Or maybe he'd find those other people. They'd probably have a woman who could explain things to Sherilyn. If Elijah's guys could find them, then he could, too. And he wanted to find them first.

He held up the seed packets.

"Good!" Sherilyn said in all her adorable childlike enthusiasm. "We'll make a garden!"

Chapter 5 - May

Sister Matthew sat at her desk preparing a report for Elijah on all the comments that had come in through the supposedly anonymous comment box she had set up in the cafeteria. Some of them were truly anonymous, but some had very recognizable handwriting. A couple of months ago, Elijah had sent out a questionnaire of every person in the community, asking them to list their "God-given gifts", in other words, their experience and any particular expertise, so that the community might make maximum use of everyone's talents. Those questionnaires and their answers were in a folder in her desk.

When she submitted her monthly report of the anonymous comments, Elijah always asked if she knew who wrote the suggestions, or more likely, the complaints, as they were almost all complaints. Sister Matthew always told him she didn't know who sent them. One of these days he would demand to see the originals, and he'd compare them with the questionnaires, and she didn't know what would happen to those people. Banned, she supposed. Kicked out, like that poor mute boy and his little sister.

"Sister?" She looked up to see Lily, one of the teenagers who helped in the school, standing in the doorway of her office, which used to be the math teacher's room.

"Yes?"

"Elijah wants to see you. Right now, he said."

"Thank you, dear." She collected her papers, put the comments back into the box and put it into her desk drawer.

Timothy and Russ were in Elijah's office when she knocked and opened the door. Elijah had his arms crossed over his chest and was leaning against his big desk. The boys stood uncomfortably silent, not making eye contact.

"There's another community in town," Elijah got right to the point. "These boys have been surveilling them for some weeks now, and it's time for us to send someone to infiltrate their organization. I want you."

Sister Matthew's hand flew to her mouth in reflex. "Me? Why

me?" The only reason she was here was to see to the health and welfare of her daughter, and if she wasn't here to keep Reyna safe, then... who knew what terrible things Elijah had up his sleeve.

"Because you'd be believable," Elijah said. "No one would suspect you."

"I can take Reyna with me?"

Elijah's lip curled. "No, she'll stay here with us."

"I can't possibly—"

"You can, and you will," Elijah said. "The boys say that some men from their group get water from the river at the same place twice a week. You're to look homeless and desperate, and see if they'll take you in. Then you can find times and ways to report back to the boys."

"Sam, no," she said.

"Elijah!" he said with force.

"Elijah, yes, of course, I'm sorry. I think I provide much more important service to the community here, as your assistant."

"Well, now you'll be my eyes and ears in the enemy camp."

"Enemy? They're our enemies? How is that?"

"Don't question me, woman." He turned to the two boys. "Take her out and tell her what you've told me. Make a plan and then execute it. You say they're there on Friday mornings?"

Russ nodded.

"Then Friday it is. You're all dismissed."

Sister Matthew tried one last time. "Elijah, please."

"I'll expect regular, very detailed reports from you," he said. "We need to know what we're dealing with. What and who." He turned his back to the three of them.

The boys left the room, and Sister Matthew, afraid that Elijah was finally going too far, closed the door firmly behind them. "I won't be used in this way," she said. "My daughter—"

Elijah turned and took a step closer to her. "You will do as I say."

"Why?"

"Why *what*?" Frustration began to show on Elijah's face. "Why will you do what I say, or why am I sending you on this mission?"

"Well, first the mission, and then the other."

Elijah took an exasperated breath as if he needed to explain things to a toddler, then sat on the edge of his desk. "Because there are few people left, and we need to all band together, that's why."

"We can't band together if you consider them enemies."

"That's just a figure of speech. We need one leader in this town, this state, this section of the world."

"And that would be you." Sister Matthew couldn't keep the sarcasm out of her voice.

"There is no better," he said.

"A real leader would go over there, introduce himself and find out how we can all work together. Why don't we try that, instead of infiltrating and spying and all that nonsense?"

"I assure you, I know much more about this than you."

"Oh?"

Elijah stared at her, his eyes hard. She met his stare, unflinching. This was the first time she had challenged him, but there were new, smaller challenges all over the compound, now that spring had arrived and people were out thinking new thoughts about going outside, breathing fresh air, talking amongst themselves about Elijah and their lives in this new age.

"You will do as I say, or you and your daughter can find your own way in the world."

"That's becoming more and more of an attractive option," she said, and turned to go.

"Wait."

She paused, hand on the door handle.

"I need you."

"You don't need me," she said. "You need power. You're becoming a very small man, Sam York. I'll go to this place, but I don't agree to report any spying."

She opened the door, a plan already beginning to take shape in her mind.

~ ~ ~

Reyna, her thirteen-year-old attitude showing clearly on her face, opened the door to Sister Matthew's office and said, "What."

"Close the door."

"It's embarrassing to be summoned out of class."

"I know, but this is important."

Reyna collapsed into the single chair in front of her mother's desk and slouched. "So?"

"I'm going to leave for a little while."

This got her daughter's attention. She sat up, worry lines between her eyebrows. "Leave? What do you mean leave? To go where? For what? For how long?"

Sister Matthew got up, came around the desk and knelt next to her daughter. She smoothed Reyna's beautiful dark hair. "There's another community in town, and Elijah wants me to go investigate it."

"Well, that can't take long."

"It shouldn't, and when I find them to be good people, and it's a good place, I'll send for you."

Reyna scowled. "That doesn't make sense. Let's just go there and see for ourselves."

"It's not as simple as that," Sister Matthew said. "Trust me on this. I know how to get us out of here—"

"Nothing's holding us here," Reyna said. "We're not in jail or anything."

Sister Matthew touched her daughter's cheek. She looked so much like her father, with those dark eyebrows and that dismissive attitude of anything she didn't quite understand. "No, but there could be trouble if we just leave."

"Trouble?"

"Reyna, I'm asking you to trust me, that I'm going to do the right thing for both of us."

"I want to go with you," she said, her face flushing. The thirteen-year-old attitude dissolved into tears forming in her lower lids. She was still a little girl. "Don't leave me here alone, please."

Sister Matthew stood up. Her decision had been made, and it was the right one. There was no way she could explain all the politics and ambitions of Elijah as well as the danger he might pose to the other community if this wasn't handled delicately. "I'll talk to Sister Ascot and she'll look after you. It won't be long, I promise, and then I'll either be back, or I'll send for you."

"How long?"

"I'm not sure, honey. A week. Maybe two."

Those tears slipped over the edges of her eyes, and she reached for her mom, grabbed her around the waist and held her tightly.

Sister Matthew stroked her beautiful daughter's long shiny hair and tried to absorb the fear the girl was feeling. "There's something else," she said.

Reyna pulled back, wiping the tears from her cheeks. "What? What else could there be?"

"Don't tell anyone about this. Let Elijah answer any questions about my whereabouts and tell no one that we've had this talk."

"You're scaring me," Reyna said.

"Look at what we've come through in the past year, sweetheart. There's nothing that could be as scary as that, ever again. You know I love you, and you know I'm going to do the very best thing I know how to do to keep you safe."

"Yeah, like leaving me here is going to be safe for me. What if Elijah just wants to get rid of you so he can get to me? Have you seen how he looks at me?"

A pang of fear threatened to derail Sister Matthew's resolve for her plan. That Elijah, or someone else would touch her daughter was Sister Matthew's first and worst fear. "You just stick close to Sister Ascot, and I'll be back. Take her or another adult with you if you need to go to Elijah's office. But nothing's going to happen between now and then. And listen…maybe we'll go to a better place."

"Like Dad? He's dead and everyone says he's in a better place."

"No. Not like your dad. I mean a community that has more and better food, and education, and not a cult like Elijah has built up around himself here."

"Elijah says there is no better place. That's why everybody stays here."

"Well, I'm going to go find out if he's right."

Reyna hugged her again. "He says the world is poison out there. I'm scared for you."

"Don't be scared for me, or for you. You just behave yourself, don't make any waves, and I'll be back."

"When are you going?"

"Tomorrow. Remember, this is our little secret."

"I hate it."

"I know, sweetie. Me, too, but sometimes we have to make brave choices in the world. This is one I'm making, and I need to have you support me."

"Okay. I'll try. I mean, I do." Reyna stood up. She had grown tall enough to look her mother squarely in the eye.

"Okay. Go wash your face and get back to class."

Reyna left and Sister Matthew sat back down in her chair at her desk and wondered if she was being truthful. It was a scary world out there, Reyna was right. She might find a better place for them, and she might be Elijah's sacrificial lamb. There was no way of knowing. Not yet.

~ ~ ~

When Parker got home from fruitlessly driving around searching for the people who lived in the cul-de-sac off Spring Creek Road, desperately looking for the community that the boys had mentioned back at Elijah's office, he found the dining room table set with actual plates and bowls, folded napkins and silverware. Sherilyn had put a single candle, unlit, on the table, and a vase of flowers. It looked so much like home that he got a cramp in his belly, missing the sound of his mom moving around the kitchen whipping up something that smelled heavenly.

"Dinner!" Sherilyn said brightly, and he saw she was wearing one of their mom's aprons. She brought out a bowl of small, white potatoes, a bowl of green beans, and another bowl with some canned salmon she had mixed with mayonnaise and crumbled up crackers. "Do you need to wash your hands?"

Parker looked at his hands. Water was scarce. He'd wash himself later. He shook his head no.

"Let's eat, then." She pulled out her usual chair and sat down. Parker sat in his customary spot, opposite her. The places where their parents always sat were horribly vacant.

"So," she continued, cheerily, as she spooned some green beans onto her plate and passed him the bowl. "It isn't hot, but it isn't raw. The potatoes and beans are cooked when they're canned, and so is the salmon."

Parker gave her a thumb's up and began to eat. Nothing he'd had at Elijah's place ever tasted this good.

"I have to tell you, though," Sherilyn continued, filling the emptiness of the dining room with her girlish chatter. "I am done with canned chili." She waved her fork around with a green bean stuck on it. "We ate enough canned chili last winter for my entire lifetime. I can't imagine why dad bought cases of canned chili. Must have been on sale. Anyway. No more canned chili. You don't ever need to bring another can of that home."

Parker agreed. As weird as her treatment of canned salmon was, it tasted amazing.

"Did you find anything interesting while you were out?"

Parker shook his head no, then pulled out of his back pocket a map of the city that he'd found in the car's glove compartment. With a red felt tip pen, he traced the roads he had investigated. Over the last week, he had covered a lot of territory, drew a lot of red lines onto the map, and saw nothing that resembled what the boys had talked about.

"Let me see."

He pushed the map across to her, capped the pen and put it back in his pocket.

"Okay," she said. "You drew me a loop with houses on it. A cul-de-sac, right? Like where the Hoffmans lived?"

Parker nodded.

"And you pointed to Spring Creek Road?"

Parker nodded again.

She traced the red line of Spring Creek Road on the map with her finger. "There aren't any cul-de-sacs off of Spring Creek Road." She pushed the map back to him. "Look. Are you sure they were talking about our town? Doesn't Spring Creek run up into Bicksburg? Maybe beyond that, even."

Parker stopped chewing and considered what she was saying.

"You should look at all the *cul-de-sacs* on the map and investigate them instead of driving up and down Spring Creek Road. Aren't you about out of gas?"

Parker shook his head. He still had a half tank. But it seemed increasingly urgent that he find that group of people.

He'd mark cul-de-sacs tonight, get up and go out again tomorrow. It was now his day job. And Sherilyn would have dinner waiting for him when he got home.

A surge of affection brought a smile. He stopped chewing and just admired her sweetness.

"What?" she asked, then blushed and looked down at her plate.

~ ~ ~

Early the next morning, with a can of peaches in his belly, a freshly marked up map of the city, and a bottle filled with strained and boiled river water, Parker started his parents' car, backed out of the driveway, and slowly idled down the street. He kept his eyes open for any movement, any sign of life besides dogs. There were a lot of loose dogs packing up and roaming around.

He wondered what he would do if he saw another car coming. Would he stop? Would he try to avoid it, or hide from it if he could? He felt as if he was living in a false sense of security, that there were likely dangers all around him, most of which he hadn't even thought about. Tomorrow he'd put his father's handgun in the glove compartment.

At a corner, he stopped, then turned left. There was a neighborhood full of cul-de-sacs ahead, and while they were nowhere near Spring Creek Drive, he might as well look them over. Those boys in Elijah's office had to be mistaken about the location of the group of survivors.

Maybe they were telling Elijah misinformation on purpose.

Still, even though he didn't know where the people were, he knew that they were somewhere. He'd seen them loading a chair into a truck.

After a few more miles and a few more left turns, he reached the neighborhood he'd marked on the map. This was another neighborhood of very nice homes, most of them two story, with lots of brick and stone facing the street. Beautiful big trees throwing cooling shade from the warm sun, many colorful rhododendrons in full bloom.

But only one house drew his eye. A white house, two story, nicely kept yard totally consumed by dandelions like the rest of the yards. There was nothing special about this house, but Parker was drawn to it.

He parked the car on the street and got out. He listened. Bird sounds, nothing else. So eerie, this silence. He looked around and saw no movement except a little breeze in the tops of the trees.

What was it about this house? Was there a chance someone was alive inside? Holed up, afraid, like he and his sister had been all winter?

The brick walk led to a three-step porch, littered with the detritus of the fall and winter. Old leaves, a little trash blown into the corners.

He lifted the heavy brass knocker on the door and banged it down three times. He cringed at the loudness.

Again, he looked around to see if the sound had attracted the attention of anybody else in the neighborhood. Still, no movement.

He tried the doorknob. Locked.

Remembering how the Zimmermans had kept their house key handy in case of an emergency, he moved the pots of dead plants around the porch, and sure enough, under one of them was a key.

It fitted into the lock. He paused for a moment to settle his anxiety about walking into another house full of corpses, then opened the door and stuck his head inside.

The taste of death on the back of his tongue was strong and sickening. Ever since dealing with the Zimmermans, and then going into the Walmart store with its rotting meat and fish counter, he was ultra-sensitive to the smell of death. He didn't think he would ever get used to that stench.

Strangely enough, this time, even though he knew the house was permeated with it, he couldn't exactly smell it. But it felt sticky on the back of his tongue.

What was he doing here? Was he going to bury the dead people inside? Was he going to raid their kitchen cabinets?

A growing feeling in his chest told him that something else was going on here. He knew this feeling, this tightness, as if he was being filled up with something that was not uncomfortable or unwelcome, just not quite familiar, although he had felt it before. Twice.

With a final look around the neighborhood, he stepped inside.

The great front room was dim; all the shades had been drawn. Morning sun came in through the windows in a room to the east; at first glance it looked like a sewing room. Nice furniture, nice rugs, pretty orange and yellow pillows on the couch. He should take one of those pillows home to Sherilyn. That would brighten up their living room.

Would it be right to take something like that? Food, he had determined, was fine, but other people's things? How was that all right?

The tightness in his chest grew. He stopped and took some deep breaths, trying to calm his pounding heart.

He moved quietly deeper into the house, toward what was surely the kitchen. It seemed darker even than the living room.

Parker turned the corner and was surprised to see a man standing next to the kitchen table. He looked to be about forty, wore a dark blue suit and green striped tie, his hair neatly combed. He stood with his hands on the back of a chair, looking out onto the back yard.

Parker didn't want to startle him, although he had knocked, and his footsteps were not silent, so he moved a stool at the breakfast bar, scraping it across the floor.

The man turned and looked at him. A faint glow of blue surrounded his face. "I need to get to work," he said, his voice slightly muffled.

Parker's heart pounded so hard he was afraid he would faint. He took another step closer to the man, and noticed that as he came closer, the view out the window dimmed. The man was standing in a cloak of shadow.

"I need to get to work," the man said again, "but I can't seem to. I can't seem to be able to get out of the house."

The feeling in Parker's chest moved up his throat and he began to understand what was happening here. He began to understand why he was drawn to this house, of all the houses on the street.

Parker opened his mouth and words came out. "Your work here is finished," he said, surprised again at the sound of his own voice. These words were not his, yet they were somehow *of* him. "You have worked long and hard and provided well for your family. You have proven yourself to be a good man, a good husband and father, and now it is time for you to go receive the rewards for your work."

"I don't understand," the man said. "I need to get to work."

"Your new work is of a different nature," Parker said. "Look over there, look over your left shoulder."

The man looked around, and a light opened up, a brilliant, soothing tunnel of golden light. Vague shadows moved in the tunnel, which seemed welcoming and safe.

"Well," the man said. "Would you look at that."

"Go," Parker said. "Your family is waiting."

The man turned and took one step in. The light closed around him and winked out.

The shadows vanished and the stench of death returned in full force.

All the energy ran out of Parker along with the heavy feeling. He was back to normal, no, not normal, vacant. He pulled out one of the kitchen chairs and sat down. The encounter had felt strangely natural, and he had no idea what to make of it.

Now the stench of death was overwhelming.

He knew exactly what he would find if he went upstairs to the bedrooms. That man, and likely his wife and children, all dead in their beds. They all went on to the afterlife, except the man who felt so responsible for them that he couldn't bear to leave his house. Had he been standing here in the kitchen since last fall?

Maybe he didn't reckon time in that in-between place where he had been for so long. Until Parker showed up.

Was this Parker's new job? Not looking for the other community, but driving around and liberating souls who had not been able to let go of their material lives and move on to the afterlife?

Well, it was better than the job of pulling corpses out of their beds and hauling them outside. Or worse, hauling them out, mattresses and all.

What a weird life this was turning out to be.

Exhausted and yet exhilarated, Parker rubbed his face, ran his hands through his hair and felt as if he had done a full day's work. The room had brightened, and he could see clearly through the window how nice and spacious the back yard had been.

Before he left the house, he drank down a warm Diet Coke, then filled a tote bag with canned food—no chili—and put one of the yellow and orange pillows on the top. He found a bag of birdseed and filled all three of the bird feeders in the back yard, then left the bag open, so the birds, squirrels, or whoever needed food could find it for themselves.

Then he put the tote into the trunk of the car, consulted the map, and began again, searching for the group of people he felt he was meant to find.

~ ~ ~

Amanda got out of Elijah's truck with the dark green garbage bag full of her belongings. She had argued with Elijah about taking a garbage bag, when perfectly good luggage was everywhere for the taking. But he was insistent that she look disheveled and unwashed and desperate. He even made her rub dirt on her clothes before leaving.

The boys dropped her off two blocks away from where they said the other people came to fill their water tanks. She walked down to the Silver River and sat on a rock, her head in her hands, not exactly feeling as good about being out in the fresh air and sunshine as she would have liked. She didn't wait long before the two teenage boys found her.

She tried not to seem too eager to join them, she made them talk her into it, after watching them pump the water. She told them she wasn't in the habit of getting into trucks with strangers, but she let them persuade her to get into the back seat with these two nice, clean-cut boys, one black, one white, both seemingly full of life.

"Hey," one of them said. Robby, she thought his name was. Maybe Robert. "Do you play softball? We're trying to get a team together."

Amanda didn't answer. She tried to act as if she had been horribly traumatized, which in fact, she had, but not in the ways Elijah wanted her to appear. In fact, she would love to join a softball team. With Reyna.

They drove a few miles to a cul-de-sac of nice homes, where the yards were well kept, and it seemed to be a hive of activity.

She could see between the houses that the communal back yards had been turned into a huge garden, with probably twenty people out there working that she could see. Others were walking from house to house with boxes of papers, baskets of bedding, or clothes on hangers.

She hugged her bag of belongings to her chest, and the boy named Robby, or Robert, helped her out of the truck, took her elbow and guided her to the central house that faced the circle. A black and white dog came to greet her, wagging its tail.

"That's Alta," the boy said. "She's a good judge of character."

Amanda leaned down and petted the dog.

The air was different here. The whole feeling was different. Everybody here was happy and healthy and working in concert and cooperation with one another. The exact opposite of what was happening in Elijah's community, where nobody smiled, nobody went outside except the youngest children and those sent out to loot stores and houses.

She tried not to grin as she thought what a gold mine she had found, and already she couldn't wait to get Reyna here to join her.

These two boys would provide great company for her daughter, and maybe help her get over her thirteen-year-old attitude. Perhaps there were some girls here, too, and she could find a social circle that was more to her liking.

She looked behind her before entering the front door of what was clearly the main house, knowing that Elijah's spies Russ and Timothy were somewhere close by, watching. She didn't care. She felt freedom. She felt hope.

"This is the great room," Robby said as they walked through the front door. The house smelled like fresh bread and something else, something delicious cooking on the stove. "This is where we have all our meetings." Clearly, walls had come down to make the room bigger, and there were couches, loveseats, chairs, and stools to accommodate a lot of people. Much more comfortable than straight chairs set up in rows in the cafeteria of the high school for Elijah's daily mandatory preach fests. A man was giving guitar lessons to a half dozen kids in the corner by a piano.

Robby steered her toward the big kitchen, again modified to make room for more people to work. "This is Mary," he said. "She owned a five-star restaurant in Portland. She's a genius with food." A nice face with light brown hair turning gray, tamed back by a blue bandana, turned to smile at her. "Mary, this is Amanda."

"Hi, Amanda," Mary said. "Would you like something to eat?"

Amanda looked at the ground. She'd had breakfast before all of this, and the deception gnawed at her. "No, thanks."

"Okay, maybe later then," Mary said. "Robby, why don't you go help with the water? I'll take Amanda to meet Castile."

"Okay," Robby said. "You're in good hands with Mary. And if she has any of that great soup left over from last night, you'll be happy that you had some."

"Thank you," Amanda said, hugging her bundle closer.

"How about a piece of pie?" Mary asked. She pulled what looked like a cherry pie from the cupboard and held it up.

Amanda's mouth watered. She nodded.

"Good," Mary said, cut a slice and set it on a plate, then returned the pie to the cupboard. "Strawberry rhubarb. The last of the season, I'm afraid. We might need to use canned fruit until the harvest comes in a little later." She pulled up a stool for Amanda to sit on and handed her a fork. Then she poured a small glass of water from a pitcher and set it down. "Go ahead," she urged. "Eat."

Amanda knew the questions would begin to come fast and furious, and already she was feeling guilty for deceiving these fine people. Maybe in a day or two, she would make a friend, someone she could trust, and she would privately come clean about where she came from and why. In the meantime, she liked watching Mary watching her enjoy the delicious pie.

"Are you moving through," Mary asked, "or are you looking to settle?"

Amanda took a drink of water. "Don't know," she said.

"Honest answer," Mary said. "Most people here are from right around here. We've just collected them. There's lots to do, and we're always looking for willing hands."

Amanda nodded and finished the pie. She had no idea what to say. She hadn't thought this through very well. Fuck Elijah for putting her in this position.

Mary took her plate and empty glass.

"That was very good. Thank you," Amanda said.

"Come now, I'll take you over to the infirmary and introduce you to Castile."

Infirmary? This place has a doctor?

She picked up her bag of clothes and followed Mary out the kitchen door into the sunshine and fresh air. Two girls, not much older than Reyna, were taking loaves of fresh bread out of a wood-fired brick oven. Two men were working on a metal tower, and a third was doing something at the base of a very active windmill. Thirty or forty people were working in the enormous garden, some weeding, some planting, some stretching trellis twine, some turning sod over to make new beds. At one end, a man and a woman stood talking quietly, and Amanda instinctively knew they were the architects of this massive project. They must rule with a soft kid glove. Everybody seemed so happy to be doing what they were doing.

"Hi, Amanda!" It was the other boy, the one who had picked her up with Robby.

She smiled and waved back.

"Jamaal," Mary said. "I love that kid. Lost his whole family to the flu like most of us, actually. He's a treasure around here."

They walked a well-worn path between the main house and the house next door. "This is where Willie and Castile live. Castile is Willie's daughter. She lost her husband and twin sons. Willie lost his wife, Castile's mom." They walked around the perimeter of the garden, Amanda feeling foolish for clutching this trash bag of belongings, but nobody seemed to mind.

"Everybody lost somebody, and most people lost everybody, know what I mean? Of course you do. We've all got scars from last year, Amanda. It's hard to believe it's not even been an entire year since the flu and the… the rest." Mary paused. "What I'm trying to say is that we have all been where I think you are now. You'll find a community here, a good community, if you decide to stay." Mary walked up to the back door of a house on the back side of the garden. "This is the infirmary," she said. "Castile is a nurse. She takes care of us. Medicine is kind of scarce, but we make do." She opened the door and Amanda walked into a cool, sweet-smelling, dimly-lighted house that felt like a sanctuary all unto itself. There were two empty hospital beds in the living room, each with a side table, each made up hospital-perfect. There was a small kitchen and what looked like three bedrooms in the back.

Mary knocked twice on one of the bedroom doors, then opened it. "Castile?"

"Mary, hi. Come in."

"This is Amanda. Jamaal and Robby found her down by the river."

"Amanda," Castile said, standing up from her desk and reaching out her hand. "Welcome. Have you had any of Mary's soup yet?"

Amanda shook her head.

"Pie," Mary said. "She opted for pie."

"Wise choice. Thanks, Mary."

"I'll leave you two to talk," Mary said, touching Amanda lightly on the shoulder.

Her calm, friendly touch burned Amanda's traitorous arm.

"Sit down, Amanda," Castile said.

Amanda sat.

"Mary told you that I'm a nurse, right? I take care of the community's health. Most people who show up here have issues. Do you need any medications?" Amanda shook her head no. "Do you need to wash your clothes? Do you need to bathe?"

Amanda shrugged her shoulders. "Not really," she said.

"Do you have any pressing needs that I ought to know about?"

"I'm okay," Amanda said. She clutched her bag of clothes closer. It worked to have the boys talk her into coming here. She didn't want to appear too eager to join this group of people, although she would gladly become a wholehearted member of this society, and she'd only been here less than an hour. "Why is everyone outside?" she asked. "Isn't the air poisoned?"

"The winds from the nuclear destruction of Tokyo seemed to go to the north of us," Castile said. "And of course Los Angeles is way far south. There are people here who know more about that than I do. I just know that I haven't seen any radiation poisoning here."

"The ground is not poison? The river is not poison?" Seems like everything Elijah has been saying was, as she had suspected, complete bullshit.

"We're eating from our garden and abandoned gardens all over the region, and it all seems to be good. As you can see, everybody is happy to be outside in the fresh air." Castile made some notes on a sheet of paper. "Hey, do you play softball? Jamaal and Robby are trying to get together a couple of teams. They've been working on rehabbing the diamond over at the middle school."

Amanda shook her head and looked at the ground.

"Would you like to stay the night? Have dinner with all of us? I can set you up with a private bedroom in a nice house about a block over. There's no electricity yet or running water, but we have a bath house where you can clean up, and we can wash your clothes, or we can even get you new clothes if you wish."

"That would be nice," Amanda said, looking up and making eye contact with Castile for the first time. She looked into soft, kind eyes and a gentle face.

"At dinner, you can meet the rest of the people and decide if you'd like to join us. We all work. Everybody has their specialty, or their interest, and everybody has their chores to do every day. We try to all get along with one another. When one succeeds, we all succeed. Know what I mean?"

This could not be more different from Elijah's group. One hundred eighty degrees. With the taste of that wonderful pie still on her tongue, the kindness that everyone had shown her so far was suddenly overwhelming, and Amanda's throat closed up with tears. She let a sob out, and one tear dropped from her eyelid onto the plastic bag in her lap.

"This is part of what we heal here," Castile said. "You're safe with us."

Chapter 6 - June

Parker pulled into the driveway and turned off the engine of the neighbor's little compact car. His parents' car had long ago run out of gas, so until he could figure out how to put more gas into it, he used Mr. and Mrs. Cameron's car.

It had been a long day, and he was ready to get something to eat and go to bed with a book. But when he opened the front door, he saw his little sister standing with her hands on her hips and fury on her face.

"What are you doing all day?" she asked. "Why are we still here? Where is that other community you were supposed to find, Parker? This town isn't so big that you can take almost a month to look around and still not find it."

Parker reached for her, but she wasn't having it. So he brushed past her and sat on the couch.

She stood in front of him. "I'm boiling the water. I'm doing laundry. I'm tending the garden. I'm making food. And I'm alone all day, while you're out doing... what *are* you doing?"

Parker took a deep breath. It's true, he hadn't been looking for the other community. He seemed drawn to house after house, at least one each day, sometimes two, or today, three, helping people cross over to the other side. Today it was a family, parents and two children huddled together in a closet, their rotting dead bodies clasped together in the parents' bed. He opened the closet door and showed them the light, liberating them from an eternity of in-between.

But how could he let Sherilyn know about this work? How could he make her understand that what he was doing was massively important, that there was no one else here to do it, and she was his support person, doing work that was equally as important?

He patted the couch cushion next to him, and she flounced onto it, arms still crossed. He pulled her arms apart and held one of her hands, felt it relax from a fist. Felt her anger dissolve.

"I'm lonely," she said, and began to cry.

The next day, he took her with him. She was wide-eyed and

excited to get out of the house, away from the chores, and see the world, empty as it was.

He was happy to have her here, she was a bright, shiny thing in his life, but she was also chatty and distracting.

"Where are we going? What are we doing? Do you ever see other people? Do you see any dogs? This car is kind of cool. Do you think we could get a dog?"

He stopped at the corner, trying to connect with the force that pointed the way, but it was silent. He looked at her and held his finger to his lips to be quiet.

She nodded, and settled back in the seat.

Turn right.

Parker followed the directions, as ephemeral and indistinct as they were, until they were in front of a house only two blocks away from their house.

"This is Cassie's house!" Sherilyn said, excitedly. "Is she here? Is she home? C'mon! Let's go see!"

This was a bad idea, Parker realized only too late. He had no idea what Sherilyn would see, what she would be allowed to see of his work, but he knew that she would see the body of her friend, she would smell her friend's death.

As soon as he had stopped the car in the street, Sherilyn jumped out and ran up to the front of the house. "Come on!" she urged him, complete with arm gestures.

Parker took a minute, felt the spirit filling his torso with language and bravery.

As he had become more adept at this work, he knew how to glean more subtle details. He knew the back door of this house was unlocked. He walked around to the back yard, Sherilyn skipping along beside him. Before he opened the door, he turned to his sister, grabbed both her arms and looked sternly into her face. This settled her down. He again put his finger to his lips to silence her and ran his hand over first his face and then hers, removing her smile. This was serious business, and she now had an idea about that.

He knocked, loudly.

No answer, but he knew that. He did it mostly for Sherilyn.

He opened the door, and the taste of death poured out.

"Oh God, I'm going to puke," Sherilyn said.

Parker shook his head no and made a show of taking a deep breath. She grimaced, but followed his lead. They walked into the family room. Someone had collapsed and died while playing the piano, and there the body still was, hands melting into the keys, flies buzzing all over it. Sherilyn grabbed Parker's hand. "What are we doing here?"

Again, Parker held his finger to his lips.

They walked through the kitchen to the living room. This house, built the same year as their house, in the same development, had much the same floor plan. One story. Master suite on one side, two bedrooms on the other side.

He tried to concentrate, to listen to Spirit, as to where he should go, who he would find there, what he should do, but again, Sherilyn was squeezing his hand so hard he couldn't concentrate. He pulled himself loose, put his hand on the small of her back and turned her toward the master bedroom.

The dead mother, fully clothed, was lying on top of her bed. The person at the piano, then, must be the father.

"I can't stand this," Sherilyn whispered.

Parker closed the bedroom door behind them and moved them back through the family room to the smaller bedrooms.

One was an office.

And Cassie was in the other, sitting on the floor, trying to put a puzzle together, the familiar blue aura around her face.

"Cassie!" Sherilyn squealed and ran to her friend before Parker could stop her, but she stopped short of touching the girl.

"I can't seem to put this puzzle together," Cassie said calmly.

"Cassie, it's me!" Then Sherilyn seemed to notice that the room was dark, though the curtains were open. Cassie's fly-blown corpse was slumped against the bookcase.

She looked at Parker with wide-eyed horror. "What is happening?"

Parker was surprised that Sherilyn could see the girl's spirit. He took Sherilyn by the arm and stationed her next to the door. Then he took a deep breath and let the spirit speak.

"Life is a puzzle that is only difficult when you try too hard to figure it out," Parker said to the girl's spirit. "It really is very simple."

Cassie looked up at him, her eyes went from Sherilyn to Parker and back. "It's an easy puzzle and I've done it many times before."

"There are new and greater challenges and rewards ahead for you," Parker said. "Your time with this puzzle is finished. You've graduated."

"Graduated? But I'm only..." Cassie seemed confused.

"Look over there," Parker said, pointing over Cassie's left shoulder.

The golden tunnel opened up, the warm, welcoming light flooding the small room.

Cassie looked in. "Mom?" Cassie said. "Is that you?"

"She's waiting for you."

Sherilyn, transfixed by the sight, took three steps toward the light before Parker got hold of her arm and stopped her. "Not yet," he whispered to her.

Cassie, however, stood up, took a step in, and disappeared.

The portal closed, the room brightened and the stench of death overwhelmed them.

Sherilyn ran out of the room, out of the house, and stood, gagging in the back yard. Parker followed, feeling drained, and sat on the steps to wait for her to regain her equilibrium.

"Take me home," she said, brushing tears from her cheeks.

~ ~ ~

Parker spent the rest of the day with his sister, helping her in the garden, helping her in the kitchen, freshening up the latrine, hanging up the laundry, taking her to the river to get more water, just being a companion in general. She was right. It had been too long since he had helped around the house like this, and she liked it, he could tell. He liked it, too.

She stayed silent except for issuing the occasional instruction.

Parker knew she was mulling over the morning's experience.

He harvested fresh snow peas from the garden and cooked them in a little pot on the hibachi. Then he drained them, added a can of minestrone soup and set the table with their mother's china.

Using the special occasion dinnerware actually made Sherilyn laugh when she saw the place settings on the table.

They sat down, and Sherilyn said. "Our peas?"

Parker nodded, gave her a thumb's up.

"Why can't you talk to me?" she asked. "I've heard you talk three times now."

Parker opened his mouth, but nothing came out. He shook his head.

"And how do you know what to say to those... what are they, ghosts?"

Parker had no answer.

"So this is what you've been doing all day?"

Parker nodded.

"Every day?"

Parker nodded.

Sherilyn spooned up some of her soup. "Soup's good."

Parker agreed.

"Okay," she said, putting down her spoon. "I have something to say."

Parker put down his spoon as a show of solidarity, wiped his mouth with his napkin, and gave her his full attention.

"I think what you're doing is a good thing, although I don't get it. So you should keep doing it."

Parker nodded.

"But you should be here, too."

Parker nodded.

"And it's summer, and soon it will be fall." She looked at him with fierce determination. "Winter is coming, Parker, and I can't be here in this house, all by myself, or the two of us, all by ourselves, for another winter." She dropped her eyes. "I'd rather go back to Elijah's."

That stunned Parker, as she knew he was not welcome there. She would go back there and leave him here alone?

"So," she said. "Here's the new plan: One day doing what you did today, one day here, one day looking for those other people."

Parker was still thinking about being in this house alone for the winter, his little sister back in that horrible place.

"Parker?"

His focus snapped back to her. Of course they could not stay here another winter.

"Seriously, those other people can't be far from here. If I go with you to look at the map while you drive around, we'll find them, probably in a day or two."

Parker was skeptical.

"We won't know what they're like until we find them. But we can't be here another winter."

Parker thought about the other communities that were broadcasting on the radio. They were far away, but he knew how to drive now, and maybe they'd only have to go as far as Portland to find a place to be. Still, it would be the same, driving around looking for them, only in a much bigger place.

"So," Sherilyn said. "One day ghost catching, one day doing chores here, and one day looking for the others. Deal?"

Parker nodded, held out his hand.

They shook on it.

~ ~ ~

Steven sat at his drawing table, but his mind wasn't on the electrical system for the high school. He wasn't interested anymore. He had lost his taste for doing anything for this group and the clown that Elijah had become.

Elijah's "flock" had split into two factions: one was all for Elijah and God and fixing the world by going backwards, and the other saw through his ridiculous act and was ready to leave, to take their chances elsewhere. Of course Steven was one of those ready to put Elijah behind him. The question was: when?

He put his elbows on his drawing board and his chin in his

hands and looked out the window. Such a beautiful day. Sun shining, blue sky, untended flowers in bloom all over the place. Why were they all inside? They'd been inside since last fall.

Fear, that's why. Elijah was keeping control of his group through fear.

Maybe it was time to go. Maybe the answer to the question of when was now. Right now. Not next month, not in two weeks. Today.

He gathered up his books and papers, such as they were and put them into a box, which he set by the door. This was right. This was the right thing, and he knew Don thought so, too.

Five minutes later, Steven knocked twice on Elijah's office door and waited until he heard Elijah invite him in. This was a conversation he was not looking forward to having, but Elijah had been increasingly erratic lately, and what the teenage boys had told him about Sister Matthew needed to be addressed by an adult. He couldn't hold back. Not another day, although he would like to. Steven was not afraid of Elijah, but his plan to leave and go south had not entirely come together yet.

He opened the door to find Elijah standing in front of his desk, arms crossed over his chest, feet apart in a very defensive stance. He was scowling. "What do you need?" he asked.

"I've been talking with Timothy, and then with Russ, and what they tell me is very disturbing."

"What right have you to talk to those boys? They have no right to divulge the topics of our private conversations."

"Elijah, you've sent a spy to another community? Why would you do that? That in itself is very disturbing."

"What right have you to be disturbed by how I manage this group? What right have you to challenge my ways?"

"Because after you sent Parker and his little sister away the way you did, after you *banished* them, some of us are questioning your mental health."

Elijah laughed, ending in a sneer. "There is nothing wrong with my mental health. You have no idea what it's like, the pressure I'm under to keep this community afloat."

"That's just the thing," Steven said. "You're not keeping it afloat. People are planning to leave—"

Elijah stood straight up. "*Who?* Who is planning to leave?"

"That's not the point. The point is that people here are not happy. I'm not happy that you've sent Sister Matthew away and kept her daughter here."

"That was a private arrangement with Sister Matthew," Elijah said.

"Well, I doubt that. Regardless, the boys, Timothy and Russ, don't like trying to connect with Sister Matthew in a clandestine manner in order to get you your intelligence, or whatever it is that you think you're trying to get."

"It's not wrong to know what those people are doing over there."

"Tim and Russ told me what that community is doing. They've got a good thing going there. A garden, and electricity, and a good working environment. They're listening to the radio broadcasts of other pockets of people. They've got a real community over there. What have we got?"

"Safety," Elijah said. "And if you don't like it, you can leave, too."

"What are you keeping us safe from?"

"All the things that brought this world to the brink, that's what. Technology. Blaspheme. Disrespect."

"There's nothing wrong with technology," Steven said. "Isn't that what you're asking us to do up in the lab? Bring in electricity?" Steven shook his head. "That's not what I'm here to talk about. I want to know why we don't just go talk to those other people. Maybe we can join forces and make a real start on civilization again."

"Never," Elijah said. "They are of loose morals and they will fail. I am strong, and our group will prevail."

"It isn't about failing and prevailing," Steven said. "I seriously don't understand you. That group has a garden. They're baking bread, and putting food away for the winter. Nobody here even goes outside the walls of this school!"

"The outside world has been poisoned. The air. The soil. The water. If you can't see what we've done here, then perhaps it is time for you to go."

"Perhaps it is. And then again, perhaps it isn't. But if I go, I'll take all the electrical plans, a half dozen men and probably three or four women."

Elijah took a step forward, his face ugly. "You will take no women."

"I'll take them if they want to come. Why? Do you have plans for the women in your twisted little kingdom fantasy? Do you think you're God, like the others have been saying?"

"Get out," Elijah said quietly, a snarl on his face.

Steven gestured around the room with its empty bookshelves. "What do you do in here, anyway? Play office? There are no books, you're not doing any research. There are no papers, you're not doing any scheduling. You're acting. You're a failed used car salesman, Sam York from Sam York Ford, acting like a ruler. A petty potentate." He turned to go. "I'm going to take Reyna with me," Steven said over his shoulder. "I don't want her here alone with you while her mother is away. And I'm taking Timothy and Russ, too. And Don."

"Go!" Elijah yelled, spittle and venom dripping from his lips.

Steven left the office shaking his head. He'd pushed the issue, and now he had to leave. Timothy and Russ stood just down the hallway, waiting for the outcome of his meeting. "We're leaving," Steven said. "Are you going with us?"

"Who?" Timothy asked.

"I'm not exactly sure. I'll make the rounds and find out. We'll head south, where the winter isn't out to kill us."

"When?" asked Russ.

"As soon as we can get packed up. If you two are coming with us, let me know now, because I need you to get the van gassed up and ready to go."

"We can't go near Los Angeles," Timothy said. "It was hit. The whole place is radioactive."

"Maybe we won't get farther than the bay area. Or head to Reno. I don't know yet. Let's get everybody who wants to leave together, get packed up and get out of here and then we'll decide."

"I'm in," Timothy said, and looked at Russ.

"Me, too."

"Great. Timothy, get the van ready to go. Russ, go tell Don to load up some supplies. And then find Reyna. We're taking her with us."

"Reyna isn't here," Russ said.

"What do you mean she isn't here?"

"Her mother sent her a note and she's gone."

"When? Gone for good?"

Timothy shrugged. "A little while ago. I don't think she's gone for good. I think they were just going to meet, but I don't know."

"Okay then," Steven said. "If she's back by the time we leave…"

"We can't leave her here," Russ said.

"We can't wait for her."

Both boys looked at their feet.

"We'll do everything we can to have her join us, but you have to know—" he cocked his head at Elijah's door "I'm not entirely in control here. Wait until he finds out we're taking the van."

Both boys nodded.

"Okay, then. Get busy."

~ ~ ~

Amanda nervously paced back and forth in the alley behind the abandoned 7/11 when she heard Reyna's voice.

"Hi, Mom."

Amanda ran to her daughter and hugged her close. Reyna began to cry.

"Listen," Amanda said, hugging Reyna close. "It's only for a little while longer."

"I don't want to be there!" Reyna pulled away from her mother. She didn't sound like a self-possessed thirteen-year old at the moment, she sounded exactly as she did when she was five, whining and hiccing, trying to hold back the sobs. "Take me with you!"

"I can't," Amanda said. "Elijah tricked me into lying to these people, and so I have to be careful about how I tell them about you, and the real me."

"Just tell them. Isn't that what you've always told me? Honesty the best policy and all that?"

"I know, sweetheart, but this is a little complicated, because it's really a nice place, and there are kids your age, you're really going to like it there, and I don't want to get us kicked out because of Elijah. Because where would we go then?"

Reyna wiped the tears from her cheeks with the palms of her hands and sat down on the store's back step.

Amanda sat next to her.

"Well, where do they think you are now?"

"I just walked away. There's a big wedding going on over there right now. A huge celebration/party. They won't miss me for a little while. Everybody takes some personal time when they need it." Amanda wiped a smudge from the toe of her new shoe, sick to her stomach that she had let Elijah put her in this position, not knowing how to tell the people who have embraced her that she has been deceiving them. "What about you? Where do they all think you are?"

"I just walked away, too. Russ gave me your note, and I just left. Nobody noticed, I don't think." She picked at her cuticles. "I miss our old life. I miss Dad. I want everything to go back to the way it was before."

"I know, honey. Me, too."

"Do you think we could bring Russ with us when we go to your new place?"

"Russ?" Amanda wasn't prepared for this and didn't like the sound of it. "No, why? Are you two getting close?"

"He's nice."

"He's what, seventeen? You're thirteen! Don't be getting close to boys."

"He's sixteen, and I like him. And he likes me."

"Honey," Amanda put her arm around her daughter. "These are strange times. I'm trying to make a really nice place for us to live. Russ can come along later if he wants. That's up to him. You're my first concern."

"That's bullshit," Reyna said.

"I beg your pardon? You don't use that language with me."

Reyna fixed her mother with a cold stare. "Where'd you get those clothes?"

"They have a closet…"

"I have two pair of jeans and I've worn one or the other every day for months," Reyna said. "And you have a nice place to live with new clothes and you won't take me there. I am not your first concern, or I'd be with you in your so-called wonderful place instead of back at that smelly building with all those weirdos. The only good thing is sometimes I can be with Russ."

"Listen, honey, this is not the best time or place to have a talk about boys, but—"

"I'm not listening to you," Reyna said, and pulled away.

"Just how close are you two?"

"None of your business." Reyna stood up.

"Honey, please. Please don't go. Please think things through, before you do something with a boy that you'll regret."

"You have no power over me anymore," Reyna said. "You've abandoned me, and I will make my own decisions from now on." She started to walk away.

Amanda sat on the step, knowing that what her daughter was saying was true, at least from her thirteen-year-old point of view.

Reyna whirled around, and Amanda saw that she was crying again. "Go back to your spectacular life without me. I don't need you." She turned and began running back to the school, and Elijah, and a boy who Amanda was positive was ready to take advantage of a temporarily untethered girl.

Damn Elijah!

Amanda sat on the step for a long time, guilt pressing down on her as she weighed her options. She needed to get Reyna to the cul-de-sac, but how would she do that? She would have to admit that she'd been lying this whole time, and that was not likely to be well received. Maybe she could have a private talk with Castile, tell her the what, and the why, and then see what happened. The worst was that they would throw her out, and she'd have to go back to Elijah's.

That thought involuntarily curled her lip. She might have to go back there, but she would never climb into his bed again. She would find a group that was ready to leave, and they'd go somewhere else. She knew from reading the comments in the suggestion box that there were many who were ready for something other than Elijah and his ways. Surely there were groups in Portland. They could take a car, any car, even one from Sam's lot, and just head out. Even if it was just her and Reyna. They'd figure it out themselves. Together.

~ ~ ~

Steven supervised the loading of the last boxes of supplies from the looted Safeway into the back of the van, slammed the back doors, and looked at the small group. Edith, Suzanne, Frances, Don, Timothy, and Russ. Each person stood on the sidewalk with the little bag of belongings they were allowed to bring when they joined Elijah's group. They looked pretty pitiful. "Let's load up and get going," he said.

The front doors of the school opened and Elijah stood on the front step, watching.

"We're taking the van," Steven called to him. "You don't need it. And we've taken some supplies, too, but not anything you'll miss."

"Thief!" Elijah yelled back. "You're all thieves!"

"Jump in," Steven said quietly, as more people came out of the school to stand behind Elijah.

"I'd shoot you all right now to save you from certain, horrible death from poisoned air. Go with Satan, you thieving traitors. See how hard it is to survive without God and Elijah, his humble servant, to keep you on the path to righteousness. The Lord will bring his wrath upon you all," Elijah yelled. "You are taking those fine people to their doom!"

Russ grabbed Steven's elbow. "Reyna," he said.

"I can't help it," Steven said. "This could get ugly."

"I can't leave her here."

Steven sighed in frustration and resignation. "Okay, then. Timothy, are you coming?"

Timothy looked at Russ. Shook his head. "I don't know."

"Make up your mind, and do it now," Steven said with considerable urgency, seeing that Don was in the driver's seat and the three women were situated comfortably. "Make up your mind or we'll leave you both behind."

"Look!" Timothy said.

Everybody turned to where he pointed. Reyna was running down the street, straight toward them.

"All right then," Steven said, and opened the passenger door for himself.

Reyna arrived, breathless. "What's happening?"

"We're leaving," Russ said. "We were waiting for you."

"Good!" she said, and hopped into the van.

"You don't need your things?" Timothy asked.

"Nope," Reyna said. "Let's get the fuck out of here."

Russ laughed, and he and Timothy climbed in after her, Don started the van, Steven waved to those assembled on the school steps, got in, and they drove away.

"Look," Timothy said, and pointed back at the school.

All seven heads turned to look back. Henry, Molly and a half dozen others were standing in the street, waving goodbye. "I bet they want to come with us."

Steven shook his head. "They'll have to find their own way. Maybe they'll take a different van and head out. I don't know. I can't help them."

"Where to, Boss?" Don asked.

"To our doom!" Edith yelled. Everybody laughed.

Everybody but Steven.

Suzanne began singing, "On the road again…" And everybody else joyously joined in.

Steven appreciated the jubilant, free-at-last feeling in the van, but all he felt was the crushing responsibility of taking care of this little band of eight.

"South," Steven said softly. "That's all I know."

~ ~ ~

Amanda walked back to the cul-de-sac, her heart heavy. She

would seek out Castile and tell her everything, and stand strong to receive her, or their, verdict on whether or not she could stay with the community. The thought of going back to the high school, in the event they kicked her out, gave her a cramp, but the thought of leaving Reyna with Elijah for another moment was worse.

Oscar and Lois's wedding reception was in full swing. Amanda stopped at her house first, to wash her face and brush her hair. She looked unkempt and felt fragile. Freshened up, she left the house and headed back through the crowd toward the infirmary. Paul was playing the guitar, Mary was singing, and people were dancing. Flowers and ribbons were scattered all over the grounds, and Lois and Oscar danced slow and close over by the brick ovens. Even Alta was dancing with one of the children. It was a joyous scene, and Amanda was not in the mood.

Willie stopped her. She found she could not meet his eyes. "Are you busy?" he asked.

"I was hoping to talk with Castile," she replied.

"She's not here right now, but I know that Mary could use a little help in the kitchen today. Everybody's kind of burned out celebrating."

Amanda nodded. For a moment, she thought about talking to Willie, but he intimidated her. Maybe she could talk to Mary. No. She should stick with her plan to confess to Castile. She'd seek her out tonight.

But Castile didn't come to dinner, so Amanda took orders, mostly washing dishes. She began to hear snippets of conversation that Frances, who had been working in the kitchen with Mary, had fallen ill. So that's why Amanda got the promotion to kitchen duty instead of laundry. Funny Mary hadn't mentioned why she was short-handed. Amanda wouldn't mind a transfer to the kitchen full time.

On the way home, she passed by the infirmary, and a yellow piece of paper was taped to the door. Do Not Enter was written in black magic marker.

Apparently, Castile suspected that what Frances had was contagious. That couldn't be good. A second round of the devastating flu? A mutation that would wipe out the rest of the survivors? She remembered all the news stories, speculating about the virus mutations. Evidently, one of them did mutate, and it cut a wide swath through the world population and then died out, rocking the survivors to the core.

Another mutation might finish the job.

But she didn't want to think about that right now. She had a daughter to care for.

Reyna would have to stay another night at the high school. It was too late to fetch her now, anyway. She'd talk with Castile at breakfast.

Eventually, the party died down and everyone said their goodnights. Amanda lay awake in the night, listening to the chatty revelers going to their homes, feeling a double dose of guilt, first knowing that her daughter resented her so, and second her deception to this community. But it would all work out in the long run. Wouldn't it? These were such strange times, who knew what working out even meant anymore? Reyna would have told her if she felt menaced in any way by anyone, including Sam. Amanda was certain she was safe at the high school, unless she got too close with that boy, but supervision seemed to be pretty tight, so she doubted that anything would happen before Amanda talked to Castile and got permission to bring Reyna here.

She looked out through the bedroom window to the trees silhouetted against the sky, lighted by the moon. She wanted to pray, she wished she could pray, but every time she tried to address God, all she could hear was Elijah's stupid voice. How could she have ever fallen under his spell the way she had?

Grief, that's how. Upset, that's how. Everyone's world had turned upside down, and Sam York, aka Elijah offered something people could cling to in their collective grief and upset. At least for the moment. But not for long. It didn't take long for Amanda to see the light, once she was far away from him. It wouldn't take the others much longer. Then Reyna would be here with her, safe from that Russ boy, here with some wholesome kids who knew how to put in a day's work under the supervision of caring adults who only wanted to make a better world.

While sleep was hard to come by, comfort was easy. Amanda snuggled down in the fresh sheets she herself had laundered and began to count her blessings.

~ ~ ~

Parker changed into his swimming suit as he listened to Sherilyn get ready for their trip to the river. "Bath day, bath day," Sherilyn sang as she gathered the old milk jugs, juice bottles, and mason jars they would take to fill. "I need a new swimming suit," she said out loud to nobody as she pulled on the elastic that was too tight around her. This would be a day when they would look for the other people, and these were her favorite days. They started with getting water from the river, and then jumping in and cleaning themselves.

The first time they did this, Parker brought soap, but Sherilyn told him no. She said that they couldn't use soap, they just had to use river water and a washcloth, because what if somebody downriver needed water? It wouldn't be right to give them soapy water. That comment was so much like something their mother would say that it squeezed on Parker's heart.

Parker picked up the gym bag with his dry clothes and thought about that for a minute. He was starting to forget what their mother looked like. And their father. Their wedding picture was on the mantle, and there were albums in the bookshelves, but it wasn't exactly the same. It's not as if he was forgetting what they looked like, or forgetting some of the things they did together, it was more like he was forgetting them. Completely.

He felt the wave of grief that occasionally rolled him over starting to overcome him, but then he heard her start to sing again. "It's bath day! It's bath day!" Instead of sitting down and giving in to the tears, he wrapped a dry towel around his neck and went into the living room where Sherilyn was putting bottles and jugs into plastic totes with handles. Maybe he'd think about their parents tonight. Maybe he'd let the tears come then, when Sherilyn couldn't see.

He missed them so much. He didn't really like being the responsible adult, but he hoped that wherever they were, they were proud of him. Them. Sherilyn included.

As soon as he got a grip on himself, he went into the living room and picked up the first box. Sherilyn ran to open the garage door for him.

All jugs and bottles packed in the trunk, towels and dry clothes in the back seat, Parker backed out of the garage and headed toward the river.

"We both need new swimsuits," she said.

Parker nodded.

She clapped her hands. "Walmart!" she said. "We get to go to Walmart!"

Parker shook his head and smiled. Such simple things kept her so happy.

Both of them kept their eyes open as they drove the familiar road to the little riverside beach under the bridge. The water was shallow there and they could easily fill their containers, and then splash around and give themselves a decent scrub before drying off, getting into dry clothes and then driving around, looking at places they hadn't been before, looking for the community of people.

Box by box, Parker brought the containers to the river and Sherilyn filled them up. Then Parker took the heavy totes back to the trunk. By now they knew how to ration their water and they knew how much they would need until the next bath day. Tomorrow, Parker would stay home and they would work around the house. The next day he would go, letting Spirit guide him to the lost souls who needed help finding their way home. On those days, he suspected Sherilyn didn't do much around the house at all. He thought she spent the day reading, and then on the third day, they would be out of water and back to the river to fill up their jugs and take their baths.

Next time they would bring laundry.

Turned out, they both liked routine, and this was one that suited them in every way.

When all the jugs of water were back in the trunk, Parker hung his towel on a branch and tip-toed into the icy water. He made a face that made her laugh. She threw her towel on top of his and ran in, splashing him as she went, gasping as the cold water caught her breath. A moment later, they were both in it up to their necks, ducking under and scratching the dirt from their hair, scrubbing their skin with wash cloths. They turned their backs to each other while they washed their private parts, Parker finding it harder to do while wearing his swimming suit that was at least two sizes too small. He assumed Sherilyn was having an even harder time.

They washed each others' backs, and then just crouched in the water up to their necks and enjoyed the feeling of the water swirling around them, and the hot sun on their faces. "Bath day," Sherilyn whispered. "I love bath day."

Parker gave her a thumb's up.

"What's all this now?"

A male voice surprised them both, and they turned to see two men standing by the car.

"Two kids taking a skinny dip? Come out and show us what you've got."

Parker stood up, but Sherilyn grabbed his hand and pulled him back down in the water.

"It's just a kid," the other man said. "Two kids. You kids out here by yourselves?"

Parker cursed himself for feeling so safe and free out here. He'd let his guard down, and now his little sister might be in danger. He still had his father's pistol, but it was in the car's glove compartment. He never thought he'd need it here, and now it was likely these guys were going to steal it and the car and their water, too. Well, they could have it all if they left them alone.

"Where'd you get this nice car?" one of the men asked. He opened the driver's side door and got in.

"Hey," Sherilyn stood up and yelled. "That's our car. Get out of it!"

"She ain't *that* much of a kid," the other one said, and walked down toward them.

"Leave us alone," Sherilyn said, and Parker heard the shiver in her voice, knew that her lips were likely turning blue from the cold, and goosebumps were up on her skin. He took a quick look around. The place where they bathed was perfect because the water was fairly calm and shallow in this bend in the river, with a steep drop-off just feet from where they stood. The river was too cold and fast to swim across, although they could swim out and float downstream a while to get away from these guys, but he didn't want to give up the car, their clothes, his dad's pistol…

He didn't want these jerks to win.

Plus, they might follow them downriver, and it would be the same there as here.

Mostly, he didn't want either one of them to get their hands on his little sister.

"We been alone too long," the approaching man said. He wore a tuxedo tee shirt with jeans and a red ball cap. He needed a bath. Needed a haircut. Needed to brush his teeth. "We'd welcome the company of some fine folks such as yourselves. Why don't you come out of the water and be sociable?"

"We don't want to be sociable with you," Sherilyn said, indignation surely warming her up. "Go away and leave us alone."

Parker admired her spunk, but didn't think it was going to do any good.

The car door slammed, and the other man came around the car toward them. Both men were dirty, as if they slept in ditches instead of in any one of the zillion empty houses in town. This one was older, his stringy hair streaked with gray. He wore dress pants with cowboy boots and a dirty white tee shirt under a plaid long-sleeve shirt. "These here your towels?" He picked them off the tree. "Come and get them."

~ ~ ~

Willie sat relaxing in his office chair, feet up on the desk, a book on electrical wiring open on his lap, a hot cup of tea in his hand, when a knock came on the door. "Come on in," he said.

Robby opened the door enough to show his face. "Hey. You busy?"

"Always. Why?"

Robby opened the door a little wider. "We need to get water, and we also need two beds. Thought we could do both things at once, but we need an extra hand.

Willie closed his book. "I could use some time away from this stuff," he said. "You know where the beds are?"

"The gleaning crew scoped out a summer camp about five miles away, said there were lots of bunk beds, which would be perfect for us. We could probably get two in the truck and fill the water tank in the trailer all in one trip."

"Who's going?"

"Just me and Jamaal."

"Jamaal and me."

Robby smiled. "Yeah. Jamaal and me."

"Okay," Willie said. "Now?"

"We're ready when you are."

Willie nodded, gulped down his tea, and followed Robby outside.

Willie got into the driver's seat while the other two piled in next to him. He checked the gas gauge. "The generator has gas?" he asked.

Both boys nodded. "We're needing more water these days," Jamaal said. "We might think about finding another water tank."

"They have them on the lot over at the feed store," Robby said. "They have trailers, too. We could get another trailer, then we'd just have to move the generator back and forth between them."

"Or get another generator," Jamaal said. "Maybe another truck."

The boys were thinking, and that was a good thing. The community was growing, no doubt, and Willie had started to think they might have to split up and let the two halves grow their own way. Maybe the whole water thing would be the catalyst. He'd talk it over with Castile, and then maybe propose the idea to the Committee. Each group needed certain things: a head cook, a head gardener, a medical professional, and some kind of an engineer. This group didn't have any of those to spare, so perhaps it wasn't time yet. This group had a lot of hard workers, but not enough leaders, and it wasn't big enough to have duplicates of the essential skills. "How many in the cul-de-sac now?"

"Well, we're way beyond the cul-de-sac," Jamaal said. "But a lot. about a hundred thirty, I think."

That sounded about right. People jammed into the main house for the evening broadcasts, and Mary now needed four people in two kitchens to keep everyone fed. He'd already heard talk about tearing down more walls in the main house—why have bedrooms?—to make more room for the evening gatherings, meals, and to expand the kitchen. But again, did they have a builder in the group who knew how to do all those things? He didn't think so, and he didn't need another job. He was trying to get the houses electrified, no simple thing. And water. It would be great to have running water and flush toilets.

Maybe next year.

He turned on the road that flanked the river, and first thing they saw was a car, a little blue car, parked on the shoulder of the road.

Willie stopped the truck. "Is this how you guys usually come to get water?"

"Yep," Robby said.

"Ever seen that car before?"

"Nope."

He let the truck idle forward, but it wasn't long before he could see what was happening. Two people in the water, two men keeping them from getting out. This was not a situation for the live-and-let-live philosophy that the cul-de-sac had adopted. There was menacing going on here. He pulled over and stopped the truck, putting the keys into his pocket.

The three got out of the truck, Willie pulling the shotgun from behind the seat. They walked, in the middle of the road, slowly toward the car.

The girl in the water saw them and waved her arm. "Hey, help!"

The two men turned.

"You boys stay behind me," Willie said quietly. "I don't like the looks of this."

"They're unarmed," Robby said.

145

"Maybe." The Marine in him began to surface.

"What's going on here?" Willie asked, leveling the shotgun at the two men standing near the water's edge.

"Nothing much," the one in the ball cap said. "Just trying to be sociable."

"Doesn't seem like it," Willie said. "You've got those kids' towels?"

The other guy threw the towels into the water.

"That wasn't very nice," Willie said. The older boy in the water picked up the sopping wet towels and tossed them onto the beach.

"Well, maybe we're not very nice," the ball cap said. "What's it to you?"

"We like people to be nice around here." Willie responded. "If you're not very nice, then maybe you need to move along."

"You the law?" The man in the plaid shirt laughed and started moving toward them. "There ain't no law anymore, mister, in case you hadn't noticed."

"There's still decency," Willie said.

"Well, maybe we're not decent, either."

The man in the ball cap laughed at that.

Willie's pulse pounded in his ears. There was a good chance he was going to have to kill one or both of these men, and that's something he had never ever thought he'd have to do, once he got out of the service. Never again.

The plaid shirt kept coming, slowly, around the front of the car, fearless in the face of a shotgun aimed directly at him, his eyes steady on Willie. The ball cap came around the back of the car. "You're going to point a weapon at me, you pussy? You and a bunch of kids? We seen lots of people like you. We ain't scared."

"Don't want anyone to get hurt," Willie said. "Just want you to move along is all."

The man took two quick strides and made a grab for the shotgun's barrel, and Willie pulled the trigger, catching the man square in the chest.

"*Holy fuck!*" the other man said and lunged at Jamaal.

Willie pumped the gun, whirled and fired again, taking off half

146

the man's head.

The world went silent, except for the sound of two shots reverberating in Willie's head.

Robby and Jamaal didn't move, they just stared at the dead men on the road.

Willie looked up at the sky, a prayer beyond words pouring forth from his soul. He heard the birds, he heard the river, he heard a little soft breeze rustling the cottonwoods. The smell of gunpowder, the ringing in his ears, the concussion of the gunstock against his shoulder, all nauseated him. He gulped air, swallowed bile, gulped more air.

Robby put a steadying hand on his arm, and the world came back into focus.

Two cold, wet kids stood on the side of the road.

"You saved us," the girl said. "They were going to hurt us."

Willie snapped back, realizing that he was the adult in charge. "You two okay?"

"Cold," she said, "but we're all right."

"What are we going to do with these guys?" Robby asked, looking at the bodies.

"Leave them here for the crows," the girl said.

"Send them downriver," Willie said. "Food for the fish, and later for the crabs."

The boys grabbed the legs of the first guy and dragged him into the water. Parker pulled him out into the current and let him go. Then they did the same with the other one. Willie supervised, sick to his stomach at the sight, at what these kids had to see. No kids should ever have to see something like that. But then these kids had seen many things no kids should ever have to see.

When they came back up to the car, Sherilyn had changed into her jeans and a shirt, her swimsuit discarded in a wet pile on the pavement. Parker ducked quickly behind the car, shed his swimming suit and dressed in dry shorts and a shirt.

When he came back to the group, Willie took a double take, then a closer look at Parker. "Hey, wait. Do I know you?"

Sherilyn's head snapped up. "Are you the guy? Parker, is he the guy?"

Parker, his eyes fixed on Willie's, nodded slowly.

Willie squinted, trying to figure this out. "Not quite sure what you mean," he said.

"We've been looking for you guys. You all live in a cul-de-sac, right?" Sherilyn said.

"Yes," Jamaal said. "About two miles from here. How do you know about us?"

"That's a long story," Sherilyn said, "but we're alone, living in our old house, and we can't be alone again this winter, so we've been looking for you." She grabbed Parker in a bear hug. "We found them!" she said.

Jamaal stuck out his hand. Parker shook it.

"I'm Sherilyn, and this is my brother Parker. He doesn't talk."

Willie, barely recovered from the shotgun blasts that still rang in his ears and the remnants of brains and blood blast on the road, wasn't quite tracking everything that was going on, but the kids seemed to be doing all right without him.

"We're going to get water," Robby said, after shaking Parker's hand, "then you can follow us back if you want."

Sherilyn clapped her hands and did a little dance.

~ ~ ~

Parker and Sherilyn followed the truck and trailer about five miles upriver, then stayed in the car while the others went to work. The two boys, obviously practiced, jumped out of the truck, pulled the generator, pump, and hoses out of the back of the pickup, and one of them took the hose with the filter end down to the water while the other one hooked up the pump and then pulled the cord on the generator until it came to life.

Willie stood by and watched, hands on his hips.

"Did you see those two men's souls leave their bodies?" Sherilyn asked quietly.

Parker shook his head.

"Is that because they had no souls?"

Parker shrugged. He thought everybody had a soul of some sort, but he didn't know.

"Maybe bad people don't have souls," she said. "But that doesn't seem right, does it? Maybe you just didn't see them. Maybe they were just little teensy, tiny souls and they flitted away like a shadow, and you missed it."

That was more likely. He was sorry his little sister had to see those guys shot by a shotgun at close range. He was sorry he had to see it, sorry they all had to see it, sorry it had to happen at all, but he was overwhelmingly grateful that Willie and the boys showed up before those men did something horrible to Sherilyn. He couldn't have stood that.

He looked over at her, as she contemplated soul life and her new ideas about the afterlife, and again he was struck with his deep affection for her. He would protect her at all cost.

"Mom and Dad went on, didn't they?" She turned to face him, and he saw sincere concern in her eyes. "I mean, you'd see them if they were still in the house, wouldn't you? And the Zimmermans?"

Parker nodded as solemnly as he knew how, trying to comfort her. He didn't think it had been a mistake to take her on one of those excursions because it opened her eyes to a whole way of thinking about life, as it had done his. But he didn't want her to dwell on it, either.

"Why didn't we die, Parker?" she asked. "How come Mom and Dad died and we didn't?"

Parker took a deep breath and exhaled slowly. This was a question that had echoed in the back of his mind for months.

"I mean," she went on, "the virus came, and it was a big deal, everyone wearing masks and staying home, all over the news, and then suddenly, everybody died. It was so fast. Remember? Dad was watching football and an hour later he died. Same with Mom the next day. And then it was over, as if it had killed everybody it wanted to kill and then it was done. Why them and not us?" She crossed her arms over her chest and set her jaw.

These were not questions he could answer even if he could speak.

These were questions that no one could answer, and she knew it. He reached over and tugged on one of her arms until she loosened up. He held her hand and stroked it.

She let him do it for a moment, then pulled her hand away and brushed tears from her face.

Surely there were girls at the cul-de-sac, too, and Sherilyn could have a social life. A good, healthy girly social life. She'd have chores to do, probably, with the others, and there would be some type of school, and that would be good for her. Not a solitary, silent, boring life of unending work and worry with him in their old, empty parents' house. Something new. Something fresh. She was excited about the prospect, and Parker was excited for her.

It didn't take long for the pump to fill the tank and for Sherilyn to collect herself, and soon they were on their way again. Sherilyn followed along on the map, trying to figure out how they never came upon the place in their searches.

The truck pulled up into the driveway of a house at the end of a cul-de-sac, and Parker saw an amazing community at work. Everybody was active. Some were mowing, some were sweeping, some were walking, carrying what looked like bundles of laundry, and he could see what looked like an enormous garden back behind the main house.

"Wow," Sherilyn breathed. "This is it. I mean this is more than it. This is *really* it!"

Jamaal jumped out of the truck and came back to them, showed them where to park. "We have to go pick up a couple of beds, so as soon as we unhitch the trailer, we'll be off again, but I want to take you to meet Castile. She's Willie's daughter, she's a nurse, and she kind of takes care of all of us. She'll want to talk with you."

Parker and Sherilyn parked in the indicated spot, got out of the car and followed him into the main house, where a couple of people were reading, a man in the corner was giving a child a piano lesson, and a tall woman with short dark hair was chopping vegetables.

"Mary, is Castile around?" Jamaal asked.

"She was here a minute ago," Mary said, wiping perspiration

from her forehead with the back of her hand. "She may be in the garden." She looked at Parker and Sherilyn. "Who's this?"

"I'm Sherilyn, and this is my brother Parker," Sherilyn said.

Mary wiped her hands on a towel and shook hands with both of them. "Are you here to stay?"

"I hope so," Sherilyn said.

"I hope so, too," Mary responded with a warm smile.

Jamaal led them out the back door into the garden that looked like something Parker had seen in magazines. Perfect rows, filled with healthy vegetables, lots of people with hoes, some on their knees, everybody moving, everybody working.

"There she is," Jamaal said, and got Castile's attention with a wave. A woman with lots of curly dark hair started over toward them.

The whole sight was a lot to take in, and Parker wasn't sure his eyes were open wide enough. This looked like paradise. To the right was a big wood-fired oven, and two girls—could they be Sherilyn's age? no, they were a little older—were taking loaves of bread out on a big wooden platter. Sherilyn would love to learn how to do that, and Parker bet that this place went through a lot of bread. There were a lot of people.

One of the girls, a long-legged girl in blue shorts and a white tank top, her blonde hair in braids, stopped and stared at them. She carefully put the bread on the table without taking her eyes off them.

She was possibly the most beautiful girl he had ever seen. She had the softest blue color around her. But why was she staring?

Did she recognize him? Or Sherilyn? Did he know her? No, he would remember that face if he had ever met her, like in one of his classes at the high school or something.

She made him a little uneasy, and he turned away to look elsewhere at the garden, but a moment later, snuck a glance back in her direction.

She was still looking at him. Then the other girl she worked with elbowed her and she picked up a bowl of dough, turned it upside down on the table, and began to knead it.

"*Sister Matthew!*" Sherilyn yelled, and ran past Castile, past the oven, where a surprised and mildly horrified Sister Matthew greeted Sherilyn's enthusiastic hug.

Castile stopped in her tracks and watched the reunion. Parker saw Sister Matthew's eyes meet Castile's over Sherilyn's head, then Castile continued on toward Parker and Jamaal.

"Sister Matthew?" She asked Jamaal.

"Don't know anything about that," he said. "But that girl is Sherilyn, and this is Parker, her brother. Parker doesn't speak. We found them in trouble down by the river. Willie can tell you the whole story. I've got to go help them pick up some beds."

"Thanks," Castile said, then turned kind eyes on Parker. "Welcome," she said. "I'm sorry you were in some trouble. Are you okay?"

Parker nodded.

"And you're mute?"

Parker nodded again.

"From birth?"

Parker waggled his head and then nodded.

"Would you mind if I ran some tests? Have you seen speech therapists?"

Parker nodded wearily. He'd been down that road many, many times.

"Okay, then, I don't want to traumatize you further. Are you looking for a new place to live?"

Just then, Sherilyn came bouncing up. "Did you see her Parker? Did you see Sister Matthew?"

Parker nodded.

Castile held out her hand. "Hi," she said. "I'm Castile. Can we talk a while?"

"Sure!" Sherilyn said, eager to get the formalities over.

A black and white border collie greeted them with similar enthusiasm.

"That's Alta," Castile said. "She's our guardian and our mascot."

Sherilyn got down on her knees to hug and pet the dog who returned the affection with liberal face kisses. "Oh, I love her! Her nose is so cold!" What a difference fifteen minutes makes in the life of a twelve-year-old, Parker thought.

Castile led them to a corner of the great room in the main house, where Mary brought them glasses of tepid lemonade that tasted wonderful. "Usually, we'd be in my office at the infirmary, but I've got a sick patient in there now and until she's better, or I know what her problem is, I'm not taking anybody inside."

"Who lives here?" Sherilyn asked. "How many are there? Do you have school? Are there any kids my age? Do you have books? I have lots of books at home that I could bring over here."

"You've been alone a while?" Castile addressed Parker, who nodded, both of them smiling at Sherilyn's excitement.

"Yes," Sherilyn said. "We've been alone at our parents' house, but we can't be alone another winter over there. We've been looking for you. We hope you have room for us."

"We certainly do have room," Castile said. "But we also have chores. Everyone here pulls their own weight."

"I work hard," Sherilyn said, her face serious, "and so does Parker. He's really smart. At the other place, he was working on a solar electricity system."

Castile's eyebrows went up. "Oh? What other place?"

"With stupid Elijah at the high school. We were there for a couple of months. That's where we met Sister Matthew. We left there a while ago."

Castile turned her attention to Parker again. "Do you read?"

"Yes!" Sherilyn offered. "And he knows how to draw plans."

"Then you'll probably want to work with Willie," Castile said. "Now let's talk about your health, in case there's anything I need to know. Then we'll find you a house to live in. With some compatible roommates."

"If we're going to move here, I need to go home to get some stuff," Sherilyn said.

"Of course," Castile replied. "I'll show you around, and you can go home and get what you need this afternoon. I'll introduce you to the community this evening at dinner."

Sherilyn clapped her hands and grinned at Parker.

~ ~ ~

Castile met the truck when Willie returned with the boys and the beds. Other men came to help the boys offload and take the beds, while he recognized trouble in Castile's face. "My office?" he asked. Castile nodded.

"There's another community not far from here," Castile began after they were settled in the little workshop.

Willie nodded. "I knew there must be."

"Amanda was part of it."

Willie frowned. "Really? Has she said anything about that?"

"No, and that's the troubling thing. The kids you brought here? They were at that place for a while, run by some evangelical named Elijah, but they left. They recognized Amanda."

"Have you talked to her?"

"I wanted to talk with you first."

"It makes sense," Willie said. "I saw that boy, Parker, once, and he was in a truck with two other men."

"So Amanda's been lying to us," Castile said.

Willie took a deep breath. "What about the kids?"

"I spent a little time with Parker. His mutism is very interesting. Sherilyn said he had a fever when he was a baby, that's all she knows. I can make him mimic me. He can say his name, or any other word by repeating the sounds I make, so there's nothing wrong with him physically. But when I ask him his name, he knows it, but can't say it."

"He has a short in his wiring."

"Exactly. I've put them in the Morrison house with Rita and Charlie. They've gone to pick up some things from their old place. They're very excited to be here. Parker reads and I think he knows about electricity. He might be useful to you here in the shop. Mary's gearing up the canning effort, so I'm going to put Sherilyn on food preservation duty."

Castile looked closely at Willie. He suddenly seemed old, pale, and not very interested in anything she was telling him. "Are you okay?"

"I need to tell you what happened at the river, when we picked up those two kids."

"Okay," Castile said, "and then we need to make a decision about Amanda."

"Let's talk with her privately before we bring her up before the Committee."

Castile nodded. "Good idea. Now tell me what happened at the river."

Willie shook his head and closed his eyes, the vision of those dead men on the road still vivid in his mind's eye. "Oh, man," he said. "It was bad."

~ ~ ~

Dinner was a whirlwind for Parker. He and Sherilyn had picked up lots of stuff from their house, mostly clothes and some canned food. Sherilyn wanted her own pillow, her stuffed elephant and their mother's pearl necklace. They unpacked their things in a nice house about a block away from the main house. It appeared as if the community was taking over the entire neighborhood. He and Sherilyn each had their own bedroom, and a nice couple, Rita and Charlie, older than their parents, slept in the other bedroom. Charlie gave him a big-handed handshake and a nice smile and welcomed them to the house and informed Parker that he was automatically part of the team that maintained the latrine for the four houses whose lots came together. He'd been doing it by himself for a while, and would welcome the help. Same with the wood for the wood stove when the weather turned cold. Parker smiled back. He was going to like this guy. He and Sherilyn had never known their grandparents, but Charlie, with his gray hair, big nose, and lots of tattoos on his forearms was exactly how he imagined his grandfather to be. Rita, with her gray hair done up in a knot on the top of her head, small and prim next to Charlie's gregarious personality, sat Sherilyn down in the living room and listened patiently to her whole long story about last winter alone in their house, and how everything changed when Parker started to drive.

In less than an hour, they all felt like family.

Dinner was another story. The main house was packed with people, and Rita and Charlie introduced them around. They went through the chow line, filling their plates with beautiful food, mostly an assemblage of colorful salads, while Mary stood by watching, satisfaction on her face. The highlight of the meal was the giant bowl of steamed snow peas, fresh from the garden. A dozen freshly-baked cherry pies sat on a sideboard, cooling.

Sherilyn tugged on Parker's sleeve and pointed at the pies. "Cherries are in season right now," Mary said to her. "We have a gleaning team that goes around town and picks fruit and berries from abandoned trees and vines, vegetables from old gardens and so forth. Is that something you might be interested in doing?"

"Yes, yes, yes!" Sherilyn said, bouncing up and down. "I would *love* that!"

Mary smiled at her. "I'll talk with Kip. He's in charge of that crew."

Sherilyn looked up at Parker with wide eyes and an enormous grin.

Castile, wanting to introduce them to the group, had saved a place for them to sit at the table next to her and Willie, and they put their plates down and ate. Most people ate with their plates on their laps or on TV trays, but they seemed used to that, and conversation filled the room, loud and energizing.

Parker looked around the room at how everyone had congregated in small groups to chat about their day. This could not be more different from the way things were over at the high school where everyone seemed to view everyone else with suspicion. These people had finished an honest, hard day's work for the whole of the community, and they felt good about themselves. He couldn't wait to find out what everybody did in the evening after dinner.

He wished he had found this group earlier. He looked over at Sherilyn, shoveling food into her mouth while she looked around the room. "This is so good," she said, and he knew she meant more than the food.

When they had finished, that same girl, the one from the bread oven came over and collected their plates. "Hi," she said. "I'm Crystal."

"Hi," Sherilyn said. "I saw you baking bread. This is really good bread. Did you make it?"

"Well, we made it," Crystal said. "Mary's in charge, I'm just on the kitchen crew. Today was bread day."

"I'm Sherilyn and this is my brother, Parker. He doesn't speak."

"Oh?" She gave Parker a smile that gave him that shy feeling in his gut. "Maybe we'll talk later."

"Okay," Sherilyn said, and after she had walked away, she whispered to Parker. "She likes you."

He elbowed her in response.

When most of the plates had been collected and returned to the kitchen, Castile stood up. "How about this meal?" The whole room erupted into applause and shouts of appreciation. Mary took a bow.

When Mary turned to attend to the dishes and the leftovers, Castile said, "I'd like to introduce Parker and Sherilyn. They're new to us as of today, and are in the Morrison house with Charlie and Rita."

Everybody clapped and said various versions of "welcome."

Parker's face grew warm with the attention.

"We have another thing to discuss before cherry pie," Castile said. "I wanted to bring this to the Committee, but Willie and Amanda and I talked it over, and we think we want the whole community to know about it."

All eyes went to Amanda, who hung her head.

"Amanda has not been entirely honest with us about who she is and where she's from."

The crowd murmured.

"She has her reasons for being deceitful, and they revolve around the safety of her thirteen-year-old daughter Reyna, who is still with the other community over at Jefferson High School." Castile paused. "We have very few rules here, but honesty and integrity are among

157

the most important. Instead of summarily asking her to leave, we thought the community should have a say."

A man in the back stood up. "Let's hear from Amanda," he said. There was a scattering of applause and nodding of heads.

Amanda stood up and faced the group. "It's true," she said. "My daughter and I were at the high school with Elijah and his group. It's Sam York, from Sam York Ford. He calls himself Elijah now. He sent me here to spy on you. He is a failed leader, who has no idea what he's doing, and I was supposed to report back to him what you are doing that makes your community a success. But I never did." She choked up on those last words. "You've all been so welcoming and so wonderful, and I have regretted my dishonesty. I would like to bring my daughter here and be contributing members of this group."

"How could we ever trust you?" a woman asked.

Amanda's voice tightened with emotion. "I'm asking your forgiveness," she said and then sat down.

"Who are we if we can't forgive someone?" a different woman asked.

"She's been a good worker, both in the laundry and in the kitchen," someone else said.

"But if we let her stay, we've brought suspicion into our community," a man countered. "Why would we want to do that? She came here to spy. I say we send her back."

Parker felt words filling him. He knew he was going to stand up and speak, and he didn't want to. He never wanted to, but once the feeling started, there was only one release.

He put his napkin on the table and started to stand. Sherilyn grabbed his arm. "No, Parker, please, please, please. You'll get us kicked out. Oh, Parker no, pleeeeeze."

He plucked her hand from his arm and stood.

Sherilyn moaned and covered her face with her hands.

He cleared his throat and let the voice speak through him. "Showing unlimited compassion and empathy is the way forward in this new world," he said.

Amanda wiped a tear from her eye and looked up at him.

"This group has a unique opportunity to create the new world. There are legions of spirit helpers surrounding you at all times, helping you to make the right decisions. All you have to do is believe, and then ask for their assistance. You will form the new world government, if you will. You will bring about the salvation of mankind, if you will. You will help rebuild society, if you so choose. We have gathered this group, and there are many leaders among you who will make decisions that will alter the fate of this planet. We suggest you begin with unlimited empathy and compassion."

Empty, Parker sat back down.

The room was silent.

Slowly, there were quiet murmurs amongst the people. Castile turned to Parker. "I didn't know you were a channeler," she said quietly.

"Channeler?" Sherilyn asked. "What's that?"

"Well," a tall blonde woman, still in overalls with dirty knees said. "I guess that's that." She turned to Amanda and gave her a hug. "Welcome!"

The entire room exhaled and began to talk and move about.

Mary came in from the kitchen. "Okay, then," she said. "Time for pie."

Chapter 7 – July

Elijah paced back and forth in his bedroom/office. This place was hot as hell and he didn't dare open a window to catch a breath of fresh air. He didn't even go outside to piss in the latrine, because he didn't want the others to see him outside, to see him with fresh air and sunshine. They had believed him when he told them the outside was full of radiation, but he had no real knowledge of that, and if they thought about it for a half a second, they would realize that there was no way he could possibly know it. Fucking followers. They were beginning to be burdensome. He hoped they were grateful, but he knew they were not. They were fussy and grumpy.

Most of them went outside to the latrine every day, more than once a day. He, himself, pooped in a bucket with a toilet seat on it and someone fetched it and cleaned it out twice a day.

This was no way to live, but he seemed to have painted himself into a corner and wasn't entirely sure what to do about it.

Something had to change, because it was July, hot as holy fuck, and it was becoming intolerable. People were leaving, and he couldn't exactly blame them. They were zooming through their food stores with no way to replenish them for the coming winter, and winter was, without question, on its way.

But before he could sit back down in his chair, put his feet up and treat himself to a little sip of the whiskey he kept in his desk, the office door slammed open and a red-faced and wildly angry Sister Matthew marched in.

"What the fuck, Sam?" she yelled. *"What. The. Actual. Fuck?"*

Elijah hurried around the desk to close the office door. "Lower your voice when you speak to me, woman," he said. "And I'll thank you not to use prof—"

"Fuck you! Where's my daughter?"

Elijah took a deep breath, hoping to diffuse the situation. "She left," he said, crossed his arms over his chest and leaned back against his desk.

"I put her in your care while I went off on your stupid mission, and you were going to take care of her."

"You failed your mission," Elijah said.

"So you failed yours?"

"I felt no responsibility to her when you went your own way. She is your daughter, you should have been here to see to her, or else done what you said you would do. This is not my fault, Amanda, this is all on you."

It worked. He saw her collapse inside of herself. He pointed to a chair behind her. She sat, and the blood drained from her face.

"Where did they go?" She asked in a small voice.

"I have no idea,"

"Who did she go with?"

"Russ and Timothy."

"Two teenage boys? What were you thinking? Oh, my God. How am I ever going to find her?"

"Teenagers have no common sense," Elijah said, contentedly rubbing salt in her wound.

"You're saying they're not likely to make it? Not likely to last? Not likely to find another group, a tolerable group to join?"

Elijah shrugged, enjoying her misery more than he thought he would. Bitch.

"I fucking hate you, Sam." Amanda closed her eyes, took a deep breath, and then stood up. "I'll see if anybody else knows where they were headed."

"You will leave the property immediately," Elijah said. "Or I will have you thrown out."

"Throw me out," she said, walking toward the door. "Just try it."

It was an empty threat, of course. Amanda walked out of Sam's office and down to the cafeteria where Susie Martin and her fourteen-year-old daughter Maria were opening cans of tuna for lunch. After hugs, a concerned Susie asked Amanda how she was. Clearly, she wasn't well after her encounter with Elijah. Fear had caught in her chest and she was having a hard time breathing. The three of them pulled chairs around and sat down. Susie gave Amanda a glass of water and waited until she was ready to speak.

"I'm living in a wonderful place," Amanda finally said. "A real community, where everybody works hard for the good of all. They've welcomed me, and I've come back for Reyna, only to find out that she's gone."

"Lots of people have left," Maria said. "People are sick of this place."

"Do you know where Russ and Timothy took Reyna?"

"Russ and Timothy? I thought she left with Steven," Susie said.

"She did," Maria said, "and Edith, and a couple of others. Don. Don drove. Russ and Timothy were with them."

"Oh, thank God there were adults," Amanda said, and felt her heart ease. God *damn* Sam for leaving out that little detail just to mess with her.

"Steven's a good man," Susie said. "He'll take care of them. He'll keep everyone safe. Him and Don."

Amanda nodded. "No idea where they went?"

Susie and Maria both shook their heads. "I don't think they knew where they were going. They were just getting out of here. Lots of people have left. Probably half the people who were here when you were have gone."

"Steven's group was maybe the first," Maria said. "More people started leaving after that. Taking Sam's cars right off the lot." She covered her smile with her hand.

"Where is everybody going?"

"I don't know," Susie said. "Some said they were headed to Portland. Others said they were going south. In fact, I think I heard Steven once talk about going south."

"South is a big place," Amanda said. "But it's a start." She felt her lungs begin to take in more air. "Are you two all right?"

"I hate it here," Maria said.

"I don't know where else we would go," Susie said. "Elijah keeps telling us about roving bands of rapists and murderers. Poisoned air and water. At least we're safe here, and we have the Lord."

"It's not true," Amanda said. "Where do you think you're getting your water? From the river, just like the rest of us. We're all outside, growing a garden."

"A garden?" Maria said.

"There are no roving bands of rapists and murderers. There is virtually nobody alive out there," Amanda said. "And how would Elijah know about roving bands of rapists and murderers? Has he been outside?"

Susie looked at her hands.

"Those who survived are congregating together in little communities all over. I've heard the broadcasts."

"Broadcasts?" Susie raised her eyebrows. "Technology?"

"There's a broadcast from Boulder Colorado every day at six o'clock. The guy relates news of other communities across the world. People are starting to be connected with information and hope." Amanda paused. "You two can come with me, if you want. It's a good place, where people actually care about one another."

"Mama?" Maria looked at her mom with hope in her eyes.

"There are other teenage girls there," Amanda said.

"I don't know…" Susie said, looking at the kitchen where lunch was only halfway prepared. "I should get back to making lunch…"

Amanda knew the look. Susie was not moving. She was probably bedding Elijah by now, and he had her total loyalty. Amanda looked earnestly at Maria. "The boys from our place go to the river about two miles east of the bridge to get water every day," Amanda said. "Tell them I sent you. When you're ready."

Maria understood and gave Amanda a hug.

Susie went back to opening cans.

~ ~ ~

Freshly showered and wearing only a pair of boxer shorts, Parker gratefully slipped into his bed. Someone, Sherilyn, probably, had changed the linens, and the clean sheets felt cool and smooth.

It had been quite a day. Last month, he and Willie redesigned the new windmill, a bigger, more powerful, sturdy windmill, and today it was installed on the tower their crew had built over the past month. Just before dinner, they had hooked it up to a massive bank of batteries they had scrounged in the neighborhood, from cars, gas stations, and auto parts stores, and then they hooked it up to the main house.

Willie stood in the main room of the house, his arm around Parker's shoulders when he gave the nod to Tony to activate it.

All the lights in the kitchen and the great room came on and a cheer came up from the people, who turned as one to see the two of them standing and grinning.

Willie hugged him, and pretty soon everybody else was hugging him, too.

Parker smiled into his pillow. He liked working with Willie. They were interested in the same things, and though Willie was not his father, he was the kind of the father he had always wanted. His own father loved him, he knew, but they had nothing, really, in common. He and Willie communicated perfectly, they had some kind of a strange alignment; it was almost as if they could read one another's' thoughts when they were working on a project.

Getting running water to the community was next, and he had a stack of books on his nightstand to go through, but not tonight. Tonight was a milestone and a celebration to go with it. He'd start on the water tomorrow. Chances are, they'd have to go to the pumping station up in the hills. The whole water system should still be operational, if only they had power. Well, power could be had. Imagine the hugs they'd get if suddenly the toilets began to flush, and water came out of the faucets!

He'd make that happen, he and Willie. They'd been charging up old cell phones so they could take photographs of what they found up in the pumping stations. That would help them figure it all out.

He turned over, ready for sleep, but sleep wasn't ready for him. In the midst of all the happiness and successes, he felt a pull, as if he should be combing the neighborhood, helping people who had died to get unstuck and go on to their next adventure. This was not something he could talk over with Willie.

Unless he took Willie with him one time. But there was no guaranty that Willie would be able to see the way Sherilyn had. That had been completely unexpected. And she hadn't wanted to go with him again after that. He didn't want Willie to look at him differently, either, if he knew about this thing that Parker did. Maybe he'd just get in his car and go, say one morning a week. Nobody would mind, he was sure.

Yes. One morning a week, he would get back to it.

Sherilyn was in heaven on the gleaning team. The team had put her in charge of marking down on maps everywhere they found fruit. They were bringing in flats full of figs, raspberries, blueberries, and blackberries now, and food preservation was in full swing. They were canning the fruit as well as produce from the garden and using the half dozen dehydrators they had hooked up to solar panels out in the yard.

Every time Parker saw his sister, she was happy and smiling, laughing easily and looking healthy. Living here felt like a return to emotional normalcy. She worked hard and was growing strong and tall and tan in the process.

Parker punched up his pillow, sent his nightly message of *all's well* to his parents, wherever they were on the other side, closed his eyes and felt his whole body relax into sleep.

At first, he thought he was dreaming that someone had opened his bedroom door, but then she stood next to his bed, pulling off her t-shirt and pajama pants, and when she slid naked into his bed, her cool skin next to his, he was suddenly very awake.

"Hi," Crystal whispered, and wrapped her arms around him.

They'd engaged in a little flirting here and there, little smiles across the lawn, secret glances during the evening meals, but he never imagined this… Her skin was smooth like nothing he had ever touched before. He wanted to feel all her skin, everywhere.

Then she was kissing him, but this was not the way he heard the boys in the high school locker room talk about kissing, and his shorts became way too tight.

She smelled delicious. He had no idea girls smelled sweet like that, with a hint of fire smoke and freshly baked bread. She tasted like minty toothpaste. His hands began to explore her, and she liked it.

Her hands were busy feeling him as well, starting at his head, and shoulders, then down his back and to the waistband of his underwear, and under, her hands feeling his butt, and moving around to the front.

He moved away and freed his hungry penis from where it was hung up on the waistband, and pulled his under shorts down to his knees, where she used her toes to pull them the rest of the way off.

He rubbed himself against her belly as their hot mouths suctioned together and it was the most glorious feeling in the world.

She squirmed around until she was under him, her legs open.

Vague echoes of his father's safe sex lectures played in the back of his mind, but he had no time for that. He was too busy trying to figure out what to do next.

But she knew what she wanted, and he let her lead.

She wrapped her legs around him, and with her hand, guided him gently inside her: moist, sweet, slippery, welcoming.

He came, first thing, and moaned his disappointment.

"It's okay," she said, and kept moving her hands around him, kept kissing him, nuzzling him, until his erection grew again. He kissed her breasts, sucked on her magically responsive nipples, and soon he was back inside her, and they rocked together, quietly, calmly, and then urgently.

She began to make noises, and he put his hand over her mouth, and then pulled the covers over their heads. He did not want to wake Sherilyn, asleep in the next room.

Crystal nodded against his chest that she understood. She put her lips on him, making little noises deep in her throat as they moved together until Parker could not stand it another second. Her vagina contracted in spasms around him, and he exploded in a burst of glory.

When their breathing slowed, he slipped from her and lay next to her in the bed.

"Was that your first time?" she asked.

He nodded.

"It was nice," she said. "You're nice."

He put his arm around her and pulled her close. Is this heaven? Is this heaven on earth?

"I remember the first time I saw you," she whispered.

He nodded.

"I couldn't stop looking at you. There's something... I don't know... special about you. Have you ever felt that? Have you ever felt that someone was, I don't know, part of your destiny?"

He pulled back and looked at her searching, sincere eyes. He kissed her lightly on the lips.

"I'll take that as a yes," she said, smiling. "There might be something special about us."

Parker closed his eyes in contentment.

When he opened them, sunlight flooded the room, and Crystal was snoring lightly, her back to him.

He gently pulled the covers back from her shoulder, and then all the way down, admiring the curve of her back, the dip of her waist. He ran his hand over her skin, that amazingly smooth skin, until she sighed, and turned toward him.

"Good morning," she whispered.

He smiled at her, his greedy penis pushing against her, begging for more.

She shook her head. "I have to go."

Disappointed, he nodded. She really should leave before the household awoke.

"I'll be back," she said, and then slipped out of bed, and he put an arm behind his head and watched her pull pajama bottoms over long, strong legs and cover those amazing breasts with a t-shirt.

She finger-combed her tousled hair, blew him a kiss and slipped out the door.

Now what, he wondered. Likely there was some protocol or standard of behavior going forward, but he had no idea what that would be.

She said she'd be back. That was all he really needed to know.

~ ~ ~

Amanda's little visit had given Elijah an idea. First, though, he needed to know who he could depend on. Miles had proven himself to be a good right-hand guy ever since Don and Steven left. He didn't know anything about bringing electricity to the building, or plumbing, but he didn't seem to question anything that Elijah asked of him, especially if he threw some scripture in for good measure. Maybe it was time to give Miles a little test.

The next morning, Miles stood in front of Elijah, flanked by Cassandra and Harrison. Elijah was not thrilled with Miles's choice of partners in this little errand, but he had given Miles the freedom to choose, and this is what he came up with. Miles, small and dark, and probably forty, had some leaderships skills. Harrison was about the same age, but taller, and kind of a dork. Cassandra was the one with the mouth. She was younger, maybe thirty, and wore clothes that were too tight and too revealing. She had been told multiple times about her provocative nature, and she had done nothing to change her ways.

This was the best of who was left? Pretty pitiful.

"I have a mission for you," Elijah said. "Take a van from the lot and go to all the stores and get all the guns and ammunition you find and bring it back here."

All three looked at him with open mouths and furrowed brows, as if they were stupid. "Guns?" Harrison asked. "We've been against guns and violence. What do we need guns for?"

"First," Elijah said slowly, as if talking to a child, "We need to keep guns out of the hands of others. Yes?" Harrison nodded his agreement. "Second, there is a rival group, and I think it's time we had some protection from them. Third, resources are beginning to dwindle, and winter approaches."

"That's true," Cassandra said. "I was over at the elementary school yesterday, and our stores are way down. We need to replenish."

"Exactly," Elijah said. "There may be resistance, so we need to be prepared. Are you familiar with the Salvation Army?" All three nodded like bobble head dolls. "Well, we will be the New Salvation Army. God's Army. And armies need arms."

"Makes sense, I guess," Miles said. "Where are we going to find guns?"

"That's your mission," Elijah said, checking his exasperation factor. You go out and find them, and then bring them back here. Guns and ammunition. All you can find. We'll turn a classroom into an armory."

"Okay," Harrison said.

"Then go!" Elijah shooed them out, careful not to speak out loud the things he was thinking about his dwindling flock.

An hour later, they had walked the half mile or so to the Sam York Ford dealership.

"Elijah's not going to like this," Cassandra said as she viewed the shattered glass walls, the keys that had been scattered around the floor, and the few cars left on the lot with their gas caps open.

Miles found a van inside the service bay with the keys in it. He pulled up the big garage door and drove it out to the front. Cassandra got into the passenger seat, Harrison in the back, and Miles drove off the Sam York Ford lot, and then stopped at the first stop sign. "Where to?"

"You mean where we haven't been to yet? This is ridiculous," Cassandra said. "Guns? Come on."

"He's scared," Harrison said.

"Of what?" Cassandra crossed her arms over her chest. This was a fool's errand to top all fool's errands.

"I don't know," Harrison said, "but it has to be something. Otherwise, why would we need guns?"

"We don't need guns," Cassandra said. "He thinks *he* needs guns. But why?"

"Well," Miles said, tapping his fingers on the steering wheel. "We better come back with something. He's getting jumpy about it."

"We've been to all the sporting goods stores," Harrison said, "looking for other things. You know there are no guns or ammunition in those places. We'd have to go a hundred miles away to find another."

"Sometimes convenience store employees keep guns under the counter. We could check all the 7/11s," Cassandra said.

"That's not what he wants," Harrison said. "He wants an arsenal." He was silent for a while as Miles tried to engage the air conditioning. "Actually, I knew a guy who had an arsenal. He sold guns. He made his garage into a giant vault, full of all kinds of guns. He even had a Howitzer. I went shooting with him a few times. I shot an AK-47 and a Tommy gun. It was fun."

"Fun?" Cassandra asked.

"Yeah, I shot guns when I was in the Army. It was fun, shooting at targets. Whatever Elijah is planning, though, I doubt will be much fun."

"Why the hell didn't you mention this earlier?" Miles asked. "Where? Where is this guy's house?"

Harrison told him.

They found the owner of the house with his wife in the back yard, both dead of gunshot wounds to the head. Considerate, Miles thought, as most of their remains had already soaked into the earth. "Let's pick up that pistol on our way out," Miles said, pointing at the revolver still in the guy's hand.

Cassandra grimaced.

The back door was unlocked.

Seemed like a regular house in a regular neighborhood. Nothing fancy.

Cassandra stopped to look through the kitchen cabinets to see what kind of canned goods they had stored up. There wasn't much. "Not much food, old appliances," she said. "Was this guy a prepper?" she asked.

"I don't know," Harrison said. "Probably."

"Then he has a stash of food and other stuff somewhere else. We should look for it."

"Guns," Miles said, reminding them that their mission was not to gather food or judge the décor.

Harrison led them through the house to a small room which had been converted to an office space. The bookshelves were full of books and magazines, all about various forms of firearms, in a range of languages. He pointed at a door. "In there."

Miles tried the door, but it was locked. He rummaged through the desk, looking for what appeared to be a standard key for a standard knob.

Cassandra picked a pretty cup with pheasants painted on it from a shelf by the door. It tinkled. She turned it over, and a key fell out.

It fit the door, but beyond that was a metal door with a push button combination lock.

"You ever see him open this thing?" Miles asked.

"Sure," Harrison said, "but I don't know the combination."

"My folks had a combination lock like that on their front door," Cassandra said. "It has batteries in it. There's a key to it, so in case the batteries die, you can still open it."

"Another key," Miles said, looking around the office. "Where would he put that key?"

"Some place safe, where he would know how to get to it, but he wouldn't necessarily need it but every five years or so," Cassandra said. "My folks had a little key thing, like a hollow book, where they kept all their spare keys, you know, the neighbor's house, the bike locks, extra car keys. That's where they kept theirs. On the bookshelf."

The three stood back and scanned the bookshelves.

"It wouldn't be in here," Miles said, and walked back into the living room to look for other bookshelves. "Check closets, too," he said.

"A key? A little key? Oh, man, it could be anywhere." Harrison went to the master bedroom and Cassandra went back to the kitchen to look around, and to see if there was maybe a basement where they would keep a stash of emergency food. Guns were stupid.

The little pantry didn't have a trap door that she could see, although didn't most of these houses have access to the crawl space in one of the closets? She'd have Miles check that.

There wasn't a basement door, and the cupboards didn't give up anything of interest. She'd take the three cans of salmon and some lasagna noodles. She held her nose and opened the refrigerator and the freezer, but there was nothing worth salvaging in either place.

Just as she was about to close the door on the disgusting mess that was the refrigerator, she saw a bit of green in the back of one of the drawers.

What could possibly still be green in this morass of soupy, fuzzy, stinking slop?

She gently opened the drawer.

A cabbage.

No, not really. She grabbed it and pulled it out. A plastic cabbage, with a little screw plug at the core end. She shook it, and it rattled.

She wiped it off with a dishtowel, and then unscrewed the plug and upended it. A wad of hundred-dollar bills unfurled into her hand, followed by an odd looking key.

This had to be the key they were looking for.

From the living room, she heard Miles pulling books off a bookshelf and tossing them into a pile. Kind of disrespectful. She hoped Harrison wasn't doing the same thing in the bedrooms.

She had a choice.

She could not mention it to the guys and they could just go on their merry way, taking this guy's pistol, or she could give them the key she was sure opened the vault door.

She didn't want Elijah to have an arsenal. He was increasingly unpredictable. Faint memories of the Jim Jones massacre floated through her mind. Could he, would he kill them all?

Maybe.

"Hey," Harrison said, startling her.

She turned around, the key in her fist. "Find anything?" she asked.

"Nope."

Feeling weirdly conspiratorial, she opened her hand and showed him the key.

"Is that it?" he asked quietly.

"Probably."

He reached for it, but she closed her fingers over it and held her hand up to her heart. "Do we really want to do this?" she whispered. "Do we really want Elijah to have an arsenal of weapons?"

"Is that our call?" Harrison had a sincere face, and she had always liked him, but he was a bit of a follower. She could tell he was going to follow Miles's lead.

By showing Harrison the key, she had made the decision. She hoped it was the right one, but at least it wasn't hers alone.

Keeping her eyes locked on Harrison's eyes, she called out, "Miles? I think I found it."

Harrison nodded, in what she could only construe as relief. He didn't want to be secretive or disloyal to anyone, ever.

At this point, she wasn't sure that was an attractive quality.

The key fit in the top of the push button keypad and unlocked it. Miles opened the door to a converted garage, filled with an astonishing collection of firearms. Pegboard lined one entire wall, and rifles, shotguns, automatic weapons of probably every type, and more hung in neat rows. Along the back were at least a hundred handguns. The Army-green Howitzer, on its tripod, sat in the corner. Metal shelving units filled with boxes of various kinds of ammunition reached the ceiling, as well as cases of military-grade MREs, or Meals Ready to Eat. There were also shelves of camping gear, space blankets, radios, candles, oil lamps, Sterno stoves, hibachis, charcoal, and gallon cans of protein powder. All carefully stored, and probably categorized and inventoried.

It was almost too much to take in. Except the smell. It smelled familiar, but she couldn't put her finger on it.

"Wow," Harrison said, taking a deep breath. "I love the smell of gun oil and gunpowder. But it wasn't like this the last time I was here. He got serious."

"And what good did that do him?" Cassandra asked. She walked over to stand in front of Miles, then turned to face him. He was clearly shocked by what he was seeing. "Miles," she said softly.

His eyes refocused on her.

"Let's not turn this over to Elijah," she said.

He blinked a couple of times as if still stunned at the sight and was having a hard time coming back to reality. "What?"

"I said, let's not give all this to Elijah."

"Why not?"

"Because I don't like what I think he might do with it," she said.

"Well then, what should we do with it?"

Cassandra looked to Harrison for help.

"We don't have to do anything with it," Harrison said, much to her relief. "We just lock it up and forget about it."

Miles walked all the way into the room and looked around. He touched a few of the rifles, picked up a handgun, felt its weight, then put it back.

Cassandra thought he was feeling the power a little too much. He seemed mesmerized.

After perusing the shelves and the boxes, he took another long look at the two walls full of guns, then came back to the two of them. "I think we should take as much of this stuff as we can fit into the van and just head out," he said. "Fuck Elijah."

This took Cassandra completely by surprise. "And go where?" she asked. She looked again to Harrison for help, but he was looking at his shoes. "I don't know if I can leave…"

"Leave what?" Miles asked. "What's back there that you so desperately need? Clothes? Check out this woman's closet. Food?" He waved his hand toward months of dried and packaged food for three people. "Friends? You got me and Harrison. We'll find others. Other people who aren't on the brink of nutso."

"What if…" Harrison started quietly… "What if we went back and got another van and another van full of people. We could take twice as much stuff."

"We'd need twice as much stuff if we had twice as many people," Miles said.

Cassandra would love to leave Elijah's place, was envious of all who had, but it was scary just leaving, not knowing where you're going, not knowing where it was safe to go, not knowing if you would ever find another group of people. She had heard Elijah talk of poisoned air and crazy people until she didn't know what to believe.

She bit her lip and looked at the earnestness in Miles's face. He really wanted to talk them into his plan. Harrison was on the edge.

"Okay," Miles said. "Forget it. Let's lock this up. I'll take you two back to the high school, and then I'll come back, load this stuff up and take off."

"No, wait," Harrison said. "I'm coming with you."

Miles nodded, and then looked at Cassandra.

Why me? She wanted to ask them. *Is it because I'm a woman? Is it because I'm here? Why would you want me to go with you anyway?*

She blinked her eyes and then looked at both of them carefully. They were good men. Safe. Smart. She could do worse than to hitch a ride with these guys, and if this was her opportunity, then maybe she should take it.

"Okay then," Miles said, clearly disappointed at her lack of enthusiasm for his idea. "Let's go."

Afraid of being left behind, Cassandra quickly made up her mind. "No," she said, the word only partially catching in her throat. "I'm in."

They argued only briefly about the priority of what to take. Cassandra wanted to take food and camping gear. Miles wanted to take guns and ammo, and Harrison waited to see who won before he committed. Miles won, with a few concessions. They loaded boxes of ammunition and boxes of food first, and then Miles insisted that all the firearms be wrapped in blankets, not only to protect them from banging around, but to protect them from prying eyes. Cassandra stripped the beds and brought the bedding to the arsenal, where Miles used it to wrap the guns and store them alongside, and on top of boxes of food and ammunition. Camping gear went on top of that.

When every square inch of the van had been packed, the three got back into the van, Cassandra in back this time, Miles driving.

He drove cautiously around the neighborhood, to make sure that nobody had seen them looting the house, and then went out onto the highway and turned toward the high school.

"Aren't you going the wrong way?" Cassandra asked.

"I have to go back to the high school and pick up a couple of things."

"Like what?"

"A gas can and hose, for starters," Miles said.

"Seriously?" Cassandra's heart began to pound. She didn't like where this might be going. "We didn't get any gas cans? Hey, wait, I don't think we should go back there."

"Relax," Miles said.

"No, no, listen." Desperation seized her. "We can get a gas can anywhere. Besides, where is there a gas can at the high school?" She didn't trust Elijah, and once the decision to leave had been made, she didn't want to see him again. She didn't want to see any of them. This didn't smell right.

"Look," he pointed at the gas gauge. There was less than half a tank. "I'll only be a minute," Miles said, and moments later, he pulled the van up to the front of the school. "If there's something you want in there, now is the time to get it. Or you can wait here. I'll be right back."

Cassandra scrunched down in her seat and chewed on a knuckle, her heart racing. She had never felt like such a traitor, like such a liar. She had made her decision to go, and now she wanted to go right now. She didn't want to say goodbye to anyone. She didn't want to see anyone. She just wanted to go. "Harrison…"

"He'll be right back. I think he's giving the pistol to Elijah."

"He has the pistol?"

"In his waistband. I saw him pick it up."

Oh, God. She was pretty sure that all the guns in the back of the van were unloaded, but she didn't know about the pistol. It'd had at least two bullets in it, enough to kill the gun hoarder and his wife, that was evident. Perhaps it had more.

"Did he take the keys with him?"

Harrison leaned over to look at the ignition. "Yep."

Nothing good was going to come from this.

A few minutes later, Miles stepped out of the front doors of the school, and with him was Elijah, who had the pistol in his hand.

"What the—" Harrison said.

"Oh God," Cassandra breathed.

They were talking as they approached the van, walked around

the front to the passenger doors.

Elijah opened the front door and faced Harrison, then looked at Cassandra behind him. "Traitors," he said. "Fucking traitors. Get out!"

Miles stood smugly behind him, arms crossed over his chest.

Harrison stepped out of the van.

Cassandra didn't want to get out, but Elijah opened her door.

"Out!" he commanded.

Heart pounding, hesitantly, Cassandra got out and stood next to Harrison on the school driveway.

She stared at Miles as clues about his behavior fell into place in Cassandra's mind like tumblers in a slot machine. Then Elijah put the cold muzzle to Harrison's temple, and she knew the truth about him.

The blast shocked her more than she thought she could be shocked. Harrison crumpled to the ground, a scream burst from her, and Elijah turned his crazy eyes on her.

"Elijah…" she wanted to beg, she hated herself for begging this lunatic for her life.

He slowly lifted the gun and pointed it directly at her forehead. "Traitor," he said quietly, and pulled the trigger.

~ ~ ~

Amanda, still frantic with the knowledge that Reyna was gone, worked harder than ever, hoping that an idea or a plan would sprout. If she left to go find her daughter, Reyna might return and they would miss each other. Also, how on earth would she find her in California? There was no way that she could see, and the knowledge that she might never see her girl again kept her on the edge of tears. Sometimes in the night, she thought she was barely on the edge of sanity with worry.

She grabbed the bundle of laundry from her house and was walking it to the laundry facility when she saw a familiar face. Maria, wrapped in a blanket, walked with Castile toward the main house.

Amanda walked quickly to the laundry, dropped the bundle off and then headed to the kitchen, where Mary was dishing up warm leftover oatmeal for the girl, who was still shivering.

"Maria?"

"Sister Matthew!" Maria got up from her stool and embraced Amanda, letting the blanket drop from her back. She began to sob.

This was not the tall, beautiful, self-possessed fourteen-year-old girl that Amanda knew. Maria seemed thin, and shrunken, shaking and frantic.

Amanda looked to Castile.

"The boys found her down by the river," Castile said. "She'd been there all night, waiting for them."

"Good for you," Amanda said, stroking the girl's hair. "I told you where to find them, didn't I?"

Maria sniffled and nodded her head against Amanda's chest.

"Is your mom here with you?"

"No," Maria said. "She wouldn't come. I sneaked out last night."

Amanda got her rewrapped in the blanket, gave her a handkerchief so she could dry her eyes and blow her nose. Maria sat again on the stool, and Amanda put a spoon in her hand. "Eat this while it's still warm," she said. "And then tell us what happened."

"He's gone crazy," Maria said. "And he's got guns. Lots of guns."

"Who?" Castile asked.

"Elijah," Maria and Amanda both said at the same time.

"Okay," Castile said. "Well, you're here now, and you're safe. Elijah isn't coming here, and if he does, we'll deal with him. You eat your breakfast and I'll get you settled."

Maria looked at her, and then at Amanda, desperate to trust.

Amanda nodded in agreement with Castile.

Maria took a spoonful of oatmeal, and then hunger took over. She dug in and ate it all. When she pushed the bowl back with a look of gratitude to Mary, she said. "Elijah shot Cassandra and Harrison. Shot them in the head and made Miles throw them in a ditch."

Amanda couldn't believe what she had just heard. "No. What? Cassandra? Harrison? When? Why?"

"Yesterday afternoon. I don't know why, but that's when I decided to leave. He's crazy!" She started to cry again. "I couldn't get

Mom to come with me."

Amanda understood that Susie wasn't interested in leaving what she perceived as the safety of Elijah's group, but this was a new development in cultish behavior. This was alarming. "You're very brave to leave there the way you did," Amanda said to Maria. "We'll get your mom here sometime soon, I'm sure."

Maria shook her head. "I don't think so."

"I'm going to get her settled in," Castile said to Amanda. "And then I'll come find you."

~ ~ ~

Willie was marking up the plans Parker had made to extend their little electric grid to other houses in the community when Amanda and Castile came into his workshop.

They seemed agitated, and after he heard both of their recounting of what they knew about Elijah, his new cache of guns, and the power trip he seemed to be on, he had no idea what to do about it. "I don't know what any of this has to do with us," he finally said.

"He's dangerous," Amanda said. "He's unbalanced, and there's no telling what he's capable of. There are people over there that are seriously devoted to him and his religious zealotry."

"Waging war on us wouldn't be consistent with religious zealotry," Willie said, and then smiled. "Well, now that I think about it, I guess religious zealotry is all about waging war."

"Exactly," Amanda said. "The other thing is that they have looted local stores for all of their supplies, and they're just eating their way through them. They're doing nothing to prepare for the winter. I don't know how much they have left, but they'll be looking to raid somebody, and soon."

Willie swiveled in his chair, looked across the workshop at Parker, who was assembling some plumbing parts. "Parker?"

Parker looked up.

"Do you think Elijah could be a threat to us?"

Parker nodded slowly, thoughtfully.

Willie turned back to Amanda and Castile. "Well, I don't know that there's anything we can do about it at this point."

"Do you think we should go talk to him?" Castile asked Amanda.

"I don't think that would do anything but antagonize him," she said.

"Well then," Willie said dismissively, not wanting to let on how disturbed he was by this news. He needed to think it over, but until he had a chance to do that, and maybe talk privately with Amanda and maybe Sherilyn, he didn't want to alarm his daughter. He picked up a length of tubing and a clamp.

Amanda put her hand on his arm. "We shouldn't just wait until he attacks. We should be prepared, because if we have food, and he needs it, he'll be coming for it."

He fixed his eyes on her. "What does that mean, prepare?"

Amanda backed down a bit. "I'm not sure, Willie. I just know that he's always been unpredictable, and now he's unpredictable with firepower. Apparently, lots of firepower. We should be wary and… well, prepared."

"Okay," Willie said. "I'll take your comments to the Committee and see what we can do. I don't see us becoming an army, or acquiring defensive weaponry, but maybe others will have a different idea."

"Just don't underestimate him," Amanda said.

Willie looked back at Parker.

Parker nodded in agreement.

~ ~ ~

Parker carried the weight of that discussion around with him for the rest of the day. Elijah with guns, and disciples who would follow him anywhere. Amanda said that people had been leaving and now he'd shot Cassandra and Harrison, which was unbelievable. They were two of the nicest people at the high school. Why would he do that?

Unbalanced, as Amanda said. Unhinged.

Parker was one of the first to leave Elijah's place and come here to the cul-de-sac. Amanda was already here, of course, but under false pretenses, and now Maria had come. Unless her mother had really drunk the Kool-aid, she was soon to follow, and she might bring others with her.

If all of Elijah's devotees abandoned him and came here, there's no question he would take whoever was left and come here, armed, to try to take over this place, or kill people, or loot their food stores, or whatever. It could be bad. Very bad.

And he felt some kind of a responsibility, somehow, to try to stop it. He didn't know what that meant yet, only that there had to be something he could do to protect this place and all the people, including Sherilyn.

That night, he lay in bed, looking at the moonlight throwing shadows across his ceiling when he heard the familiar footsteps, and the opening of his bedroom door. Crystal didn't come every night, but it was a regular thing, and he loved having her with him.

She looked spectacular in the pale moonlight as she stood next to his bed shedding her clothes. When naked, she slipped in next to him. He ran his hand across her cool skin, and felt it healing whatever ailed him.

"Hi," she said, and then snuggled up. He put his arm around her, and they lay together, in silent companionship. "What a day," she said. "I'm so tired." They lay together, her head on his shoulder, fingers entwined, just being quiet together.

Parker had never known such peace.

And then he knew something else.

Crystal brought with her a difference this time. There was someone else in the bed with them.

He closed his eyes and tried to ascertain what he was sensing, and it came from her body. From her belly.

A tiny little consciousness.

Parker felt emotion rising up his chest. She had told him it was safe to have unprotected sex because nobody was getting pregnant anymore. She'd even talked with Castile about it. Plenty of people were having sex, but there weren't any pregnancies. There weren't any babies born that she knew of, just the ones that had been conceived before the flu. She said they didn't have anything to worry about.

Well, this was nothing to worry about, but this was certainly a new development.

He hugged her close and tried to connect with the mind of the baby, but it was too small, too unformed. Likely Crystal didn't even know yet.

He untangled his fingers from hers, and rested his hand on her smooth tummy, and he could feel the tiny whisper of life humming in there.

"What?" she asked.

But the emotion filled his throat, up to the back of his eyes, and leaked out as tears. He buried his head in her sweet-smelling hair and felt the promise of a new generation, he felt the responsibility to his parents for bringing about the new creation, he felt completely inadequate to the task at hand, and he felt profoundly grateful that he and the beautiful Crystal had created a new life, a life completely unique, a life like no other.

Anxiety lay just on the periphery of his thinking, but he kept it out for the time being. This moment was too important, this oh-my-god-I-love-you-already moment was so precious he wanted to keep it sacred.

But he needed to share it.

He wiped his face, then looked up at the beautiful Crystal, and saw the concern in her face, in her shiny blue eyes.

"What is it?" she whispered.

He moved his hand back to her belly, tenderly drawing a little circle on her skin.

She smiled, and then understanding crossed her face. "You're kidding."

She jerked away from him, as if she wanted to bolt, to run from the room, but he held her until she relaxed, and then she settled back down, eyes wide open, staring at the ceiling.

"This changes everything," she said. "Oh, my God."

He pulled her close, and soon she was crying too. They clung to each other, sharing the enormity of what they had done, and they were still entwined when he woke up in the morning.

~ ~ ~

Sam York closed the door to the classroom that had served as his bedroom since last fall. He looked at the empty bookshelves, the desks and chairs that had been stacked and pushed up against the walls, at the white boards that could never be completely wiped clean of their blue and red word stains. He looked at the miserable little unmade pull-out couch bed with the disgusting sheets that hadn't been changed in weeks, and he felt sick.

He opened one of the massive windows and pulled off his clothes, leaving them in a pile on the floor. They would be wrinkled and smelly in the morning, but he didn't care. Amanda would have taken them and washed them, and his sheets, too, but she was gone like a traitor, like a tramp. Like many of the others, going and leaving him alone.

He kicked at the clothes, but that was less than satisfactory. It would be better to punch somebody. To bite somebody with all the strength in his jaws. To twist, to hurt, to dig his fingers in until someone screamed with pain. That's what would make him feel better, not kicking clothes around. Not even shooting Cassandra and Harrison was enough. That had been too fast. Bam, bam, and it was over. He needed to inflict some pain, some real pain, up close and personal.

He got the bottle of whiskey out of the bottom drawer of his desk and took a long pull on it. And then another. And then he got into bed and lay, nerves taut, muscles tense, fists clenched.

At first, it had been good. Everybody was scared in the early days of the great die-off of humankind. He found them and brought them all together at the school, and they were so grateful, they did everything he asked of them. He was their leader. He took care of them. He got food and made this high school a refuge for the refugees. They had water, they had safety, they had Bible lessons. All he wanted in return was a little loyalty, but loyalty was in shorter supply than fresh salad greens.

They adored him, and he loved that. They obeyed him, they were grateful to him, they came to him for everything. They depended on him for their very lives, and he saved them. And then the good weather came, and people started leaving. First, it was just a couple, and then Steven and his group left, and that was the beginning of the exodus.

Now he had very few left, maybe twenty, and only one person he could trust, and that was Miles. Miles had proved himself, but it never hurt to continue the testing of one's loyalty. He could find another test for Miles, and if found worthy, he could take him on as a second-in-command. He'd send Miles over to bring Amanda back, and Susie's daughter, and whoever else that belonged to him that was over at that other place, and to bring back whatever they had that he needed.

He began to relax a little at the thought of Miles going over there, armed to the teeth with automatic weapons, to kick ass and take names, and the thought of it made him smile. He'd make Miles a general.

Then the dark thought came seeping in, the one he kept under wraps, but like an interloper peeking under the bottom of the circus tent, this one thought came to him in the middle of the night when he was vulnerable to his own dark thoughts.

They would all leave him, all his people, all his followers, they would leave him defenseless. Everyone would leave him, and he would have no food, no water, no people to lead. And then what? What would he do? Where would he go?

He was useless in this new world. His only strength is to keep people around and motivated to do whatever it was that he needed. He did that at his Ford dealership, and he had done that here.

But now he seemed to be failing at that task.

No. He was no failure. His body tensed again as he reaffirmed that over and over again. No failure! No failure!

He opened his eyes to see the moonlight shining in the big windows, casting the room into black and silver relief.

He couldn't be the one raiding the grocery stores, finding the beds and bringing them back. He couldn't be the one doing the laundry, splitting the wood, and tending the boiler. He couldn't be the one doing the shit work. That was for someone else to do. He was the leader, for God's sake.

And at times he actually thought God had appointed him as *his* second in command. Those were the times when he could relax, knowing that God was testing him the way that he intended to test Miles, and if Miles could pass his test, he could pass God's test, no problem.

God. A laugh barked out of him. God. Ridiculous. God was for controlling the crowd, not for the leaders. The leaders *were* the gods.

Maybe *he* should lead an exodus. Maybe everyone could get on board with leaving here and finding a new place to take up residence. Maybe that would be more attractive, get more people to join in, add more sheep to his flock.

But first things first. Miles and Amanda. Maybe Amanda deserved to be hurt. She could be the example for the others. It would be very public, and very painful, and there would be no doubt as to who was in charge. Would Miles do it?

Maybe.

It would be a fitting test, that was for sure.

Chapter 8 - August

Parker slid open the big window in what had become kind of a cramped workspace in Willie's garage. A slight breeze wafted in, but with it came the distracting sounds of people working outside. But it was just too hot without a fan or something to move the air in their workspace.

He went back to his drafting table, making subtle changes to the schematic he was designing. The solar-powered system he and Willie had set up at the closest water pumping station was working, but it was only one segment of the network that had to be redesigned and implemented before they could get running water to the houses, or at least the kitchen and the bath house. The next part was bypass the filtration system. The water they would receive wouldn't be drinkable, without treating, but it should come out of the faucet. That's what he was determined to figure out today.

The door opened, and Parker heard a familiar voice. He looked up to see Crystal talking quietly with Willie, who then motioned him over.

"Thanks, Willie," Crystal said. "I'll bring him back in a few." She took Parker's hand and led him out into the August heat. Alta, who had become Parker's constant companion, followed, as usual.

"We're going to talk to Castile," she said.

He shot her a questioning look.

"I've missed my period, so I guess it's official. She's the nurse. She needs to know."

This will make it not only official, but public. Parker took a deep breath. Actions have consequences.

He opened the door to the little yellow house that served as the infirmary, and held it for Crystal.

A woman lay under a white sheet in one of the two hospital beds in the main room. It was Patty the Cake, one of the funniest and most outgoing of everyone in the compound. She was in her sixties, vivacious and hilarious at all times. She kept a party going around her, even if she was working latrine duty.

She had collapsed in the great room last night after dinner and brought immediately to the infirmary. She appeared to be asleep.

Castile's office door was partially open. Crystal knocked briefly and pushed on in.

"Hi!" Castile said softly. "Close the door."

"How's she doing?"

"She's yellow," Castile said. "So it's something with her liver." She waved a hand at the books open on her desk. "I don't know. She doesn't seem to be in any pain. At least she's sleeping now, so that's good."

Crystal sat in one of the two chairs facing Castile's desk, and Parker took the other.

"What brings you two here?"

"We're pregnant," Crystal said.

Hearing the words said out loud startled Parker. To hide his nervousness, he reached over and took Crystal's hand.

"Really?" Castile said with a smile. "You sure?"

"My period is two weeks late, so I'm pretty sure."

Parker nodded.

Castile sat back in her chair and looked at them. "There haven't been any pregnancies since the pandemic," she said. "So this is a new development. This is very exciting to me, because clearly we need to get going on some repopulation around here. However. We don't know what effect the flu had on either one of you. I mean, I know you didn't get the flu, so you, and the rest of us have some kind of immunity, but I have no idea what that means to your health in the long run or to your baby's health. There is just so much we don't know. I hope you won't mind if I monitor your pregnancy very closely."

Crystal shook her head, and Parker saw the glint of a tear.

"I didn't think I could get pregnant," she whispered, her voice husky. "I didn't think anybody was getting pregnant. I'm not prepared."

"It's not like you have to leave home and go find jobs to support yourselves," Castile said. "You're safe here, your baby will be safe here."

Crystal squeezed Parker's hand. "I don't think I want to be a mother yet. I mean I'm only seventeen. And Parker is what, sixteen?"

"We're redefining everything," Castile said, "including our roles in society. And that includes what it means to be a parent."

Parker heard her talking, but his attention had strayed to the room on the other side of the door. To the woman in the hospital bed.

He stood up.

Castile stood, too, and came around her desk to take Crystal's hands and talk to her, woman-to-woman.

Parker left the room.

Patty was snoring, her mouth open, her thin gray hair swirled on the pillow. A yellow cast to her perspiring skin gave her a translucent appearance.

Parker saw the problem immediately. It was as if he could see beyond the white sheet, through the skin, right to the dark purple cluster of what looked like grapes inside. These were malevolent, and not supposed to be there.

He laid his hand on the side of her stomach, closed his eyes and envisioned a syringe poking each one of the tumors, drawing out its poison until it was just a deflated bit of tissue. One by one, he dealt with the trespassers, until they lay flat, and he could see the blood supply that connected them to one another and to her liver. He severed those connections with an idea like a cauterizer.

When he was finished, he opened his eyes, surprised to see Patty looking at him. She reached for his hand.

"I don't know all of what gifts you've been blessed with, young man, but I thank you for looking after me."

He gave her hand a squeeze. She closed her eyes again, and Parker went back into Castile's office, where Crystal was crying into a towel.

He sat at Castile's desk and flipped through her books until he saw a picture that looked somewhat similar to what he had seen in his mind's eye and held it up to show her. When he had her attention, he drew on it with his finger, showing her more tumors, then pantomimed draining them and snipping off their connections.

"You did that?" she asked.

Parker nodded.

Castile got up and went out into the main room, leaving the office door open.

"He's something, that young'un," Patty said. "I think he might have fixed me."

"What do you mean?"

"I woke up, and he was standing over me, and now I feel better. That's all I know."

"Well," Castile said, putting her hand on Patty's forehead, and speaking with a hefty dose of skepticism. "You stay put for now, and we'll see."

"I'm telling you," Patty said. "And for that, I'm going to throw a dance party in his honor. As soon as you let me up." She raised her voice. "Hear that, Parker? I get the first dance with you."

Parker looked at Crystal, who had composed herself, and returned his gaze with affection. If he was going to do any dancing, he wanted it to be with her.

Castile promised no official announcement of the pregnancy to the community, and Parker breathed a sigh of relief at that. If Crystal wasn't ready to be a mother, he certainly wasn't ready to be a father, nor was he ready to be thought of as one. He needed to tell Sherilyn himself, not have her hear about it through some rumor grapevine.

Dinner that night proceeded as usual, with Mary and her crew outdoing themselves with fresh fruit and vegetables from the very bountiful garden and neighboring fruit trees and vines. Sherilyn was flushed and happy, talking and joking with her friends on the gleaning crew, and the whole room seemed to be in a good mood.

After everyone had eaten, before Mary served the cakes with raspberry sauce and before the 6 pm broadcasts, Willie stood to make a few announcements, mostly about their progress on bringing running water to the community.

He started with saying that Patty the Cake was feeling better, and that brought cheers from the floor, but Parker was barely listening. He was feeling the tightness in his chest and knew that whoever it was that spoke through him had something to say, and she/it was not to be denied.

His heart began to pound in that very distinctive way, and he stood up.

A hush fell over the crowd. From across the room, he heard Sherilyn whisper, "Oh, Parker, please no."

Willie saw him stand and sat down.

"I bring you greetings from the unseen realm that is here to help you through this very difficult transition," Parker said. "It is true that we have restored your reproductive powers. When these world civilizations collapsed, it was due in large part to the overpopulation of the planet by two-thirds, squandering resources and bringing burdens of great stress upon parents. Many parents were accidental parents, and they gave rise to accidental children, who were not taught to think, to prepare, to plan, to live intentional lives. We trust that as you begin to have children, you do so with intention and preparation. Parents must be educated in the ways of rearing children, and the privilege of procreating should never be taken lightly."

Frederick, an elder, stood up. "Are you saying people should be, what, *licensed* to have children?"

Parker replied, "We are saying that community needs and resources be consulted before procreating, and that proper education and preparations be made to welcome the child."

"So who decides all of that?" Frederick pressed, clearly annoyed with the concept.

"The new civilization is in your hands," Parker said. "You must decide these things. We are here to teach you and guide you and help you not make the same mistakes as before. We wish you strong, healthy families, a strong, healthy economy, and good, common-sense government, based on the highest possible values." And with that, Parker was empty.

He blinked a couple of times, always surprised at how fast these things came on, and how when they were over, they were over. He sat down.

Crystal laid a cool hand on his hot cheek and it felt so good.

Then Alta came over and licked his hand, and somehow, feeling the love from the two of them, he knew that all was right in his world.

He opened his eyes and looked at Crystal's beautiful face, scratched the top of Alta's silky head, then searched for Sherilyn, just to smile at her and let her know that everything was all right. She was sitting in the back, next to Robby. He raised his hand to wave to her the way they used to wave to one another across the cafeteria at the high school, but she and Robby were deep in conversation, and she didn't see him. She only looked up when Lois and Oscar made their way past them to talk with Castile.

~ ~ ~

Willie set his mug of tea on the side table and looked around at the ten people he had asked to assemble in the great room. This was the Committee, the heads of the various groups, appointed by the members of those groups that made the whole cul-de-sac work. He trusted them, trusted their opinions, trusted that they would voice their views, and that whatever was said would be kept in confidence. He trusted that they would come to a reasonable conclusion about the problem facing them.

"There is," Willie started, "what I consider to be a credible threat against us by the group headed by Sam York of Sam York Ford. He now calls himself Elijah and has set up a group at Jefferson High School. He knows about us, he has an arsenal of firearms, and apparently religious zeal, and I think we ought to be prepared for some kind of an invasion."

"*Prepared?*" Mary asked. "For an *invasion?* What does that mean to you? *Guns?*"

"I don't know," Willie said. "That's why I'm bringing it to this group. I don't like the idea of guns, but if you think about it, we are completely defenseless against marauders coming in and taking over."

"What else do you know about him?" Frederick asked.

"Amanda used to be there," Willie said. "Parker and Sherilyn came from there. And Maria, you know, the new teen? Her mother is still there. She's the one who told me that he had a new cache of guns, and that he's gone off the deep end. She also said that people are leaving his little enclave, and he's getting increasingly desperate."

"Seems kind of thin," Frederick said.

"There have been murders there," Willie said.

This information was met with silence.

"Nevertheless," Kip said, "we should be prepared for this type of an emergency. All sorts of damaged and desperate people come through here, you know that. One of these days there is likely to be a bigger group and they're going to be harder to deal with."

"My thoughts exactly," Willie said.

"We could build a fence," Kathy said. "An electric fence."

"Not really practical," Kip said, "because we're growing all the time."

"We could move to a gated community." Bob offered.

Groans all around.

"No, seriously," he said. "We could still come here to tend the garden. We'd just move the…"

"The windmills, the solar panels, the big ovens, recalibrate the whole water system, which is due to be online soon, start over with electrifying the neighborhood…" Willie responded. "No, I don't think moving is a viable option."

"Besides," Mary said, "If people want in, a fence and a gate isn't going to keep them out."

"It's a deterrent," Bob said, a little defensively.

Opinions began to circulate. Willie held up his hand.

"This is a good place to start," he said. "All in favor of moving?"

Only Bob's hand went up.

"Opposed?"

All other hands went up.

"Okay then," Willie said. "It wasn't a bad idea, Bob. There are no bad ideas here. We're examining all the possibilities. Let's keep going. Let's talk about Kathy's idea of building a fence."

The discussion continued for another hour before Maxwell brought up weaponry. "If this Elijah character has an arsenal of firearms, we ought to be able to defend ourselves against that. I don't know a way to do that, except by arming ourselves."

"I hate the thought of that," Mary said. "I really... I really want no part of that."

Willie heard the kitchen door open and saw Parker come in and sit in the back, behind the circle of decision makers.

"Neither do I, Mary," Willie said. "But there are no bad ideas here. Let's explore it."

Willie didn't expect a consensus or a definitive conclusion to come of the day's discussion, and one didn't emerge. They did agree to post sentries at night, and Kip, the only one in the group besides Willie who had had military training, volunteered to make up the schedule and rig up some kind of an alarm system, maybe even just an air horn, in case the sentry needed to rouse everyone.

Everyone left an hour later, with food for thought. Some were worry-free, thinking nothing bad could ever happen to them again; others were deeply troubled at the thought of an attack.

When he got back to his workshop with a fresh mug of tea, he found a handgun on his papers and Parker sitting back at his worktable.

"Is this yours?"

Parker nodded.

"Is it loaded?"

Parker nodded.

"Okay, then," Willie said. "I'm putting it in this drawer." He opened the second drawer of a filing cabinet and put the gun way in the back.

~ ~ ~

The discussion about defending the community against marauders gave Parker dark, shapeless, disturbing dreams. Crystal came to sleep with him, but he didn't want their child's development to be influenced by his negative thought stream, so when she was fully asleep, he crept quietly out of bed and stayed on the couch for the rest of the night.

He remembered the guy who came to their door when they were still holed up at their parents' house, the guy who grabbed Sherilyn and tried to take her. He knew there were desperate people out there, desperate for many things, and if they banded together, they could be a terribly destructive force. Add to that Elijah, his instability and guns, and Parker could see that this community could be in grave danger if they didn't do something to prepare.

He was neither responsible nor powerless, yet he felt as though he was.

At dawn, he went back to his bed and wrapped his arms around his warm, cuddly girlfriend and stared at the ceiling, hoping that whoever it was that talked to him, talked *through* him, was watching over them and keeping them safe.

But they also had to act to keep themselves safe. The celestials, whoever they were, whatever they were, couldn't do everything.

After breakfast, he got into his car for his weekly session of roaming the town and let Spirit guide him. The first place he stopped was an auto mechanic's garage with a dozen cars in the parking lot. Before going in, Parker siphoned gas from one of the cars and filled up his tank.

Inside, he found the owner's body in his office, with his head down on his desk. A mechanic was on the ground next to the hydraulic lift. The spirits of the two men stood in the corner by the coffee machine, talking. They turned to look at Parker.

"We're closed," the owner said.

Parker felt his chest fill. "You both have worked hard at your craft for many years. You have brought calm to many people. It is time now for you to receive the peace you have earned."

"I said we're closed," the owner said.

"Wait," the mechanic said. "Let's hear him out."

"Look behind you," Parker said, and the beautiful portal opened between the men and their coffee machine. "Just step through."

"I don't know what kind of trick you're trying to pull..." the owner said.

"Jack. Look, it's my wife!" The mechanic took a step over the threshold and vanished.

"Your loved ones await you as well," Parker said.

"You better go peddle your bullshit elsewhere," the owner said.

"Just *look*," Parker said, and pointed behind him.

The owner turned and looked. "Oh," he said. "Oh, wow." He looked back at Parker with wonder on his face, then turned and stepped through.

The portal closed and the fullness left Parker's chest.

He stood in the greasy shop that smelled like motor oil, tires, and death, and wondered why anyone would bother preserving themselves if the afterlife was as glorious as it appeared to be. Why did people cling to life so desperately? Didn't they know?

No. They didn't know. They didn't see the rapture on the faces of those who peered into the portal. And yet, where were the celestials when the nuclear missiles were launched? Where were they when the pandemic ravaged the world, killing everyone? Couldn't they have done something?

Maybe not. Maybe they were doing something now. Maybe there was a reason for life, and this was the purpose for his life.

There had to be some kind of an inborn sense of purpose, or there would be no humans trying their best to live their eighty or ninety or whatever years here. Everything would be heaven, and that made no sense whatsoever.

It was all such a mystery.

He got back in his car and waited to be guided to his next stop.

~ ~ ~

"Come in!" Elijah shouted when Miles knocked on his office door. He had a plan, it was a good plan, a brilliant plan, it came to him in the middle of the night, and he needed to convey his vision to his second in command and together they would execute the plan. The Lord's plan. Maybe the Lord's plan. Who the fuck knew anymore?

Elijah jumped up from his chair and came around his desk. "Walk with me," he said. He picked the handgun up from the desktop and tucked it into the waistband of his pants, then led Miles through the empty and silent school hallways, flanked by empty lockers, out the front doors of the school into the bright sunshine.

"I have a plan," Elijah said. "And you will be my right hand."

"Say more," Miles said as they walked down the front steps and turned right on the sidewalk. Silence greeted them, the sounds of birds and their footfalls the only thing to be heard. Sometimes Elijah thought the world was so quiet he could hear the high-pitched whine of sunshine.

"Morale is low," Elijah said. "Stores are running low. People have left, but you and I both know that where they're going means only a terrible death from the poisoned air, poisoned water, poisoned land. Death by radiation poisoning is not swift, nor is it easy."

"Yes," Miles said. "You've said these things before."

"And still people are leaving," Elijah said, noticing that by acknowledging that he had said those things before, Miles wasn't exactly agreeing with him. "They're leaving because they don't believe me. But they will find out. Whether they come running back to us or not is none of our concern. We will welcome them, of course, if they are not diseased. But our first responsibility is to take care of those who remain." He stopped and turned to Miles. "And to keep those who remain from leaving."

Miles nodded his agreement, but Elijah questioned his loyalty.

They crossed the empty street and turned left toward the Sam York Ford dealership.

When the building came into view, Elijah stopped and gazed at it. The glass walls of the showroom had been shattered, the showroom was vacant, half the cars on the lot gone, the rest of the vehicles with their gas caps open. "Look at what they've done to my life's work," he said, feeling his blood pressure rise at the sight. They walked through the broken glass into the building. Vehicle keys, with their color-coded tags were strewn about the floor. The pop machine had been pried open and cleaned out. "They've taken probably fifty cars," he said.

"This is terrible," Miles said.

"Chances are," he turned and faced Miles, feeling fury build inside him. "Chances are, most of these missing cars are over at that place they call the cul-de-sac. I want us to go over and get them back."

"Why? What use do you have for them?" Miles asked.

"I don't need a reason. I don't need a use. Why? Because they are thieves and vandals, and they have my property, that's why."

"But—"

"Don't 'but' me! Those cars and vans and trucks are mine and I want them back. And this is exactly the thing that will bring morale back to my flock. We will go over there with might, and the truth of the Lord, and we will reclaim our property, reclaim our women, both Amanda and Maria, and we will replenish our stores for the winter."

"Replenish our stores?"

Elijah spun around. "They must pay for the use of these vehicles. They have food, and we need food, so they will pay us in food. We will go there with a mighty cause, and the Lord's backing, and—" he raised his fist as he raised his voice ""—--we will be victorious! My people, my flock will see the might of the right, and they will no longer want to go south to the valley of death."

"How are we going to do all this?" Miles asked.

"I have a vision," Elijah said. "I need to share that vision with you so that you have the same vision. It's a vision of purpose, of rightness. Of righteousness. It's a vision of victory," his voice again began to rise, "it's a vision of ascendancy, of power. The right kind of power, the power that is all to the glory of the Lord. Do you see it, Miles?" He opened his arms to the heavens, pointed his face to the ceiling. "Do you see the vision?"

Miles nodded, hesitantly, and Elijah knew he didn't have it, and likely wouldn't get it. The best he could do was to convince him to do what had to be done next.

Elijah put his hand on Miles's shoulder and turned him back toward the high school. "I have set the date of retaliation against the evil for next Monday at noon. We will gather in the chapel on Sunday and enlist the angels of the Lord to our cause. And then on Monday, we will seek justice."

"What would you have me do?"

"We need to put gasoline in the remaining vans, get them ready for the incursion, and teach our people how to use the firearms."

"I'm not sure I know how to use all the firearms."

"Do your best, my friend," Elijah said. "The Lord will guide you, and it will be enough. Remember that we go to defeat evil, because—and trust me on this—if we don't strike first, we will face their attempt to dominate us. And that cannot happen. We cannot let that happen."

Miles nodded as he walked.

"They must never be allowed to dominate us. Right? Are you with me?"

"Yes, of course. Always."

Elijah heard no conviction in Miles's pledge of loyalty. "Good man. We have five days. Make certain we are ready. You are the new General in God's Army."

~ ~ ~

After an amazing lunch at the talented hands of Mary and her kitchen crew, with the great room full of chatter, life, and laughter, Parker took a walk around the garden, just to see what was happening. His life seemed to revolve around his desk in Willie's workshop, his car as he cruised farther and farther from home seeking those in the borderlands who needed assistance crossing over, and his calm, sweet nights with Crystal, where they lay together in companionable silence. Sometimes she talked, sometimes they made love, or toyed with each others' hair, most often they just enjoyed holding hands or touching feet as they drifted off to sleep. He had not really visited the garden, really looked to see what everybody was doing there, in a long time.

Parker knew little about gardens, but he knew a masterpiece of planning and execution when he saw one. The beds were situated lengthwise to maximize the arc of the sun across each entire bed. There was not a weed to be seen. At this time of year, everything was lush and green, even the remarkable variety of salad greens, and Mary had been serving generous salads at every meal. Giant red tomatoes hung from tall plants firmly staked. Many different kinds of cucumbers, squash, and pumpkins were either hanging from their trellises or sprawling along the ground on the outskirts of the garden.

Bean vines climbed twine, giant-leafed collards, kale, and chard had one whole bed to themselves. And twenty to thirty people were there digging, weeding, watering, fertilizing, trimming, discussing, and mostly, taking pride in what they had done.

Parker had designed the irrigation system himself, and he was gratified to see that it was working properly. The boys filled the gravity-flow tank every day now in the hot August weather, and closely monitored how much river water each section of each bed needed and received.

As his stroll took him around the far side of the garden, near the infirmary, he heard trucks and vans pull up.

"We need muscle!" someone yelled, and everyone dropped their tools and went to help the gleaning crew bring in their harvest.

Parker followed them and saw the kids unloading totes full of fruit. He picked up a box of plums.

"Those to the dehydrator," Jackie told him, then pointed at a second tote. "Those to the kitchen."

Parker nodded and took a heavy load to the solar dehydrator. He delivered both totes of fruit and picked up a big, purple plum from the top.

On his way back, he saw Sherilyn, her hair falling out of its ponytail, dirt streaked across her forehead, wearing shorts, a long-sleeved man's plaid shirt and men's work gloves, laughing with someone as she hauled boxes of peaches out of one of the vans.

His heart squeezed. She had found her home. She had found her people, her tribe. She seemed so adult, so self-possessed. Looking at her bright smile and confidence it was inconceivable that mere months ago she was a scared little girl in their parents' home trying to survive the winter by rationing a single can of chili. And here they were now, amid all this abundance of food, good will, laughter, and friendship. Where once had been fear and pain, now was joy and purpose.

"She's thriving," a voice said to him, and he turned to see Castile smiling at the sight. He nodded with pride at his little sister.

"As are you," Castile said. "And everyone else. Healing and

thriving." Parker had to note that indeed, he felt better about himself, better about everything than he had, maybe ever. These people didn't care that he couldn't talk. He had something to add to the collective, and that was enough. He bit into that sweet, juicy plum and thought about how good life was at this very moment.

And yet, there was a tiny dark spot in the back of his mind that told him not everything was as perfect as it currently seemed. There was another shoe to drop, though he didn't know what it was.

Amid all the activity around the trucks and vans unloading produce the crew had gotten from local orchards and overgrown, abandoned gardens, a new face emerged. A man, a stranger, with dirty, raggedy clothes and a beard, a walking stick, backpack, and a wide-brimmed hat stopped to survey what was going on, and then walked up to the front door of the main house.

Castile walked over to meet him on the front step.

Is this guy a threat? Is he the dark spot? Parker followed her.

"Hi," Castile said.

The man sat down. "My feet are killing me," he said as he pulled off his boots. He looked up and smiled at her. "And I'd give my soul for one of those peaches."

No, Parker decided. This man was no threat. He had a calm color around him. Parker went to fetch a peach while Castile talked with the new guy.

~ ~ ~

Elijah heard a couple of random gunshots and knew that Miles was trying to train the crew that would be storming the opposition in the morning. He got up from his desk and walked through the silent halls out back to the overgrown football field, half afraid of what he would find.

He saw them, standing in a line, most with some type of a rifle or shotgun, a couple with handguns, Miles shouting orders to them from behind, as they all took aim at the scoreboard.

Thirteen people, including Miles. What a piss-poor showing of support from his supposed army. This was no way to storm a stronghold.

With a barrage of gunfire, pieces fell off the scoreboard, wood splintered, lights exploded in showers of glass, and windows broke in a few of the houses on the other side of the field.

Elijah caught up with them just as Miles was handing out ammunition so that they could reload. Marjorie wordlessly handed him her gun, shook her head and walked back to the school, not making eye contact with Elijah as she passed him on her way.

Twelve, including Miles.

Well, he thought… Twelve apostles. Look what they accomplished.

But before Miles could get them all back into a line for a second go, Rex, with a high-powered rifle, started shooting randomly.

"No, no, Rex, stop!" Miles went over to him and shook his shoulder.

"This is fun!" Rex said, never the brightest in any group.

"Stop!" Miles said and grabbed the barrel of the gun.

Rex kept firing, bullets going in crazy directions, some even close to the people standing on the line, watching.

Miles let go, and Rex fired into the air until his gun was out of ammunition. "Jesus Christ, Rex. This is not a toy."

"Reloading!" Rex shouted and walked over to where the cart of ammunition sat.

Miles caught Elijah's eye and shook his head.

"We need him," Elijah said when he got close enough to speak privately. "You're doing a good job. We want them to be wired up, enthusiastic. We want them to be their best."

"In no way is this anything close to a best," Miles said.

"Carry on," Elijah said. "The point is for them to become familiar with their weapons."

While Rex was reloading his rifle, Elijah stood in front of the group with their various firearms. They had no idea how to handle them. "Please don't point those guns at me or at each other," he was surprised he had to say, first thing. They all adjusted their posture. "Tomorrow morning," he said, "we move on the enemy."

Rex fired off three rounds as punctuation marks.

"That's not necessary, Rex," Elijah said.

"It's fun," he said.

"Tomorrow," Elijah continued, "we will return victorious as God's Army is always victorious. We will return with food and supplies, and the two women who were kidnapped from us."

"Women!" Rex yelled and fired off three more rounds.

Elijah tightened his lips but said nothing about it. He took a deep breath. "So become familiar with your weapons, because you will be the on the front lines when we storm the evildoers."

"Do they have guns?" Cassie asked, letting her handgun dangle from slack fingers.

"Does it matter?" Elijah said. "Their weapons are nothing against the might and fury of God's Army. We will not be denied. We will prevail in everything that goes to the glory of God."

She seemed unconvinced, but there was nothing for him to do about that now.

"Carry on," he said, and turned to go back to the school.

"Don't you think we've been out here long enough?" Cassie said. "I mean poisoned air and all."

Elijah turned. "Miles knows when you've been out here long enough. He is your general."

"Our general! All right!" Rex fired three rounds into the air.

"Jesus Christ," Elijah said quietly to himself as he walked. "We're all going to die."

~ ~ ~

After Sherilyn finished sweeping out the van, Kip came to her with his clipboard in hand and told her that she was off for the rest of the day and tomorrow, too. She was ready for a day off but wasn't certain exactly what she'd do that wasn't work with one crew or another.

She put the broom away, then headed back to her room to gather up a fresh set of clothes, hoping to beat the crowd at the bath house.

On the way, Robby stopped her. "I'm going to go feed the goats. Want to go with?"

She'd do anything Robby asked. "Sure," she said, "I'm kind of stinky, though."

"Not nearly as stinky as the goats," he said. "Come on."

They walked quietly the few blocks to the park, which had been fenced to hold the five goats.

Just outside the gate was a series of metal garbage cans with tight-fitting lids. "Grain," Robby said, opening one of them. "Get a double handful and follow me."

Sherilyn followed him through the gate, then held one hand full of grain out and a goat nibbled it from her palm. She wanted to squeal with delight, but didn't want to scare the goat. More, she didn't want to seem like a little kid to Robby.

"That's exactly right," Robby said. "That's Ophelia." He handed her a piece of carrot, which Ophelia immediately grabbed out of his hand. The other goats nosed in to see what was going on.

Sherilyn laughed as they jockeyed to get a piece of the carrots Robby brought with him. She petted them all, brown and white, scratched the coarse hair between their horns. The horizontal pupils in their eyes gave them a comical look, as if they were playing a trick on her by being so interesting.

"I think they all must have a sense of humor," Sherilyn said.

"Oh, definitely," Robby said. "They're very fun." Robby was quiet for a moment as they both petted the nannies. "They're still pretty skinny, but we're feeding them up. Making progress." He pointed to a goat with enormous horns on the other side of the fence. "That's the buck. He'll breed them in the fall. Until then, we have to keep them separate. He can be very ornery, and I don't want the little kids around him."

"How do you know so much about goats?"

"I didn't. But I asked Katy, in the library, to find some books, and I've been reading up on them. They're pretty great. After they have their babies, we can start milking them. Have you ever done that?."

"Milked a goat? Oh my god, no."

"It'll be an adventure, because none of us has. But I'm pretty sure we can figure it out. When that happens, I might try to steal you away from the gleaning crew to work with the goats."

Sherilyn would like nothing more than to be stolen away from anything by Robby, but she held herself in check. Instead, she moved to a different goat and began stroking her. She was afraid she would fall totally in love with Robby if she worked with him. He was seventeen, though, and she was only twelve, and she didn't need anybody, especially Parker, to tell her that she shouldn't get too close to a boy. Even if he was the coolest guy in the cul-de-sac. And that he paid this kind of attention to her made it particularly difficult. Parker would not approve.

"No," she said shyly. "I'm pretty happy with my job."

"Wait until the baby goats are born," Robby said. "You might change your mind."

"Baby goats? Yeah, well," she said, "we'll see." What she wanted to do was jump up and down at the idea of taking care of baby goats, or jump into his arms, even better, but she knew she couldn't do either one of those things.

As they walked slowly back to the cul-de-sac from Goat Park as it was now known, Robby asked her questions about Parker and their life before coming to the community. Sherilyn answered as completely as possible, telling him about their parents, and the horrible winter and canned chili, and then going to the high school with stupid Elijah. Then she stopped. Stopped talking, stopped walking. "We got thrown out of that place because of the things that Parker says sometimes. You know like when he speaks at night in the great room? He can't talk. He has never talked. And suddenly he talks and says these things, and sometimes people get really riled up about it. I'm scared that we're going to get thrown out of this place." Against her will, tears began to push against the backs of her eyes, and she was afraid to say anything more, afraid she would begin to sob. Her chin began to tremble with the effort of keeping it all back. She loved her life so much now and couldn't imagine the thought of going back to their old house.

Robby put his arm around her shoulders. "Relax," he said. "Nobody's going to kick you out. Everybody loves you." She wrapped her arms around his waist and turned it into a full hug. This was the first hug she had had from a man other than Parker since her father died, and she liked it. She felt small and protected.

"And everybody loves Parker," he continued. "Those things he says, they're good for everybody to hear." He put his hands on her shoulders and pushed her back, looking into her eyes. "Who knows why he can suddenly speak? I don't know. I doubt Parker knows. Everything is upside down, Sherilyn, you know that."

"I'm so afraid for him," she said, and took a ragged breath as a tear escaped down her cheek. "I wish he wouldn't do it."

Robby pulled her back into a hug. "Don't be afraid. You're you and your brother is who he is. And nobody's going anywhere."

"Promise?"

"Promise."

~ ~ ~

By the time Parker finished helping with the unloading, Castile had handed the traveler—Bodie Jones was his name—over to Patty the Cake, who was still recovering from her illness and remained on light duty.

Patty took him to the communal closet, where he picked out new clothes, a few extra pairs of socks, and some tennis shoes. Then she got him into the bathhouse, asked Mario to give him a haircut and a shave, and by the time dinner rolled around, Bodie Jones was a brand-new person. Maybe forty, nice looking, trim and fit, and moved with the grace of a man confident in himself.

Willie set two stools at the front of the group after dinner, sat on one and introduced him. "Tell us your story, Bodie."

Bodie sat on the stool Willie offered. He seemed comfortable and relaxed talking to a group of people. "I've always wanted to see this country," he started. "This seemed like a good time. I started off from Boulder, Colorado, in March, needing to go to a warmer climate. So I walked through Utah, and part of Nevada and California, and then turned north."

"Why are you walking?" someone asked.

"Why not?" Bodie replied. "I'm in no hurry." Everyone chuckled.

"Where do you sleep?" someone else asked.

"Anywhere I don't have to share a space with a—shall we say—former inhabitant," he said. "You know, the dearly departed. I've actually had it pretty good. Found food, toothpaste, beds, changed out my boots a few times, but these—" he showed off his new tennis shoes from the communal closet "—these will be great for a long time. Good socks and traveling light are key. And finding good water," he added. "I find myself following waterways. Rivers. Streams."

"We get the daily broadcasts from Boulder," Willie said. "Do you know Roger Miner?"

"He's my brother-in-law," Bodie said. "Good man. An engineer. We worked at the same company, him in engineering, me in logistics. Course he lost his family to the flu like most of us. But Roger is an engineering genius and has a little community there in Boulder not too different from what you have right here. His is a little bigger, but it's the same idea. You folks have done real well for yourselves here. Next to Boulder, this is the best I've seen."

The audience applauded themselves.

"Especially that dinner," he said. "Wow." Parker saw Bodie glance over at Mary, with a little grin. She blushed and turned away.

Parker looked for Crystal, but he couldn't see her. Sherilyn was sitting close to Robby. Too close, maybe. And she was wearing their mother's pearl necklace. He'd see if Castile would have a chat with her. Clearly, it was time. Sherilyn and Robby both.

"Tell us what you've seen in your travels," Willie prompted the visitor.

"Well, it's tough," Bodie said. People are struggling. You all know that. There are little pockets of folks, all trying to survive. I kept well north of where I thought the radiation would be blowing east of Los Angeles, and I didn't see any signs of that kind of sickness. But there's sickness. Lots of doomsday talkers, which I consider a kind of sickness. And a lot of superstition. Man, you can't imagine some of the things people have talked themselves into believing about what happened and what is coming in the future." He took a drink of water. "One group has built a giant concrete pad for the aliens to come rescue them. Painted some weird symbol on it. Said that their leader saw it all in a dream, and they wake up every morning expecting to be whisked away to a planet with two moons and a green sky. I mean that's what they live for!" He gave a chuckle and a shake of the head. "And there are lots of animals. Feral cows wandering around, goats, sheep. The sheep aren't faring so well, mostly because of the packs of dogs, and cougar getting bolder. Horses strolling along the empty highways. But the packs of dogs are the worst. I had to get harsh with them a couple of times or they would have had me for dinner. Some folks opened all the doors to the zoos as it got bad, so I hear there are monkey colonies, zebras, tigers, giraffes, and so forth, but I haven't seen those. Did see a pair of camels in Nevada. There are some bad guys, too, who just think that since humanity's been shall we say, culled, that they can forget all about their own humanity. You learn right fast how to recognize and avoid those guys. You should be prepared for them, because they're out there, and they'd love to find a place like this to plunder."

Parker remembered his and Sherilyn's encounter with bad guys at the river, and he didn't want to repeat anything like that. He knew Willie didn't, either. Bodie Jones was right. Security should be reinforced. Or put into place, as they essentially had none except a new sentry post, which really didn't mean much.

"For the most part, though," Bodie continued, "it's all good. Good people. As I've traveled, I've told them about communities near to them so they could maybe partner up and do a better job of it with more people. But I haven't been back down there, so I don't know what's happened with all of that."

Parker found himself envying this worldly man who had seen so much, experienced so much, just in the last few months. He wondered if Bodie would be interested in having company. No, surely he'd been asked that before. Besides, why would he want a companion who couldn't even talk?

"Have you listened to any of Roger's broadcasts since you've been on the road?" Willie asked.

"Now and then," Bodie said. "I'm glad he's keeping it up."

"Used to be daily, but now it's weekly. There are groups all over the world, listening and responding to him on short wave. He's the global news anchor now."

"Do you connect with them?"

Willie shook his head. "We don't have a ham radio system. I haven't had time to figure it all out. We just got basic electricity here and are working on flush toilets."

Bodie smiled. "I'm not sure Roger's group has flush toilets yet.

"Do you know how to set up a short-wave system?"

"Not me," Bodie said, "But I bet if you keep your eyes open, you'll find a big antenna or a tower in someone's back yard, and inside the house, you'll find the gear."

Willie looked at Parker with raised eyebrows. "It would be good to be able to connect."

"Mandatory," Bodie said, "if we're going to rebuild this country." Then he paused. "What's happening north of here? Do you know?"

"There used to be a pretty big group east of Vancouver, British Columbia, but we haven't heard from them on the broadcasts for a while. They had a hard time with the winter, so they may have taken the summer to relocate. Or disband. Or who knows what. Dirty winds from Tokyo, maybe."

"I plan to make it up there before I turn south again for the winter," Bodie said. "I don't know if I'll pass this way again but if I do, I'll let you know what I find."

"You're welcome to come and go and stay as long as you like," Willie said, and shook Bodie's hand while the rest of the people applauded their guest and then looked to the kitchen for dessert.

As Mary dished out fresh peach cobbler, people mobbed Bodie, bombarding him with questions of a more personal nature. Parker heard a lot of sentences start with "Do you know," and "Have you seen," and "Have you heard," and "If you come across". His answers were almost always a sad shake of his head, and a reiteration of the importance of getting a short-wave system set up so that loved ones could reconnect.

Parker took his dish of cobbler back to the workshop where he found Willie and a book on shortwave radios sitting on his table.

"I saw these in the library the other day," Willie said, holding up a different book on the same subject, "and I thought to myself that this should be our next project. Now I'm convinced of it."

Parker settled back into his chair and opened the book.

"Don't use too much battery with lights," Willie reminded him, then book in hand, left for the day.

Parker brought the oil lamp and matches over to his workspace, although he probably still had an hour of late summer light before he'd need to light it. A quick skim of the book told him that the ham radio concept was very simple, and it couldn't be at all difficult to set up a system here in the workshop.

When he left to go home for the night, Alta ever present at his heels, he saw a light in the kitchen. Mary had a candle burning in the middle of her big worktable. She and Bodie Jones sat close together, each with a steaming mug, and were very deep in conversation. It didn't take a genius to see the connection between them, and Parker wondered if she would go with him now or wait until he came back through.

Either way, she will be hard to replace.

As he walked around the perimeter of the garden toward his house, he looked up at the sky ablaze with stars. For a moment he felt completely insignificant in a universe so vast, and in the next moment, he felt as if he, and the rest of the life on this world was the whole point of the vast universe.

He had never seen the stars, on this moonless night, look so bright, so deep, vast, phenomenal. He sat on the ground and put his arm around the dog's neck, lost, for a moment, in the wonder of it all.

After a while, he took himself to bed, thinking about going places where monkeys lived in the wild and camels roamed the Nevada desert. *Am I looking for reasons to leave the area?*

Maybe.

But then there's Crystal and the baby.

And Sherilyn.

How could he leave them?

~ ~ ~

Parker awoke at sunrise, alone in his bed, and found no reason to linger there.

This was his weekly morning to roam the city streets looking for opportunities to help those in the borderlands cross over. It seemed, though, that people had been finding their own way through the portals, as he had to go farther and farther from the cul-de-sac to find anyone who needed help crossing over.

His weekly mornings on this detail had become an almost-endless monotony of driving around and around, looking for that telltale sparkle of blue, or an internal nudge that told him where to turn.

Another reason to leave the area, he thought, his head still full of Bodie Jones's stories of what he saw in his travels.

He dressed quickly, brushed his teeth and hair, and left as quietly as he could, planning to grab one of Mary's famous pastries or a hard roll, and be on his way.

He was surprised to see Mary in the kitchen this early. She was putting loaves of cinnamon bread in the oven and cooking aromatic oatmeal with applesauce on the stove.

"Hi, Parker," she said. "You're up early."

Parker pointed at her.

"Yeah, I know. Me, too." She looked as if she had been crying.

Parker pointed at the two stools, still close together, at the big table.

"Bodie? He's gone. I made him breakfast, packed a lunch for him, and then he took off." Sadness drew her face into an unfamiliar expression. "I mean I knew he wouldn't stay. He's not that way. Not anymore, if he ever was. But a girl can dream, eh?"

Parker tapped his wrist.

"Yeah, in time he might come back this way, but I can't count on that. I'm not going to sit here and pine for him." She took a deep breath and pressed a kitchen towel to her face.

Parker walked over and put his arms around her. She felt so

different from hugging Crystal. She was older, thinner, taller. Yet, she clung to him. "I could love him," she whispered. "I could make a life with him, that Bodie Jones."

Parker nodded and held her until she collected herself.

She dried her eyes and blew her nose on the towel then tossed it into the laundry pile. "Anyway," she said, dismissively. "Breakfast for you?"

Parker sat on the stool recently vacated by the traveler who had stolen Mary's heart, and for the first time saw an envelope on the table. Amanda's name was written on it.

He pushed it away when Mary brought him a steaming bowl of breakfast and a leftover pastry.

Mary pointed at the envelope. "Yeah. Interesting, eh? That's how Bodie found us. He ran into Amanda's daughter down in California and she told him where to find us. He delivered that letter from her, just like a regular mailman." She smiled wistfully. "A mighty fine mailman, that guy."

~ ~ ~

Spirit directed Parker to drive directly to a place he had been avoiding, but it was clear that he couldn't avoid it any longer.

The county jail.

The ghost of a woman sat on a bench in front of the steel-reinforced door, her physical body disintegrating in the corner where she had been sitting when overcome by the virus.

Parker parked his car and walked up to her, feeling the familiar fullness of Spirit, and he welcomed it, because he would have no idea how to go about doing what he thought needed to be done here. The jail was a fortress, and whoever had not died of the flu had long ago died of something else.

"Hello," the woman said as he approached. "I'm hoping they'll let my son out today. He's a good boy, but I can't get anyone to answer the door."

"You are the epitome of loving motherhood," Parker said. "Your faith in your son is an inspiration. He has one last request of you."

"You know my son?"

"He is one of those inside who has lost his way, but you can help him come back to the path."

"I'll do anything!" she said, hope filling her face with light.

"You must go inside and gather everyone together. I will open a door, and you must see them all through that door, and then follow them in."

"The door is locked," she said, "how can I get inside?"

"Believe," Parker said. He reached out and took her hand. When his physical hand touched her ethereal one, he found that he knew her, knew everything about her, mostly how much she loved her family, especially her son who had done a bad thing. She loved him still, with overpowering, unconditional love.

Parker led her to the locked steel doors.

She walked right through.

He stood, waiting, holding the space and seeing it all in his mind's eye as it unfolded, watching and listening to the inner workings of Spirit as the boy's mother walked the halls of the jail. She called to all of those left behind and gathered them into a queue of about ten, jailed and jailers alike. Several had to be coaxed; they didn't believe they were worthy of any attention from anyone, ever again. But she persisted, speaking to them about those who love them still. Parker saw it all as the men walked through the barred doors, as the woman embraced her son, and walked them all to the portal and encouraged them to step through.

As she looked into the portal herself, just before she stepped across, he felt her energy signature send him a wave of gratitude.

She stepped beyond and the portal closed.

It was done.

Spirit retreated, and all the energy ran out of him like warm water. His knees buckled with the sudden lack of adrenaline, and he sat down on the bench where he had first found the woman. The mother. The savior of her son and all those imprisoned in that cold building.

It was enough for one day.

He went back to his car and closed his eyes, resting.

This is the type of mail that I could deliver, he thought, *to people all across the country.*

~ ~ ~

Elijah waited while five people took their seats in the van, Miles slammed the van door, and climbed into the passenger seat. All seven of them, and the six in the other van wore bulletproof vests and carried the weapons they had learned to use the day before. Miles turned to say something to Elijah, but Elijah held up his hand for silence. He didn't want to hear it, whatever it was.

The remaining dozen or so people left in the high school, mostly women and children, stood on the front steps and waved them away. Some were crying, and that didn't help. Elijah set his jaw and pulled out of the driveway in front of the school, made certain that the second van was following, and turned left, per the instructions he got long ago from the boys on how to find these people he was determined to overpower.

The directions were not entirely correct. It turned out that nobody in their van had actually been to the place. They took many wrong turns, and Elijah's jaws got tighter and tighter every time they had to turn around or look for a different street. He blamed Miles for not getting the directions perfectly clear before they started. But he said nothing, knowing that morale was already thready at best.

Eventually, they saw vehicles: vans, trucks, and a few cars, parked in a cul-de-sac in front of a house, and there were several people and much activity between several of the houses in the circle.

This was the place.

He hoped that Miles had not noticed that none of the vehicles were from his dealership.

He pulled up into the next block and parked. The other van pulled in behind him.

He jumped out and put his finger to his lips, so they wouldn't slam their doors. He gathered them all together in the middle of the street. "Silently," he whispered to them all. "Surprise attack."

Everyone nodded. Some were wide-eyed, breathing heavily, clearly scared out of their minds. He singled them out and put them in the back of the pack. Rex took it upon himself to be at the very front. Elijah knew it would be futile to put him at the back, so he let it be.

In formation, and with no respect to his request for silence, they walked around the corner and headed toward what looked like the main house at the end of the cul-de-sac.

~ ~ ~

Willie sat at his worktable reading electricity and antenna requirements for a ham radio setup when his workshop door opened. Richard stuck his head through the door. "We've got trouble," he said.

"What do you mean?"

"Just come," Richard said.

Willie stepped out into the morning sunshine and saw an armed band of what looked like a ragtag militia walking toward them. They carried a variety of guns, with clearly no idea how to handle firearms, and they wore bulletproof vests over t-shirts and sundresses.

Amazingly enough, word was spreading throughout the community, and people came out of the houses, came out of the garden, Daniella even carrying her baby, and amassing at the area in front of his garage workshop next to the main house. Nobody was running, nobody was hiding. This was a brave group of people ready to protect what they had created, even if they met shotguns and rifles with hoes and rakes.

Mary came out the back door of the kitchen, drying her hands on a towel. She looked at the approaching group, and then met Willie's eyes. This was something she wasn't going to be able to put down with a delicious bowl of barley vegetable soup.

Elijah raised his hand and paused. "We have come for our women," he called.

Willie made his way to the front of the crowd. "We don't have your women," he said. "You're mistaken."

"Amanda and Maria," Elijah said.

So this is Elijah, Willie thought. *What a jerk*. He assessed Elijah's group and they were all accountants and housewives and so forth,

216

ill-prepared with any kind of training, and zero confidence in their mission. And yet, they had weapons. He was painfully aware that Parker's handgun was in a filing cabinet in his workshop, and his shotgun was behind the seat in his truck. He stood with empty hands, trying to assess how dangerous this group really was.

This could go very badly indeed.

Maria ran up to the front of the group. "Mama?" she asked. "Mama, what are you doing?"

"Come home," Susie said.

Amanda emerged from the crowd and stood next to Maria and Willie. "I am not your woman," Amanda said. "And I will not return with you."

"Me neither," Maria said.

Elijah seemed unsure of where to go next, as he had convinced his followers that the women had been kidnapped, not that they had left of their own accord.

Just then, Parker's car pulled up front and he got out.

"You!" Elijah pointed an accusatory finger at him. "You're the one making all the trouble. You're to blame for all of this, you fraud, you… you evil *fuck!*"

Willie saw that Elijah had found his enemy, and this could go sour quickly. He took a step forward. "Stop," he said. "He has done nothing to you."

Elijah also took a step forward, and so did his crowd, feeling the energy surge of betrayal that Elijah had fed them about Parker. "He's got the mark of the beast," Elijah said. "Satan speaks through that boy's mouth, and you would do well to be rid of him."

"That's not how we think about him," Willie said. "He's a fine young man, and soon to be a father."

"Evil spawn!" Elijah spat. He pointed at Parker, who had come to stand next to Willie, and Miles leveled his rifle at Parker's chest.

"Evil spawn!" Rex yelled and fired two shots into the air.

People screamed and ducked down.

This is the darkness Parker had been expecting. Elijah's entire group was surrounded by a very ugly color.

Parker felt Spirit begin to fill him. He resisted, as he wasn't sure he had the energy to endure another session this soon, but his objections didn't matter. His chest filled with confidence, and he stepped in front of Willie.

"*Parker, no!*" Sherilyn screamed and ran through the crowd to the front, where Rex took aim and shot her squarely in the chest.

Pandemonium broke out.

"Stop!" Elijah yelled, but he had lost control of the situation.

Miles grabbed the gun away from Rex, who seemed bewildered by what had just happened.

Some ran to Sherilyn, some hit the ground, and all of Elijah's people, except Rex, took steps backward. Susie and another woman turned and ran back to the vans.

Parker took a step forward and addressed Elijah directly, in a voice so commanding that he didn't even recognize it himself. "Do you think it was an accident that you and your group were spared death from the bombs and the virus?" Everyone quieted. Those in Parker's community who had cowered on the ground, began to stand and move forward behind Parker and Willie. "Do you not understand how massive your role is in rebuilding civilization?" Parker asked. He raised his hand and called to the retreating members of Elijah's motley group of wanna-be fighters. "Come closer," he said, and they came. "Division and competition are no longer valid," he said. "This planet has been given a new chance, a fresh start, but it will take everyone, working together, *together*, to create a new civilization, a new society, a new world order. These little games of power and control will not be allowed to continue." He paused. "Do you want to perpetuate the old ways? Look around you! Do you want to keep the ways that resulted in pestilence, war, and death? Of course you don't. This is your opportunity. You can join together and accept the great task ahead, that of fostering this new way of living, the way of peace, of empathy, of compassion, the way of equality, with a love of all your brothers and sisters, a love of humanity in general, in all your governmental and social affairs. The way of the golden rule. Or you can be distractions on the outskirts of civility, and eventually banished from society altogether, where you will surely perish."

"Who are *you* to lecture to *us*?" Rex said.

"We are interested in receiving souls weighty with the experience of service," Parker replied.

"Fuck them," Rex said to Elijah. "They have food. We need food."

"Shut up," Elijah said.

"Give us food!" Rex yelled and wrested his gun back from Miles. He fired two shots into the air. "I'll fucking kill you all!"

Nobody paid attention to him.

Someone behind Elijah dropped a rifle, and then another gun hit the pavement. The sound of Velcro ripping open as bulletproof vests were thrown aside met the sounds of birds and the sobbing of those tending to the lifeless body of Sherilyn.

"Go now," Parker said, "And see to your souls." He felt a massive wave of blue energy flowing out of him, so powerful he could see it in his peripheral vision. It swept over Elijah and all those who still stood near to him, but also touched those who had retreated. "What has happened here is but a trifle, if you see it for what it is and repair your relationship with the one who made you. We welcome those who choose to serve. Those who choose to persist in error may leave."

And with that, Spirit departed, and again Parker's knees grew week with the effort of standing.

Willie helped him as Elijah took steps back, and Miles again grabbed the rifle from Rex's hands.

Those who had shucked their guns and vests moved forward to mingle with the very people they had come to dominate, and they were welcomed.

The rest turned and went back to the vans, Elijah bringing up the rear.

Parker turned to the body of his sister. Those around her moved away to allow him to put his hands on her, to heal her, for surely he could. But he saw her spirit linger just long enough to lay a loving hand on his cheek, and then the portal opened behind her. Their parents stood just inside waiting to welcome her as she turned to her left and stepped through.

The portal closed, and Parker laid down next to the body of his sister and pulled her close. He buried his face in the crook of her neck, still smelling like fresh baked cinnamon bread, and began to cry. He cried for her, cried for his parents, cried for the world and all the grief that had come to it in the last year. He cried for the young Parker who was thrown into an adult world too young and given a power far too great for his immaturity to manage. He cried for the loss of his sweet sister, just learning what it meant to become a young woman in a realm of infinite possibilities. He cried for the world his baby would be born into, he cried for all the misguided Elijahs out there, all the bad guys Bodie Jones had to circumvent, and their victims. He cried for the domestic animals suddenly turned into the wild with no way to know how to care for themselves. He cried for the people who were not equipped to do what Spirit would have them do: create a new civilization that was true to values, set upon ashes of the old civilization that was built upon greed, political expediency, ego, and self-aggrandizement.

Parker cried for the first time since his parents died. He laid on the grass, cradling the body of his dead sister and sobbed until he fell into an exhausted sleep.

~ ~ ~

That night, in bed, Parker heard the voice of his angel for the first time. She woke him by calling his name.

At first, he thought Sherilyn needed him in the night, and he was immediately alert, but then he remembered and sank back down into his pillows.

She said his name again, and Parker recognized her.

"Don't talk to me anymore," he said to her in his mind. "I can't do it. This is too hard."

"Your road is a long, difficult one," she said. "We understand that. We see that. We honor your willingness to help us this far."

"My sister..." he said.

"She is safe here with us," Spirit replied. "We know that what we ask is challenging. We are with you."

"You weren't with my sister."

"We do not interfere with free will," she said. "And therefore, we will abide by your decision to step away from this work, although we respectfully request that you not do so. You are instrumental to our plan."

"Find someone else." Parker felt his muscles tighten, his hands formed into fists.

"We have much invested in you."

"What do you want from me?"

"We want your willingness."

"But you can't protect me. You couldn't protect my sister. I miss her so much... And my parents..."

"There is no death, you know that. You are doing a tremendous act of service to your world, and your work continues, should you choose."

Then Parker was shown a vast desert landscape, with hot sun, sand, sagebrush, cactus, and little tin-roofed shacks at the end of dry, dusty driveways. In the distance a small city gleamed, although he knew that while it looked like civilization, he might find it abandoned. He hefted the heavy backpack that was cutting into his shoulders and calculated the time it would take to get there, took a drink from his water bottle, and kept walking.

It was a flash-forward moment in time, time which didn't exist for Spirit. They could call up events from the future as easily as they could call up events from the past.

"So this is all preordained?"

"We have a plan," she said, "but you humans are unpredictable. You always change things. Nothing is foreordained. Your free will is sacred and will always be respected."

Parker knew that he could never refuse them. He knew then what he needed to do, and he knew when he needed to do it. "Okay," he said, and while it seemed like some sort of personal defeat, he also felt a warm flush of angelic affection flow through him.

~ ~ ~

Two days later, they buried Sherilyn, tightly wrapped in a

flowered sheet, on the periphery of the garden. Parker gave permission for them to plant an apple tree on that spot, which would not only nourish the bodies of those in the community, but eventually provide shade for his child to play on the grass.

Everyone in the community, including the new arrivals, attended the simple ceremony. Parker looked around at those who had loved his sister, and he saw tears and swollen eyes, drawn faces and emotionally scarred auras. People had been subdued since the attack by Elijah's group. They didn't want to talk about it, but they couldn't stop talking about it, quietly, one-on-one.

After Sherilyn's burial, Mary and her crew whipped up a special buffet lunch. Willie tried to engage the community with Richard's proposal that they establish a security council. Everyone seemed to agree, but there were no volunteers to staff it. It was too soon. It was too late, and it was also too soon. People sat around in the great room, comforted in the shared experience of their grief, yet still muted and downcast.

After lunch, Parker sat on his bed, thinking of all the next steps he needed to take, not knowing how to take any of them. It was impossible for him to believe that Sherilyn was not in the bedroom next to him, and whenever he remembered, a fresh wave of grief threatened to paralyze him.

Crystal knocked lightly on his bedroom door and then came in. "Hi," she said.

He smiled at her, the best smile he could muster, which wasn't much, and patted the bed next to where he sat. She put her arms around him and tipped them both back onto his bed, where they arranged themselves comfortably, familiarly, and she kissed his cheek.

He held her, and felt as if he wanted to cry, but had no tears left.

They lay together quietly, the secret in the pit of Parker's stomach seething like a ball of acid becoming heavier and harder to bear with each passing moment. He was leaving her, leaving his baby, and didn't know how to tell her, didn't know what to tell her, didn't know how she would respond, or how he would respond to her response. The secret ached all the way to his fingertips.

"I've been talking with Oscar and Lois," Crystal said quietly.

Parker tried to separate to look at her, but she held him so tightly he couldn't see her face. "We're too young to be parents, Parker. I don't want to raise a child right now, and I don't think you do, either. Oscar and Lois are older, and they're so ready to have a baby."

Parker felt the stone in his gut dissolve in a flush of gratitude.

"I'm going to move in with them until after the baby comes," she said.

He brushed her hair away from her face and kissed her on the temple.

"Really?" she asked, and then she pulled away from him and looked deeply into his eyes. "You're okay with this?"

He nodded, and then pulled her close again.

His future opened up for him, and he saw the hand of Spirit guiding him. Guiding them all.

He pointed at the backpack sitting on the chair in the corner. He'd gone to the community closet just before lunch and picked it out.

Crystal broke away from him and sat up. "What's that? Parker, what does that mean?"

He sat up next to her and unwavering, met her questioning gaze.

"You're leaving." Tears filled her beautiful eyes and one tripped down off her lower lid and skidded down her cheek.

Too many tears, Parker thought. I'm finished with all these tears. He wrapped his arms around her and held her until she nodded against him. "I've known you'd be leaving," she said. "I knew it when I saw you speak to that gang of thugs." She stopped, her voice clotted with emotion. "I knew it when I heard that you had healed Patty the Cake. Is that true, Parker? Did you really heal her?"

How could he tell her that it wasn't him, it was Spirit, that he was just an instrument? He couldn't tell her. Instead, he kissed the tear from her cheek.

"You'll come back and see our child?"

He nodded, hoping to God that this wasn't an empty promise.

"Are you leaving today?"

Parker nodded.

"Okay," she said, wiped her cheeks with the palms of her hands. "You have to say goodbye to Oscar and Lois."

A half hour later, his little backpack was overfilled with his essentials, and he threw it into the back seat of his car. He went with Crystal to Oscar and Lois, standing in the corner of the garden, and saw their faces light up when they approached. They loved Crystal, and they would love this child.

As if drawn by some magnetic force, Willie and Castile joined them in the corner of the garden, and Crystal brought them all up to date on events.

Willie shook Parker's hand. "Thank you for all you've done for us," he said.

Oscar and Lois pulled Parker and Crystal into a group hug, no words were necessary.

Castile hugged him last. "Save the world, my friend," she said. When she pulled back, she said, "You should go tell Amanda."

"Amanda?" Crystal asked.

Castile nodded cryptically.

"Okay, then," she said, and led Parker over toward Amanda's house. Halfway there, they saw her coming toward them, wearing a blue backpack. "You're leaving?" Crystal asked.

"I know where Reyna is, in California," she said. "I'm going to her."

Parker fished the keys to his car out of his pocket and held them up.

Amanda's eyes grew large. "A ride? Now?"

"Yes," Crystal said. "Parker has to go spread his special gifts to the greater good of us all."

"Are you going south? I would love to travel with you," Amanda said. "I've already said my goodbyes."

Parker took her backpack from her and carried it to the car.

Amanda got in the passenger seat and gave Parker and Crystal a private moment.

"I love you," Crystal whispered in his ear. "Take my love with you. And the love of our little critter here." She put his hand on her swelling stomach.

Parker drew a heart with his finger, first on her chest, and then again on her belly. Then he hugged her close, kissed her, and got into the car.

Alta tried to jump in with him, but he stopped her, looking deeply into her eyes and scratching her ears.

"C'mon, Alta," Crystal said, and pulled the dog away.

Word had spread. A crowd of people, still raw with grief, gathered to share a new type of grief as two of their number, two very special members, were leaving the community.

Parker pushed aside his second thoughts. This way was his destiny. The cul-de-sac was the easier, more comfortable way, and it was not for him, not anymore.

He looked over at Amanda, who gave him an uncertain, tentative smile, then he started the little car and waved at his past as they drove out of the cul-de-sac and toward his next assignment.

Epilogue – 5 years later

Parker was helping Crystal sort mail for Kentuckians when Bodie Jones pulled the big motor home into Jacobson Park lot. Crystal put Lexington mail into one bag and other Kentucky mail into a different bag and got ready.

A group of a hundred or so people met the motor home on a beautiful, if humid, June afternoon.

Parker watched out the window. It was the same everywhere they went. People eager for the mail, eager for word of what was happening elsewhere, eager to hear what he had to say.

Bodie opened the big door and stepped out. He shook hands with the tall, thin man who met him, and Parker knew this was Salim Abbas, the guy who coordinated Lexington communications with Willie via ham radio. Willie had sent Bodie the instructions for this event when they left their last big stop in Nashville.

Crystal picked up the small table and took it outside along with the two small bags of mail and a basket for people to drop in outgoing mail, then set it up while Bodie encouraged everyone to make an orderly queue.

Mary followed her out and set up a different table for donations. Food had become the currency of choice for most people, and she stood quietly, gratefully accepting donations of beautiful produce.

Parker closed his eyes and prepared. He no longer had to help borderland spirits cross over; he had come to understand that there were many people doing that work now. In the last five years, he had grown accustomed to Spirit speaking through him, and he felt that today there would be some type of an announcement, something other than the usual talk about raising children with the core values that would eventually transform society and bring peace to the world.

He relaxed and closed his eyes, welcoming the feeling of partnership with the celestial entity who spoke through him, while he also listened with half an ear to the excited chatter outside. He heard squeals of delight as letters actually found their intended recipients, and lots of encouragement from Crystal to take and deliver any mail they could, all across Kentucky.

When the mail had been scrutinized, and the donations table filled, Salim encouraged the people to assemble on the lawn, away from the weedy parking lot. The noise moved away with them, and the motor home became very quiet.

Parker could hear Bodie's voice as he addressed the crowd. Although far enough away that he couldn't make out the words, he knew from experience that he was giving news of the world as he knew it and talked about their experiences in Nashville, and Atlanta before that.

Then Spirit nudged him, and Parker stepped out of the motor home into bright sunshine.

He took Bodie Jones's place in front of the throng and noticed how many children were in attendance. Almost half of those here were very young, very attentive, their little faces turned toward him just like their parents'.

Parker took a deep breath, felt his chest expand with the presence within him.

"Peace be upon you," he said, feeling the love and encouragement of the crowd. "I am here to announce that a great new source of energy is about to be revealed on this planet. You have all seen and actually experienced the destructive forces of great energy. This first generation has learned experientially how, when used in the wrong way, energy can devastate this planet. Subsequent generations will forget, which is why we are revealing this now. We have faith that you all now know this and will put this new technology to use in the best possible way to rebuild your civilization. See to your families. See to your children. See to it that they all learn the values of what makes a civilization prosper into the next one thousand, five thousand, ten thousand years. Then you will surely utilize this new energy source to its best advantage. We have given permission for your scientists, your engineers, your mathematicians, your physicists, to come together and connect the dots, for all the building blocks of this new energy source are already known to them.

"See to its careful distribution. See that a few don't make slaves of the many by attempting to control this energy. See to your governments for wide disbursal and decentralized control. See to your souls. Make wise decisions." Parker paused. "We are here, we are here to help you. We love you and we believe in you."

Spirit fled, and Parker stood alone in front of a very quiet crowd. He never knew what they expected to hear from him, but whatever it was, it clearly wasn't this. They seemed stunned to silence.

Then a woman stood up. "Will you heal my son?" she asked, pointing at a young man lying on a blanket. "Please?"

A chant arose from the crowd. "Heal him! Heal him!"

Parker wished with all his might that he had that ability, but he didn't, no matter how many times he was asked. He shook his head and turned away. The chant faded.

Salim Abbas took his place and thanked the crowd for coming while Bodie led Parker safely back into the motor home.

Mary was making soup. A beautiful loaf of fresh donated bread sat on the countertop. Crystal was trying to sort the new mail, while cradling a fuzzy brown and white puppy in her lap that kept stealing the envelopes. "Look," she said when Parker came in. "She was a donation."

"Thought we'd call her Harmony," Mary said.

Parker picked up the warm puppy and sat down. Harmony licked his chin, and liking what she tasted, struggled for access to more of his face to lick. Parker fell over backwards and let the pup have her way with him.

Bodie pulled a paper from his pocket. "Our new marching orders from Willie," he said. Everyone stopped what they were doing to listen. This was how the four of them reconnected three years ago, and they'd been traveling and doing this work peacefully together ever since. Whenever Willie sent a message, they all listened.

"Dear ones," Bodie read. "You've been requested in Cincinnati, Ohio on July 6 at the new Center for Families and Children, formerly the Paul Brown football stadium parking lot. Louise Kim will meet you. She will tell you where to find diesel and propane."

Crystal reached for the well-worn road atlas and began flipping pages.

"In other news," Bodie continued reading, "trains are moving from Chicago toward Sacramento and from New Orleans toward Chicago. The going is slow because they have to clear the tracks, but this is good progress. Eventually, they will take over the delivery of mail and other goods. All is well at home. Little Sherry Lynn has a new friend that only she can see. Says her name is Juliet and that she is an angel. Juliet has told her that you will all be back for Christmas. We hope this is so. Love to all. Willie."

Parker looked at Crystal, who looked back at him with big eyes, beginning to fill. He moved over and wrapped his arms around her. Harmony was happy to enthusiastically lick her face, too.

"Sherry Lynn has an angel for a friend," Crystal whispered. "That's our girl."

The motor home was silent for a long moment. Then Harmony grabbed Parker's shirtsleeve and tugged, growling, too adorable to be taken as fierce.

"Home for Christmas," Bodie said quietly. "Sounds good." He gave Mary a squeeze.

"Lunch in ten minutes," Mary said with a smile.

About the Author

Elizabeth Engstrom is the author of 17 books and hundreds of short stories, articles and essays. A former editor and publisher, Engstrom lives in the Pacific Northwest with her fisherman-husband, where she puts her pen to use for social justice. She is always working on the next book. To learn more: www.elizabethengstrom.com

To learn more about celestial planetary management, visit:
www.bigmacspeaks.life

To learn more about how to make values-based decisions, go to:
www.7corevalues.org

Parker's address to Elijah's group on page 89 is a direct quote from *The Urantia Book*.

IFD Publishing Paperbacks

Novels:
Of Thimble and Threat, by Alan M. Clark
Baggage Check, by Elizabeth Engstrom
Bull's Labyrinth, by Eric Witchey
The Surgeon's Mate: A Dismemoir, by Alan M. Clark
Siren Promised, by Jeremy Robert Johnson and Alan M. Clark
Say Anything but Your Prayers, by Alan M. Clark
Candyland, by Elizabeth Engstrom
Apologies to the Cat's Meat Man, by Alan M. Clark
Lizzie Borden, by Elizabeth Engstrom
A Parliament of Crows, by Alan M. Clark
Lizard Wine, by Elizabeth Engstrom
The Door that Faced West, by Alan M. Clark
The Northwoods Chronicles, by Elizabeth Engstrom
The Prostitute's Price, by Alan M. Clark
The Assassin's Coin, by John Linwood Grant
13 Miller's Court, by Alan M. Clark and John Linwood Grant
Guys Named Bob, by Elizabeth Engstrom
Fallen Giants of the Points, by Alan M. Clark
The Itinerant, by Elizabeth Engstrom

Collections:
Professor Witchey's Miracle Mood Cure, by Eric Witchey

Nonfiction:
How to Write a Sizzling Sex Scene, by Elizabeth Engstrom
Divorce by Grand Canyon, by Elizabeth Engstrom

IFD Publishing EBooks

(You can find the following titles at most distribution points for all ereading platforms.)

Novels:
The Prostitute's Price, by Alan M. Clark
The Assassin's Coin, by John Linwood Grant
13 Miller's Court, by Alan M. Clark and John Linwood Grant

Guys Named Bob, by Elizabeth Engstrom
Apologies to the Cat's Meat Man, by Alan M. Clark
Bull's Labyrinth, by Eric Witchey
The Surgeon's Mate: A Dismemoir, by Alan M. Clark
York's Moon, by Elizabeth Engstrom
Beyond the Serpent's Heart, by Eric Witchey
Lizzie Borden, by Elizabeth Engstrom
A Parliament of Crows, by Alan M. Clark
Lizard Wine, by Elizabeth Engstrom
Northwoods Chronicles, by Elizabeth Engstrom
Siren Promised, by Alan M. Clark and Jeremy Robert Johnson
To Kill a Common Loon, by Mitch Luckett
The Man in the Loon, by Mitch Luckett
Of Thimble and Threat by Alan M. Clark
Jack the Ripper Victim Series: The Double Event (includes two novels from the series: *Of Thimble and Threat* and *Say Anything But Your Prayers*) by Alan M. Clark
Candyland, by Elizabeth Engstrom
The Blood of Father Time: Book 1, The New Cut, by Alan M. Clark, Stephen C. Merritt & Lorelei Shannon
The Blood of Father Time: Book 2, The Mystic Clan's Grand Plot, by Alan M. Clark, Stephen C. Merritt & Lorelei Shannon
How I Met My Alien Bitch Lover: Book 1 from the Sunny World Inquisition Daily Letter Archives, by Eric Witchey
Baggage Check, by Elizabeth Engstrom
D. D. Murphry, Secret Policeman, by Alan M. Clark and Elizabeth Massie
Black Leather, by Elizabeth Engstrom

Novelettes:
Mudlarks and the Silent Highwayman, by Alan M. Clark
The Tao of Flynn, by Eric Witchey
To Build a Boat, Listen to Trees, by Eric Witchey

Children's Illustrated:
The Christmas Thingy, by F. Paul Wilson. Illustrated by Alan M. Clark

Collections:
Suspicions, by Elizabeth Engstrom
Professor Witchey's Miracle Mood Cure, by Eric Witchey

Short Fiction:
"Brittle Bones and Old Rope," by Alan M. Clark
"Crosley," by Elizabeth Engstrom
"The Apple Sniper," by Eric Witchey

Nonfiction:
How to Write a Sizzling Sex Scene, by Elizabeth Engstrom
Divorce by Grand Canyon, by Elizabeth Engstrom

IFD Publishing Audio Books

Novels:
The Door That Faced West by Alan M. Clark, read by Charles Hinckley
Jack the Ripper Victim Series: Of Thimble and Threat, by Alan M. Clark, read by Alicia Rose
Jack the Ripper Victim Series: Say Anything But Your Prayers, by Alan M. Clark, read by Alicia Rose
Jack the Ripper Victim Series: The Double Event by Alan M. Clark, read by Alicia Rose (includes two novels from the series: *Of Thimble and Threat* and *Say Anything But Your Prayers*)
A Parliament of Crows by Alan M. Clark, read by Laura Jennings
A Brutal Chill in August by Alan M. Clark, read by Alicia Rose
The Surgeon's Mate: A Dismemoir, by Alan M. Clark, read by Alan M. Clark
Apologies to the Cat's Meat Man, by Alan M. Clark, read by Alicia Rose
The Prostitute's Price, by Alan M. Clark, read by Alicia Rose
The Assassin's Coin, by John Linwood Grant, read by Alicia Rose
13 Miller's Court, by Alan M. Clark and John Linwood Grant, read by Alicia Rose

Novelettes:
Mudlarks and the Silent Highwayman, by Alan M. Clark, read by Alicia Rose

www.ingramcontent.com/pod-product-compliance
Lightning Source LLC
Chambersburg PA
CBHW032042240626
47154CB00003B/1036